THE LAST
WAGON RIDE

THE LAST
WAGON RIDE

RANDY STEPHENSON

MOUNTAIN ARBOR
PRESS

MOUNTAIN ARBOR
PRESS
Alpharetta, GA

ISBN: 978-1-63183-677-0 - Paperback
eISBN: 978-1-63183-678-7 - ePub
eISBN: 978-1-63183-679-4 - mobi

Library of Congress Control Number: 2020902954

Printed in the United States of America   0 2 1 8 2 0

⊗This paper meets the requirements of ANSI/NISO Z39.48-1992 (Permanence of Paper)

For all of the descendants of
Willis Albert and Mary Frances (Fannie) Stephenson

A voice we loved is still, a vacant place in our home,
no other one can fill-still seems lonely for we have
Missed you so much since you have been gone.
Our abiding love.
—From "A Poem" by Fannie Stephenson
Zion's Landmark, Volume CVI, No. 14
June 1, 1973

PREFACE

The Last Wagon Ride is loosely based on the life of Willis Albert Stephenson, my paternal grandfather. Because he passed away long before I was born, I never knew him; however, after reading his obituary, which was written by his brother, Leonard H. Stephenson, I developed an interest in knowing more. That led me to begin my work at the Johnston County Heritage Center in Smithfield, North Carolina, where I waded through old issues of *The Smithfield Herald*, as well as clippings from other local newspapers. I looked at land and marriage records from the time period. I read books on topics pertinent to the story, including books on the influenza pandemic. I learned what I could about some of the farming practices of the early 1900s through old issues of *The Progressive Farmer*. From there, I used the aforementioned obituary as the framework for building the story, which is a combination of fact and fiction.

Although many of those who appear in the story were real people, some characters and all conversations are products of my imagination. Because those who lived at that time are no longer with us to give firsthand accounts, I used my "best guess" as to the motives and actions of those involved. There were a couple of stories that my father told me, and other family members were able to share a few things they knew. For the most part, however, I had to create situations that might have occurred based on events that were known to have taken place during the time period from 1882–1919.

ACKNOWLEDGMENTS

A work of this nature is not done in isolation, and I have many to thank for their assistance as I worked through the process. First of all, I must thank Mark Valsame, who published the *Nimrod and Amanda (Johnson) Stephenson of Pleasant Grove Township, Johnston County, NC: Their Ancestors and Descendants*. Mark published this volume in 1991 and later updated it in a CD format. Another valuable resource was *Pleasant Grove Township, Johnston County, North Carolina: The First Hundred Years, 1868-1968* by E. Joan Jones. Without these reference sources, my work would have taken much longer.

Secondly, many thanks go to Todd Johnson and all the staff in the library of the Johnston County Heritage Center for answering my questions and assisting me with the research.

I am also in gratitude to those family members who shared their knowledge and, in some cases, loaned or gave me materials and pictures. I especially want to thank Grady Stephenson Jr. for his contributions, and Lola Delbridge, who shared much about her father, Leonard Stephenson. Lola has also helped to keep the Stephenson family history alive.

Finally, I want to express my thanks to the staff at BookLogix for being willing to work with me on the publication of my work and for all the assistance provided along the way.

CHAPTER ONE

THE SHAKING

It was almost September and well past dark, but there was the light from the kerosene lamp—not a bright light, mind you, just enough to be able to read—on a small, faded-blue table on the front porch. Wooden columns and elaborate latticework adorned the porch of the white farmhouse, where a family was gathered to listen to the biblical story of David and Goliath. The father sat on one of the birch rockers he had brought in the wagon from Smithfield, the mother in the other. Three boys—the oldest being five and named Charles Edward—sat on the floorboards facing their father. Then there were four-year-old Albert and Alonzo, aged three. The boys were shirtless and barefoot on this sultry evening, the kind of evening typical of late summer in Pleasant Grove Township. Occasionally a thunderstorm would bring some temporary relief to the muggy air, but not this evening. Callie, a little over a year old, leaned against her mother's legs. Her eyes alternated between being open and shut. Their mother, Amanda, nestled Leonard, the newest addition to the family, in her right arm. Light from the lamp had cast shadows, mostly of the mother and father, on the front wall of the house.

Shep, a brown-and-white feist who had taken up residence under the front porch when he'd first appeared a spell back, curled up next to Charles. Nimrod, the father, had forbidden the dog's entry into the house at first. "You ain't bringing that fice dog in this house," he'd said. Yet when winter had come, he'd given way to his boys' pleas that the dog at least be allowed to sleep on their bedroom floor during the worst of the cold. That soon led to Shep being on the floor next to Albert every night.

The only sounds that evening were a chorus of humming cicadas and Nimrod's slow, steady reading from the thick, black family Bible, which had begun to show signs of wear on the corners of the cover. The three boys had just finished eating the last of their mother's apple jacks fried in a big cast-iron skillet that morning. Albert's eyes widened as his father read about Goliath. He wondered if Goliath had been bigger than his daddy.

"Therefore, David ran, and stood upon the Philistine, and took his sword, and drew it out of the sheath thereof, and slew him, and cut off his head therewith."

Albert didn't always understand everything his father read from the Bible, but he'd seen his daddy cut off a hog's head at hog-killing time.

"Is that story true?" asked Charles.

"It's in the Bible, son, so that means it's so," replied their father. Amanda nodded her approval.

"Still, I don't know how David kilt that big man." Charles narrowed his eyes and tilted his head to the right.

"That's because David had God on his side. It's in God's power to decide what'll happen," Nimrod answered. There was an undeniable conviction in his voice.

"So, God's planning everything that happens. Even to Shep?"

Nimrod smiled, reached out, and patted Charles Edward on the head. "Even Shep," he answered.

Albert, who still had the vision of the bloody hog's head mixed in with Goliath's decapitation, drew his legs up to his chin.

"Time for bed," Nimrod announced, and he stood to gather up Callie, who was by then sound asleep. Amanda rose with Leonard in her arms, and the boys jumped up to head inside. The oldest boys slept in the same bedroom. Charles slept alone in a small metal-framed bed, while Albert and Alonzo shared a similar, larger one. Amanda kept colorful, homemade patchwork quilts on top of each bed, but during the heat of the summer, the boys often slept with just a sheet to cover their legs.

The boys pulled off their knee pants and pulled thin white nightshirts over their heads before climbing into bed. The bedroom windows were almost always raised at night in the hopes of catching a breeze. Sometimes, if the breeze came from the east, the smell of the farm animals and manure wafted in. A milk cow, a couple of mules, and a horse were housed in an unpainted barn to the right side of the house. A few sheep, goats, and pigs roamed freely; there was no fencing law. A gaggle of geese, several chickens, and a rooster milled about during the daylight hours. The chickens and even some of the geese stayed under the house at night.

Across the hall from the boys' bedroom, Nimrod and Amanda—or "Mandy," as folks liked to call her—laid the babies down in two cradles that Nimrod had fashioned from some pine boards he had picked up at a nearby sawmill. He'd attached rockers to the bottom of each and stained them a dark-brown color. Mandy had padded both cradles with small blankets and quilts for cover, as needed.

"Going back on the porch to get the lamp," Nimrod told his wife.

Mandy, who had pinned her long, straight brown hair up in the back, reached back to remove the hair pins. As her hair dropped to her shoulders and back, she reached for her hairbrush on the antique oak dresser opposite their bed. She looked in the square German plate mirror, and as she began running the brush through her hair, she heard the sound of loud voices coming from the boys' bedroom. Without hesitation, she walked over to their room and thrust open the door.

All three boys were out of bed. Shep was running amok and whimpering. "What's the matter, boy?" asked Albert. Albert always talked to Shep as if he were going to answer him back. Albert tried to grab hold of Shep, but the dog just wrestled his way out of the boy's arms.

Through the open window, Mandy could hear the high-pitched bellow of the milk cow. "Y'all stay here," she commanded the boys. "I'm a-going to find out what's happening." She stepped out into the hallway and headed toward the front porch. Yet before she could open the screen door, the house began to shake.

3

Nimrod, who had heard the uncustomary bellowing of the cow, had stepped off the front porch to stride toward the barn when the shaking began. Sensing that his family was in danger, he did an about-face and ran back up on the porch, almost tripping when he reached the overhang of the floorboards at the top step. The kerosene lamp fell and shattered. What little kerosene left in the lamp ran out and seeped through the cracks in between the boards. With no time to think about the broken lamp, he threw open the screen door and raced toward the bedroom, where Mandy had retreated to try to get the babies out of the cradles. Dishes, pots, and pans rattled in the kitchen. The cradles rocked to and fro, and the metal-framed beds rattled on the wooden floor. Mandy had already grabbed up Leonard and was trying to lift Callie with her other arm.

"Lord have mercy!" she cried. "I got them! Nimrod, you go see about the boys!"

Nimrod, hardly knowing which way to turn, ran across the hallway where Charles, Albert, and Alonzo stood at the bedroom doorway as if they were in a trance. He yelled, "Let's get out!"

Mandy, ahead of them, went on the front porch and down the steps. Nimrod lifted Alonzo and carried him while Charles and Albert followed onto the porch and into the front yard. Shep scurried behind them.

And just like that, it stopped.

Out of breath, Mandy asked, "What in the world was that?"

Trembling, Charles and Albert clung to their father's legs. Leonard had slept through it all, but Callie started to wail. Trying to calm her, Mandy held her tight to her chest. The shaking had caused much anxiety among the animals, and they wandered about aimlessly amidst a plethora of sounds. Pigs squealed, chickens squawked, geese honked, goats bleated, and from the barn the cow continued to bellow. Meanwhile, the horse and mules whinnied and brayed in such a manner that one would have thought the barn was on fire.

"Ain't no telling," said Nimrod, shaking his head from side to side. The family stood transfixed under the dim light of a waxing crescent moon and the small white dots of light that populated the night sky. "I don't know what that was," Nimrod continued, "but whatever it was, let's hope it's over."

"I reckon it's the devil's work." Mandy pursed her lips and looked at her husband. "We may be a-looking at the end of time."

"I don't know what we're looking at, but let's get these children back to bed. To be sure, it's over."

As Albert and Charles followed their father back onto the front porch with Shep trailing behind, Albert recalled that he'd heard that word *devil* before. From everything he'd heard, the devil must be something frightful. Charles Edward had told him that the devil was ugly and had horns like a cow. Albert sometimes wondered if the devil might try to come and get him.

While Mandy returned to the bedroom to lay the infants back down, Nimrod stood at the doorway to the boys' bedroom until they climbed back into bed. "Everything's all right now. Y'all go on back to sleep." Shep curled up once again on the floor next to Albert.

Nimrod and Mandy had barely gotten into bed themselves when another jolt caused him to spring out of bed and head back over to the boys' room. Around midnight, they were awakened twice more by similar tremors, but none was like the first that had driven them outside. Finally, exhausted from the excitement of the evening, the family surrendered to sleep.

***

A couple of days later, Mandy stood in the kitchen preparing a midday meal of fried chicken and vegetables from the garden. Nimrod read from *The Smithfield Herald*. "Says here that no major damage was done around here, but that at Selma and Raleigh the shock was more severe. Says some thought the last day had indeed come."

"You see, I was not the only one who thought that," Mandy said as she filled up an oval platter with fried chicken.

"Says too they was a earthquake in Charleston, South Carolina. Some people killed, it says."

"I ain't never heard no telling of earthquakes here in North Carolina. Looks like the devil's work to me." Mandy placed the platter of chicken in the middle of the table and began dipping up butterbeans to put in a bowl. The smell of the fried chicken coupled with the smell of the homemade biscuits in the oven caused Albert's mouth to water, even though he was confused. His daddy had said God planned everything, but now his mother said the shaking was the devil's work. Just who was responsible, he couldn't quite figure out.

"What's a earthquake?" Charles asked.

"I've heard about them in other places," said Nimrod. "It's when the ground shakes and trembles like it did the other night."

"Will they be more shaking?" asked Charles.

Nimrod shook his head and looked down at his sons. "Probably not. That's not something that happens all the time." There was no mistaking the relief that appeared on both boys' faces. Three-year-old Alonzo just fidgeted with his hands, oblivious to it all.

Charles spoke up. "God must've planned it, Daddy."

"Maybe so, son. But y'all don't have to worry. Most likely it won't happen again."

At this, the boys turned their attention to the food their mother had put on the table. Some years later, when the children were older and talk turned to the events of that night, they understood more clearly that what they had experienced was a rare event for eastern North Carolina. They were thankful that no one had been hurt or killed in Pleasant Grove, and they were most grateful that the end of days had not yet come.

CHAPTER TWO

PICKING COTTON

Willis Albert Stephenson loved October. It was when the summer's end gave way to the soul-invigorating coolness of fall, and he delighted in the way that nature slowly segued from the lush greenery of the warmer months to the radiant display of orange, yellow, and red colors of autumn. He especially loved October because it was cotton-picking time on the farm. Now that he was eleven, he was old enough to drag a burlap sack all by himself up and down the rows of cotton that ran along the sides and back of their farmhouse.

In the spring, his father had shown the older boys how to drop seeds in the plowed rows. Later, after the cotton plants had sprung up, he demonstrated how to use a hoe to thin out the plants. Everybody called this "choppin' cotton." During the summer months, they learned to pull unwanted weeds from around the growing cotton plants. When fall arrived, Albert delighted in how the cotton bolls would pop open to offer up their snowy-white prizes from within.

The Stephenson family had grown since the earth shook mightily back in 1886. The birth of two girls, Mittie Catherine and Mary Valeria, and another boy, Nimrod Vasper, brought the number of children in the household to eight. Mandy certainly had her hands full with feeding and taking care of a crowd of children. In spite of the responsibilities she faced, she did so with a kind demeanor, and she rarely showed signs of stress. No matter the season, she was generally attired in a long dress or skirt with an apron tied around her middle.

One crisp October morning, Nimrod walked into the kitchen where the children, except for baby Mary, were already seated at the table for breakfast. Mandy was just spooning scrambled eggs into a bowl. She had already placed a bowl of steaming-hot grits and a large plate of ham biscuits in the middle of the table. Callie and Leonard had their eyes closed while the others yawned and perhaps wished they were still in bed.

"Liven up, boys, we start picking cotton today," Nimrod said. Instantly, eyes opened and yawns were replaced by exclamations of "Yay!" and "Yippee!"

"Soon as we finish breakfast, we'll get started. Now, who'll say the blessing?" Nimrod asked. Of course, Albert already knew the answer.

"I will!" replied Leonard. Unlike most children, Leonard paid attention in church services at Rehobeth Primitive Baptist, and it was no surprise that he frequently volunteered to say a prayer.

"Let's bow our heads," he began. "Lord, we ask thy blessing on this family and this food. Amen."

Amanda and Nimrod, both strong believers in the Primitive Baptist faith, regarded their son's interest in the church with pride. A chorus of "amens" followed Leonard's short prayer. Nimrod took his seat at the head of the table, and now that Amanda had placed all the food in the middle, Nimrod began passing around the eggs, grits, and ham biscuits.

In between bites of food, Nimrod spoke directly to the older boys. "Charles, you and Albert will be carrying a sack apiece. Alonzo, you and Leonard will share a sack."

Albert figured this was because Leonard was only seven and couldn't be expected to be as fast as he and Charles. Albert felt proud that his father was entrusting him with more responsibilities. They had learned how to feed the chickens and the geese, and his daddy had even shown him how to milk one of their goats. "Is they anybody else helping today, Daddy?" asked Albert.

"Yeah, I got five colored men and women that's coming. We got a lot of cotton to pick, so we need a lot of help."

"How they getting here?" Charles wanted to know.

"I 'spect they're walking. They live not far away, down around Middle Creek."

Albert had observed that the colored help were never invited inside the house. If they needed water, they got it at the well; however, they always drank from a separate tin cup than his family did. He'd also noticed that when they went into town, the colored folk never shopped in the same stores that they did.

After breakfast was over, Callie helped her mother clear the table while the boys—except for Vasper, who was too young to pick— went back to their room to change into long-sleeved shirts, overalls, and boots. Albert was the first to be dressed, so he walked out onto the front porch, where he saw that the first rays of sunlight were beginning to break over the horizon. There was a light frost on the ground that looked as if a trace of snow had fallen the night before. One of Albert's favorite spots had always been the front porch. He loved listening to stories that his father told there and to the adult conversations that took place when company came.

Shep, now stiffening with age and unable to run and fetch as he once could, spent most of his days either lying on the porch or, if the weather was hot, sleeping underneath. This morning he lay next to where Albert stood as he watched the five cotton pickers walking up the dirt path to their house. The three men walked in front. They were dressed much like Nimrod in overalls and straw hats. The two women wore long-sleeved shirts and long skirts, and each had tied a wrap in a knot at the crown of her head.

Albert threw up his hand and waved at the group as they passed to the right side of the house and toward the back, where Nimrod had emerged from the kitchen. Albert could hear him explaining where they needed to start, how the cotton would be weighed, and how they would be paid. Albert's brothers joined him on the porch.

"Race y'all to the back!" Charles exclaimed. He always loved to race, because more often than not, he won. All four boys jumped off the side of the porch and sped to the back, where their father was handing out sacks to the workers.

As the hired workers walked away to begin picking, Nimrod looked down at his four sons. "Now, y'all follow me. I'm gonna show you again how to do a good job."

Albert practically had his father's cotton-picking directions memorized, since he had started picking at age eight, but he knew to stand and pay attention as if receiving those instructions for the first time.

Nimrod handed each boy a small sack with a strap sewn to each side. "First, hang the strap around your left shoulder and put the sack on the right side." He demonstrated with Alonzo. "When you're picking, be sure to get as much of the cotton out of the bolls as you can. And be careful. Sometimes the sharp ends o' the bolls will stick your fingers." He pointed to where he wanted them to start, and the boys began picking. Nimrod stood for a moment observing his sons as they pulled the cotton and put it in their sacks. Nimrod knew that they wouldn't be able to pick a lot of cotton in a day's time, but the most important thing was that his sons were getting the experience.

Meanwhile, the three men and two women had already made headway down their rows, leaving only wisps of cotton fibers remaining in some of the bolls. Nimrod turned his attention toward the barn and the animals that had to be fed.

By midmorning, the initial excitement Albert had felt had waned some as he and his brothers settled into the monotony of getting all the cotton off one plant before moving on to another. The boys passed the time bantering back and forth, occasionally laughing, occasionally complaining about the bolls sticking their fingers or how long it was taking to move from one plant to the next.

"Y'all want a drink of water?" Nimrod called from the edge of the cotton patch. The boys threw off their sack straps and ran to the well next to the back door. Nimrod lowered a bucket attached to a rope and threaded through a pulley to draw up some fresh water. He handed each boy a tin cup, and one by one they dipped their cups into the bucket of water and gulped down the water.

"I was about par-ished," said Alonzo as he dipped for a second cup full.

"Uh huh." Leonard nodded in agreement.

After all four had drunk at least two cups each, Nimrod said,

"Now, y'all get on back in the field. Before you know it, it'll be time to eat. Mama's cooking a chicken stew." Nimrod knew this would motivate them to keep working until midday. Everybody knew that Mandy's chicken stew was the best around. The boys walked briskly back to where they had stopped, and began again.

The boys didn't have to be called twice when, with the sun high in the sky, Nimrod called them to the house for the midday meal. He yelled for the colored folks to come, too. Mandy had placed a small wooden tub of water on the back steps and a cake of lye soap next to it so that Nimrod and the boys could wash their hands. When the boys finished and went into the kitchen to take their places at the table, Nimrod showed the tub and soap to the hired workers, then told them to wait under the nearby oak tree.

Earlier that morning, Mandy and Callie had gone outside to the garden and cut plenty of turnip salet to feed the family and the hired hands. She had boiled the cut leaves in a big pot and seasoned them with ham hocks. Now, Mandy began dipping up helpings of chicken stew onto a plate, to which she added a big slice of fresh-baked cornbread. "I need for you young'uns to take these plates out to the men and women that's a-sitting under the oak tree. Careful and don't spill anything. Vasper, you take them these forks." She handed him five of the plain everyday forks from the set they used unless company was coming. Charles, Albert, Alonzo, Callie, and Leonard each took a plate and walked slowly out the back door, followed by Vasper with the forks.

"Look here!" said one of the men upon seeing the plates piled high with food. "That looks like some mighty fine eating."

"Bless you, chile," said one of the women after receiving her plate from Callie.

"Lord have mercy! Look at all this," added one of the other men while flashing a row of perfect white teeth.

After all the plates had been handed to the workers and Alonzo had given each a fork, the children hurried back into the kitchen, where Mandy had placed a big bowl of chicken stew and a slightly smaller bowl of turnip salet in the middle of the table. She had baked the cornbread in big cast-iron skillets, cut it into slices, and set it on a big white plate alongside the other food. Callie had set a plate for everyone and filled small glasses with water from the well.

This time, Mandy asked everyone to bow their heads, and she said a brief prayer before Nimrod began passing around the bowls and the plate of cornbread. "How's the picking going?" he asked the boys.

Albert spoke up. "It's going all right. Takes a long time to get much in the sack. Wish I could pick as fast as them men and women under the oak tree."

Nimrod swallowed the mouthful of chicken stew. "Them folks has been picking for years, one place or another. The more times you do it, the faster you'll get. Don't worry about going fast. Important thing is, you boys is learning."

Albert's brothers were eating as if they hadn't eaten in a week. At that moment, cotton picking was far from their minds. Albert, however, stopped eating for a moment and looked at his father. "How late we going to pick?"

"Well, as you can see, we still got a lot of picking to do, so I imagine it'll be late before we stop. Soon as y'all finish, you better rest up a little bit before we go back to the field."

As soon as the boys were finished, Mandy said to them, "Now, y'all go back out and get them plates and forks from the colored folks. Callie and me will wash everything and get it put away."

When the boys got to the back door, the men and women were already standing there with their now-empty plates and forks. One of the women said, "Please tell y'all's mama that we want to speak to her."

Charles called back to the kitchen, "Mama! They say they wanna speak to you!"

Mandy wiped her hands on her apron, walked to the back entrance, and opened the screen door. Five grinning faces were there to greet her. The woman who had asked to speak to her said, "We all want to thank you kindly for the food."

One of the men took off his straw hat and added, "That was

some good cooking, Miz Mandy. Done revived me back up so's I can pick some more."

"Well, I'm glad y'all liked it, and I'll see to it that y'all get a good plate every day that you come here to pick." At that, Mandy took the plates and forks one by one and headed back to the kitchen. The boys headed out toward the front porch to await their father's signal that they could begin picking again.

After about half an hour, Nimrod called for the boys to start working. The hired workers were already back in the cotton patch, bending over and picking with renewed energy. Other than taking a short break to drink water a couple of times in the afternoon, everyone—including Nimrod, who had now joined them—picked steadily. They filled their sacks, and the cotton was dumped into big burlap sheets spread out at the beginning of the rows. When Albert finally filled his sack and dumped it into a sheet shared with his brothers, he marveled at how much the hired workers had picked compared to them.

Late in the afternoon, Nimrod called for everyone to stop picking and to come tie up their sheets for weighing. Each of the hands helped one another by bringing together the four corners of their sheets and tying them in a knot in the middle. The sheets were then dragged to what looked like a giant sawhorse, where an iron weigh scale hung from the middle of the wooden bar. The men lifted each sheet and attached it to an iron hook. Nimrod moved a heavy metal weight along the scale until he got a balance. At that point, he announced the weight and wrote it down in the little notebook he kept in the front pocket of his overalls. "William, you picked two hundred and eighty-six pounds, Lenora two hundred and sixty pounds . . ." He continued until he had weighed and recorded each of the pounds picked.

Albert paid close attention to how his father weighed the cotton. As he watched, he thought, *One of these days, I'll be doing the weighing.*

After the hired workers' sheets had been weighed, Nimrod told them to wait outside the back door. He went inside and got the wooden cigar box that he kept in the bottom dresser drawer in his and Mandy's bedroom. Albert loved to watch how his father figured out how much to pay each of the workers, reached into the cigar box and drew out a dollar bill or a dollar bill and a few coins to give to each. One by one, each of the men and women held out their hands to receive their money.

After each one had been paid, Nimrod spoke to them. "Good work today, everybody. Y'all plan on coming back tomorrow morning, and we'll keep at it 'til we get it all picked. 'Less it rains, of course. In that case, wait 'til we get fair weather."

After thanking Nimrod, the men and women turned and headed back down the path, made a right turn, and walked back in the direction from which they had come in the morning.

"Now, let's go weigh your sheet," Nimrod said to the boys, who had been hanging around waiting until their father had finished paying the workers.

Albert could clearly see that their sheet would not be as heavy as the others that had already been weighed. After helping their father bring the corners of the sheet together to be tied, they helped by dragging it to the scale. "Y'all grab hold of one side, and I'll grab the other," ordered Nimrod. The boys strained, their faces turning red, as they helped their father lift the sheet up high so that he could hook the knot to the scale. After moving the weight to get the balance, Nimrod said, "One hundred and fifty-five pounds. That's pretty good." The boys stood back from the hanging sheet, their faces still flushed.

"We done better than I thought we would," said Charles.

"We done good," Albert added with a look of pride in their accomplishment.

"I 'spect by the time we get finished with picking all of it, y'all will be picking close to two hundred pound a day," Nimrod said in an effort to encourage his boys.

Albert thought about that and imagined that indeed it could be possible.

Nimrod looked at the setting sun as it had its last gasp before sinking into the distant horizon. Then he turned his attention back to his sons. "All right then, y'all get on in the house and get ready for supper. We need to be in the bed early so you can be up and ready to go again tomorrow."

Before he went in the house, Albert stood on the porch picking off the cockleburs that had stuck to his clothing as he had moved up and down the cotton rows. Even though he was tired, the smells from the kitchen drifting out through the front door meant that a good supper awaited him in the kitchen.

CHAPTER THREE

HURRICANE

The remainder of the week was pretty much a repeat of the first part. Every morning just after sunrise, the hired workers arrived ready to get started in the cotton field. The boys began to see the weight of their sheet going up each day, so that by the time Thursday afternoon's weigh-in came about, they had collectively picked almost three hundred pounds in one day. After their sheet had been weighed, Nimrod told the boys, "Ain't got but just a little more to go. I think we'll be finished sometime tomorrow."

Over the course of the week as the sheets of cotton were tied and weighed, the men who had come each day to pick assisted Nimrod with putting each sheet in a stall in the barn in case of rain. Later, the sheets of cotton would be loaded onto wagons and taken to a nearby cotton gin.

Albert was worn out every evening when quitting time came, but he felt a sense of pride in what he and his brothers accomplished. At the end of Thursday, he said to his father, "They sure is a lot of cotton in the barn, Daddy. I think you gonna make a lot of money." Albert beamed as he said this.

"Depends on the market. Sometimes a bale of cotton will go for a good price, and then again not."

"Why's that?"

"Sometimes they's a lot of cotton being sold, and maybe the demand is not as much. Prices then go down. If they's a high demand, then maybe prices will be higher."

"Uh huh." Albert thought about that for a moment to try to understand. He wasn't sure he completely comprehended it all, but he already had his sight set on having his own cotton crop when he got older. It would be important to know everything he could about planting, growing, and harvesting cotton, as well as how to get the best price.

On Thursday evening, as soon as the family had eaten supper, Albert and his brothers practically fell into bed from exhaustion. Very early the next morning, Albert was awakened by the sound of rain falling on the roof accompanied by a light wind. "Uh oh," Albert said out loud. "Won't be no cotton picking today."

Later at the breakfast table, his father confirmed what Albert had thought. "Too rainy and windy today to pick cotton, boys. Maybe if it blows over, we can get back out there tomorrow or the first of the week to finish."

For some boys, that announcement would have been a welcome respite from a day of hard work in the field. Albert preferred being outside, though. Besides, he supposed that his mama would put them to work doing household chores, something he was not fond of doing.

After breakfast, Mandy looked at the boys and said, "Callie needs a day off from washing and drying dishes. You boys can pitch in and do that today."

"Awww, Mama, do we have to do that?" Alonzo pressed his lips together and lowered his shoulders. Charles lowered his head, Leonard sighed, and Albert frowned.

"Now, y'all look here," began their mother. "I ain't having sour looks this morning just 'cause y'all got to do a little something in the house."

Albert felt guilty. "All right then . . ." He made a feeble attempt to smile. "What you want us to do?"

"Well, y'all can start by clearing the table, and washing and drying the dishes. Then I want you to clean up some in your bedrooms."

The boys stood, pushed their chairs in, and began clearing the table. Outside, the wind had picked up even more and was driving the rain against the windows.

Their father put on his overcoat and boots, and came back through the kitchen as the boys began washing and drying the dishes. "Going out to get some of the animals inside the barn, if I can," he told his sons. "Y'all stay inside. It's too rough for you out there." He then opened the back door, upon which a rush of wind came into the house. Albert peered through the kitchen window as his father braved the wind and rain to head toward the barn. Albert surmised that the chickens and geese had taken shelter under the house, but some of the goats and pigs were outside in the elements. He could see his father trying to shoo them inside the shelter of the barn where the cows, mules, and the horse had apparently already taken refuge.

Having been successful in getting some of the animals housed in the few stables in the barn and ensuring that at least the others had shelter, Nimrod made his way through the driving wind and rain to the back door and into the kitchen. "I ain't seen no storm like this one in a long time," he said while wiping his face with a rag. "I wonder if we'll even be able to pick the rest of the cotton that's left when this is over."

The boys were just finishing up with the dishes and getting them put away. Albert hadn't thought about the rest of the cotton in the field since the rain and wind had begun, but now, as he looked out the window, he could see nearby trees bending over in the now-intensified wind. It sounded to Albert like tree branches were falling on the roof, and the wind and rain were blowing against the house with such force that the windows were rattling.

Mandy, holding baby Mary, went to the front parlor to sit by the fireplace with the younger children. Shep, who spent most of his days curled up next to the fire, was so unnerved that he began pacing about the room. Occasionally, the noise created by the storm caused him to whimper as he moved about.

Just as Nimrod was about to walk down to the front parlor to join his wife, a big thud and then a crash sounded in the kitchen. Rushing back in, he could see that a huge limb from the big oak tree had fallen, and the end of it had crashed through the window on the back side of the kitchen. Charles, who was standing closest to the window when the branch hit, had barely escaped the broken glass that spewed all over the counter. A burst of wind and rain through the broken window sent the boys scrambling to get out of the kitchen.

Mandy came down the hallway, holding Mary tightly to her chest. "What was that?" she called out.

"The kitchen window busted! Glass everywhere!" responded Albert.

"Are y'all all right?" Mandy tightened the muscles around her eyes. "Where's Nimrod?"

"I'm back here!" Nimrod called from the kitchen. "Y'all go back to the front and stay there. I'm gonna try to put something over the window. Wind and rain is a-coming in hard!" Nimrod tried to think quickly of what he could do. First, he would need to go back outside and pull the tree limb out through the windowpane. He put back on his overcoat and boots, and opened the back door. The wind was now so fierce that when he opened the screen door, it flew back with great force against the side of the house.

Pushing through the blinding wind and rain, Nimrod managed to grab hold of the fallen limb and pull it backward. The end of the branch popped out of the window and landed with a thud on the ground. Meanwhile, the screen door flapped madly back and forth in the wind. He decided to let it go. After opening the wooden door and forcing it shut, he spotted a burlap sheet that would have been used for the remainder of the cotton picking. Grabbing up the sheet, he moved quickly to the broken window and stuffed as much of the sheet as he could into the rectangle where the windowpane had been. This he did carefully to avoid being cut by the remaining glass around the edges of the frame. The sheet immediately stopped the howling wind and relentless rain from coming inside. Then, he spotted the broom in a corner of the kitchen. With much care not to get cut, he picked up the pieces of glass that had shattered onto the table where the boys had put the dishes. He used the broom to sweep the glass that had fallen on the floor into a corner.

Satisfied that all the glass was out the way where no one would be injured, Nimrod walked back up to the front parlor. "Well, looks like I've got a windowpane to replace, but it could have been worse," he announced. "Nothing we can do but stay in and do the best we can until it's over."

Albert and his brothers spent most of the afternoon dividing their time between playing checkers and jacks. Callie started a game of Hide the Thimble with her sisters.

Finally, as the afternoon began to fade into the darkness of the evening, the wind and rain began to subside. It wasn't until the next morning when Albert went outside with his father that they saw the extent of the damage. In addition to the broken window-pane and downed tree limbs, the cotton plants that had not yet been picked had been flattened to the ground by the storm. Water puddled in between the rows, and the remaining cotton was now a soggy mess. Albert kept quiet as he watched his father squint his eyes to look upon the surreal scene.

"Well . . . it's good we got most of the cotton picked. I reckon you're learning a big lesson here, Albert. When it comes to farming, sometimes the weather works to the good, and sometimes it don't. Pays to always plan ahead in case of a loss like this."

Albert wasn't very sure about how he would have to plan ahead, but he knew that now was not the time to get into that. He could see the look of concern on his father's face and realized there would be plenty of time later to ask questions.

CHAPTER FOUR

A TRIP TO BENSON

By the time the 1890s came to an end, the family had grown yet again with the birth of Hettie Viola in 1894 and Irving Henry in 1898. Albert was now sixteen, and the older brothers in the family and he were "feeling their oats," so to speak. In their younger years, they had walked to school during the four-month term, wherein they learned to read, write, and do arithmetic. Now that they had advanced to their teen years, Charles, Alonzo, and Albert no longer attended school, although opportunities to continue one's education had sprung up in Johnston County. Albert figured that he could learn everything he needed to know by watching his father and reading *The Progressive Farmer* and *The Smithfield Herald*. Some children had struggled with reading and writing when he was in school, but Albert had been smart enough to learn to read rather easily. This ability benefited him greatly, as he was able to glean much farming information through reading magazines and newspapers.

Most of Albert's days were filled with farm work, including tending to the livestock, working in the cotton or cornfields, or picking vegetables from the garden for his mother. Sundays were generally a day of sometimes attending services at Rehobeth Primitive Baptist Church, followed by an afternoon of leisure and fun.

One Sunday after church and another one of their mother's delicious meals, Albert, Charles, Alonzo, and Leonard took off for Middle Creek, which bordered their land on the north side. When they reached the creek, they saw a large gathering of people on the south bank.

"Looks like a baptizing," said Charles, pointing at the gathering.

"Sure does," Albert agreed.

There was a throng gathered on the north bank of the creek, as well as a group of about six or seven men and women from some nearby congregation, all dressed in white and standing knee-deep in the cool waters of the creek. The preacher and another man stood together, and one by one they took the arms of the person to be baptized. Each person being baptized fell backward into the water, and the preacher and the other man, holding on to the believer's arms, rapidly pulled the born-again member of the flock back up. Each time, this action was greeted by a chorus of "Praise the Lord!" and "Amen!" from the group on the bank.

The boys stood and watched until all the born-again believers had been submerged and had waded out to join the others. Albert noticed that his younger brother Leonard was particularly interested. This did not surprise Albert, since Leonard had been getting up on tree stumps to preach to whomever was willing to listen since he was about ten years old.

As Albert stood engrossed in the scene before him, another small group of boys around his age emerged from the trees behind them, and they, too, stood watching the baptism. After the congregation on the riverbank dispersed, Albert and his brothers met up with the other group, upon which it was decided that they would play stickball in a clearing just a short distance away from the creek. Albert saw that they had come prepared. One held a red rubber ball in his right hand, while yet another carried a long wooden handle, perhaps broken off from a farm implement.

Entertainment on Sunday afternoons for Albert and his older brothers included games like stickball or marbles. Sometimes they ended up exploring the vast acres of land owned by their father. Another Sunday sometime later, Charles, Alonzo, and Albert convinced their parents to allow them to miss church service so they could take one of the farm wagons to Benson. Reluctant at first because he had never allowed the boys to take the wagon on a daylong trip before, Nimrod finally gave in and helped hitch Toby, one of their three mules, to the wagon, and gave them strict instructions to be home by dark.

Benson was a relatively new town at that time, having sprung up along the railroad line running through Johnston County. Many of the original buildings had been destroyed in a fire in 1894, but now they were being replaced by brick structures. Charles, being the oldest, held the reins as the three boys left out early in the morning to head south into town. The several hours' ride passed uneventfully, but that all changed as the mule began pulling them through the main part of the town. Out of nowhere, a short, disheveled man with a beard and straw hat appeared behind the wagon. As the man approached the rear of the wagon, Albert recognized the smell of liquor. He had only smelled it once, when a boy with whom he and his brothers sometimes played had offered Charles and him a drink down by the creek one Sunday afternoon. Both Charles and Albert had refused to drink from the bottle out of fear of what their daddy might do if he smelled it on them.

"'Kin ye boys gimme a ride?" the man asked as he grabbed hold of the right side of the wagon.

Alonzo and Albert let Charles do the talking. "I don't think so, sir. We just going down to visit somebody we know . . . just right down close to the railroad."

This was a lie, Albert knew, but none of them wanted that drunk man in the wagon.

"Maybe you boys 'kin take me wid you then." The man's hands held tight to the side of the wagon. Albert had never been around anyone drunk before, and was taken aback by the smell of alcohol and the inability of the man to stand up straight.

"No, sir," Charles answered. "Our daddy told us never to let anybody we don't know in the wagon."

This was another lie, as far as Albert knew. He did not recall his father ever telling them that, but he knew Charles was trying to get them out of a difficult situation.

"But y'all don't understand," the drunk man insisted, and then he went to the back of the wagon and started trying to climb in. Thankfully, Charles realized quickly enough that he needed to urge Toby forward so that the man could not get in, at which point they would have had a bigger problem on their hands. As Toby continued down the street, the man, who had managed to get one leg in the back of the wagon, lost his balance and fell flat in the dirt. As the wagon moved farther away, the man started yelling words Albert had never heard before. The man repeatedly tried to rise to a standing position. Suddenly, another man appeared, whom they learned later was a policeman by the last name of Johnson. Charles stopped the wagon several yards ahead of the fallen man, and the boys watched as the policeman put handcuffs on the drunk and led him away toward a nearby building.

"That must be where the jail is," said Alonzo in awe of what he was seeing.

As the mule plodded down the street, Charles looked at his brothers and said, "That's what licker does to some folks."

"I never seen anything like it," added Albert.

"We better not say nothing about this to Mama and Daddy," Alonzo added. "They won't never let us come back again."

"You probably right," responded Charles. "I wonder if they's more drunks than him. Can y'all believe that? And on Sunday, too!"

What the three brothers really wanted to do that Sunday was go down to the train station to wait and see if a train might come through. They had heard about how townsfolk and those who lived nearby would flock down to the train station when it was time for a train to pass through. If it was a passenger train, folks liked to wave to the travelers inside, and if a freight train passed through, it was fun to watch the loading or unloading of produce, fresh fish, ice, or other products.

The boys were in luck that Sunday. Shortly after noon, after peering down the tracks toward Dunn, they saw the locomotive appear, first as a tiny speck. As the sights and sounds of the oncoming train gained proximity to the depot, excitement grew in the crowd. Many had arrived as the boys had: either by wagon or by buggy pulled by a horse or mule. The arrival of the train was accompanied by a cloud of billowing smoke from the engine and the screeching of the wheels as the engineer applied the brakes. A man with a cart containing bags of mail appeared, and the mail was quickly lifted up into the first passenger car. Since it was a warm day, windows on the passenger cars were lowered, and the boys could easily see the passengers who, as their mama would have said, were dressed in their "Sunday go-to-meetin' clothes."

"I wonder where they going," Albert said to Charles and Alonzo as they sat watching in the wagon.

"I 'spect they're going to maybe Richmond or Washington," Charles replied.

"I wonder what it's like up yonder," Alonzo said.

"I imagine they is a lot more people. Them cities are big," Albert offered.

After a few minutes, the engineer blew the train's whistle, signaling that they were ready to move on. Those in their buggies or wagons waved their good-byes to the passengers, and the locomotive, with a great deal of noise and smoke, made its departure from the depot. The brothers watched as the full length of the train rolled past, and they gazed until the last car disappeared into the distance on the northbound side.

Mandy had packed her sons a basket lunch of ham biscuits and collard greens. For dessert, she had included three apple jacks fried that morning. After the ride, the boys were famished from the excitement that came from dealing with the drunk man and watching the arrival and departure of the train.

After they finished their meal, they realized that it was getting a bit too late to do much more and have time to get back home well before dark. So, Charles took the reins once again and coaxed Toby back through town and onto the dirt road leading north toward Pleasant Grove.

They arrived back home to find everyone sitting out on the front porch awaiting their arrival. Alonzo and Albert jumped out of the wagon as Toby pulled Charles back toward the barn, where the boy would unhitch, feed, and water the mule. Alonzo and

Albert took turns telling of the train's stop in Benson, but there was no mention of the drunk man. Albert missed having Shep greet them with his tail wagging. He had gone outside one morning in the winter to find the dog curled up lifeless at the front door. Albert had found it difficult to fight back the tears that morning, for Shep had been a part of the family for many years.

CHAPTER FIVE

THE BOXCAR

A few months later, when the cold and dark of winter had given birth to the refreshing hopefulness of spring, the boys managed to get permission once again to take the mule and wagon out on a Sunday. It was a welcome respite from preparing the land for spring planting. This time, they were accompanied by younger brother Leonard. Charles, Alonzo, and Albert were surprised that Leonard was willing to miss church, but their younger brother seemed genuinely excited about going.

They told their parents that they wanted to go to Four Oaks. This was because they had heard that the boys in Four Oaks really liked to have fun down at the railroad. Like Benson, Four Oaks was another town that had been founded along the Wilmington and Weldon railroad running through Johnston County.

Mandy, always thinking about her boys' stomachs, once again packed a basket lunch. As the rest of the family prepared to go to Sunday church services, Charles and Albert hitched Toby to the wagon. On this occasion, Albert held the reins as they rolled down the path to the main road in front of their house. The time it took them to get to Four Oaks was a little longer than it had taken to get to Benson, but they managed to arrive just outside the town shortly before noon.

Albert reined Toby in under a big sweetgum tree that stood to the side of the road leading into town. Leonard said a brief blessing, and the four brothers feasted on the fried chicken and biscuits that their mother had packed in the basket. After the boys finished their lunch, they climbed back on the wagon. As the wagon rolled along toward town, Albert expressed to the others that he hoped the train would come while they were there. Leonard broke in excitedly, "I never seen a train before. Can't wait to see that!"

After finally arriving in Four Oaks, the boys went straight to the depot. Unlike the Sunday in Benson, where people had been gathered at the depot to watch the train's arrival, hardly anyone was to be seen. As they edged closer, they spotted a man who, by the sight of his uniform and cap, appeared to be a railroad worker. Alonzo called out to him, "Excuse us, sir, but is a train coming through today?"

"Not until late this afternoon," he answered with a smile. "If you young fellers is a-looking for something to do, you might want to walk beside the tracks toward Smithfield. Usually they's a lot of young folks out and about in that direction."

"Thank you, sir!" the boys replied in unison. Albert slapped the reins on Toby's back, and the mule began plodding in the direction of the tracks.

After they had ridden a short distance alongside the tracks, Charles interjected, "Why don't we stop and tie the mule here at this tree?" He pointed to a thin-trunked pine to the left, which was a good enough distance away from the railroad track that no harm would come to the mule should a train pass before they got back.

"What're you thinking?" Albert wanted to know.

"I thought it might be fun to do what the man back yonder said. We could walk on the tracks that way," Charles replied, pointing in the direction of Smithfield.

Alonzo seemed a little unsure and asked, "What if a train is coming?"

"Well, then we'll get off the tracks," Charles said good-naturedly as he patted Alonzo on the back.

After tying Toby to the pine tree, they took off down the tracks, sometimes walking on the railroad ties and sometimes trying their hand at maintaining balance by walking on the rails. Not long into their walk, Leonard, who was in front with Alonzo, belted out, "Look! Somebody's coming!"

Sure enough, as he peered in the distance, Albert saw a boy and a girl walking toward them. As they got closer, he could see that they were holding hands. Not too far behind the couple appeared yet another young pair walking in their direction. As the first couple approached, Albert could see that they were about the same age as Charles, or perhaps himself. The boy was dressed in a dark-colored suit, white shirt, and bow tie. The girl, who appeared to be about three or four inches shorter in height, had curly brown hair that fell down to her shoulders. She wore a flowery print dress that went down below her knees and black stockings.

"Hey, where y'all been?" Charles asked the pair.

The boy responded, "We walked all the way down to Holt Lake. On Sundays a lot of us likes to walk down to the lake and back. Gets us out of the house and away from the prying eyes and ears of the family." He looked at Charles and Albert as if to say, *I know you know what I mean.*

As Charles questioned him further about the walk to Holt Lake and the possibility of a train's passing, Albert tried to glance at the girl without being noticed too much. Mostly she kept her eyes lowered and allowed her boyfriend to do the talking.

The boy introduced himself. "My name's Rufus, and this here's Sarah." Sarah did not speak, but looked at the boys and smiled as an acknowledgement of their presence. After all introductions were made, Rufus continued, "If you boys want some fun, when you get to the sidetrack a little further down, they's a group of boys there that can give you a little ride on one of them cars."

Leonard practically jumped with excitement. "How can we do that?"

"Well, y'all will see when you get there. You can only do it when a train's not coming."

By this time, the other couple walking on the tracks made it up to where Albert and his brothers were, but they were obviously not interested in stopping and talking much. Beyond offering a brief hello as they approached and passed, nothing else was said. Albert and his brothers quickly said their good-byes to Rufus and Sarah, and Rufus took her hand once again as they continued their walk back toward Four Oaks.

Now that the boys knew a possible adventure awaited them, they began walking rapidly. After about ten minutes, Albert spied the sidetrack and boxcar to which Rufus had been referring. Hanging around the boxcar was a group of about fifteen or twenty teenaged boys. As the brothers got closer, one tall, lanky boy with blond hair called out, "Hey, you boys want to ride?" Sensing the brothers' puzzlement at the situation, the boy with the blond hair said, "My name's Luther, and all of us boys here goes to school in Four Oaks. We done this before a time or two. What we'll do is this—I'm gonna open the switch, and that way we can push the car onto the track. It's not that hard, because they's nothing in it, and besides, they's a bunch of us. Then, you can all get in and ride down to the bridge."

The bridge was down at the Neuse River. Luther signaled for the brothers to follow him so they could see, and just as Luther had said, the track indeed made a sharp descent to the bridge below. Albert thought to himself that he loved an adventure as much as any other boy, but since he had never been on any part of a train before, he wasn't quite sure that they should be part of this little prank.

"What if a train comes and we're on the track in the boxcar?" Charles wanted to know.

Luther, without hesitation, replied, "They ain't no trains coming 'til later. We've done it before, and they's been no trouble."

The blond boy's confidence didn't do much to placate Albert's worry that something bad could go wrong. Nevertheless, neither he nor any of his brothers could suppress their excitement to try it.

Luther continued, "Since this the first time y'all are doing this, we'll let y'all ride and we'll push."

"What y'all think?" Charles looked at his brothers. Albert knew by the expression on his brother's face that he had already decided he wanted to try it. Alonzo and Leonard were quick to say they wanted to ride, but Albert was a little more hesitant.

"You sure we'll be all right?" Albert directed this question to Luther.

"Never had a problem before, have we, boys?" He looked at the rest of his group for confirmation. Several negative responses erupted from the boys as they gathered along the sides and rear of the boxcar. "Y'all just jump in," the blond boy instructed, "and we'll do the rest."

The boxcar doors were open, so Charles put his hands on the floor of the boxcar and then lifted first one leg and then another inside. Then he held out his hand to help each of his brothers up. By now, Albert's heart was beating faster in excitement and nervousness.

As the other boys took their positions on the sides and the rear of the boxcar, Luther called out, "Watch your legs and feet! We don't want any cut-off parts!"

Albert knew he meant this as a joke, but all at once he imagined bloody, severed limbs. It was too late to back out, though, as Luther began counting to three. The boys pushed with all their might, and the boxcar gradually started moving forward onto the main track. After the boxcar was clearly off the sidetrack, the boys pushed a few yards more, and the car began its descent. Though it wasn't that far to the Neuse River bridge, the boxcar was still able to gain a pretty good speed. Not knowing what to expect, Albert held on for dear life just inside the doorway.

"Woo-hoo! Boy, that was fun!" Alonzo practically yelled when the boxcar finally came to a stop just shy of the bridge.

"Can we do it again?" Leonard said. They had all clearly enjoyed their little adventure.

Albert was just glad they had made it without loss of life or limb. "They'd have to push the boxcar back up the hill, and I don't think they can do it," Albert responded.

When the boys arrived downhill to greet the brothers, Luther announced, "Y'all wanna hang around? When the next freight train comes later from Smithfield, we're planning to jump on and ride in to Four Oaks and jump off at the depot."

Albert, Alonzo, and Leonard all looked at their oldest brother, Charles. "Don't think we can do it," he told Luther. "We gotta get back into town. We left our mule and wagon tied to a tree, and we'll need to be getting back home before dark."

The brothers expressed their thanks for the fun, said their good-byes, and started walking back up the hill alongside the railroad track. Privately, Albert wondered what was going to happen when the train came and there was a boxcar sitting on the tracks. He thought his brothers were probably wondering the same, but none of them spoke about it.

After about fifteen minutes, they arrived back at the wagon, where Toby was grazing on some grass under the tree. For Albert it had been a fun day, but he couldn't quite escape the fearful feeling that had accompanied his excitement.

***

A few weeks later, when Charles and Albert accompanied their father to Benson on some business, they found themselves once again hanging around the train depot, where a crowd had gathered to watch the next train's arrival.

While waiting for Nimrod to finish his business, the boys decided to go over to the post office across from the depot, where a man was getting bags of mail ready to load on to the next train. As Albert got closer to the post office, he nudged Charles and said, "Look over yonder." He pointed in the direction of a group of people standing near the train tracks. "That looks like that boy Luther, don't it?"

Charles nodded his head, and they quickly walked to where Luther was standing.

"Hey, you was at the train tracks the other Sunday, and you and some other boys pushed us down the hill a boxcar. You remember us? I'm Albert, and this here is my brother Charles."

The boy peered at Albert's face and said, "Oh yeah, I remember. Y'all live here in Benson?"

"No, our house is a few miles up from here. We come into town with our daddy. Did you boys jump on the train and ride that day?"

Luther glanced down, and his face appeared to redden just a little. "Yeah, we did, but it was a bad decision."

"Why's that?" asked Charles.

"Well, it was a freight train. We hid behind some trees down near the bridge, because we knew the men on the train would be mad once they seen the boxcar on the tracks. Well, anyway, the engineer was able to stop the train just before it hit the boxcar, and after that some men got off the train and was cussing like you never heard before. Only thing they could do was use the engine to push the car back up the hill. Just before they started the engine, we crept out from our hiding places and climbed inside a couple of the open cars near the end of the train. They never knew we was on the train, and the way we figured it, we'd get a ride to the depot, where we'd jump off just before the train stopped. Only problem is, the train didn't stop. It kept right on a-going, and we all got worried we'd end up no telling where. So, after we realized the engineer wouldn't stop, we decided to jump out of the boxcar. Thanks be to Gawd that none of us was kilt, but it shore could of happened. Most all of us had tore pants, and they was a lot of scraped hands, arms, and knees."

"Glad you all didn't get hurt worse," Albert offered, feeling bad for the boys but at the same time feeling pretty good that they hadn't been part of their scheme.

Realizing that their father was probably looking for them, Charles and Albert said their good-byes and ran toward where their father was sitting on the wagon seat, ready to head home. "Now, where you two been?" Nimrod asked.

"We was just talking to a boy we know." Albert quickly changed the subject by asking his father if he had taken care of what he had needed to do. The less his father knew about the boxcar ride, the better, he thought to himself as the mule pulled the wagon back through town.

CHAPTER SIX

A DEATH AND A PROPOSAL

In the latter part of the nineteenth and into the beginning of the twentieth century, much was still unknown about the causes and cures of many diseases. There had been a smallpox scare from 1901 to 1903, and many died as a result of contracting illnesses such as diphtheria or tuberculosis.

Nimrod had been very sick back in 1892, so much so that he was bedridden for several days. Even a small article appeared in *The Smithfield Herald* about his illness and recovery. By the time late March rolled around in 1903, he had once again fallen very ill. The family never understood fully what ailment took siege of his body, but his condition grew worse by the beginning of April. Mandy, frantic with worry, managed to summon a doctor to the house to see if there was anything that could be done. Unable to confirm a definite diagnosis, the doctor left a variety of concoctions popular at the time for her to administer to her husband, but it was all to no avail.

In pain and growing weaker by the day, Nimrod slipped into a coma a couple of days before finally drawing his last breath on the morning April 9. Mandy and all their children gathered around him as he passed. Albert had never been around a dying person before, and because this was his father, the depth of his sorrow was overwhelming. Despite having to deal with his grief, Albert knew they had to act quickly. Thankfully, Charles knew of an undertaker by the name of Morgan in Smithfield who sold coffins. Not wanting to leave their mother and rest of the family. but realizing the pressing need, Charles and Albert hitched Toby to the buggy to make the journey to Smithfield to purchase a casket.

Meanwhile, word of mouth traveled rather quickly, and soon

a stream of neighbors and fellow church members began to appear in the front parlor of the farmhouse to express their condolences. Many stayed throughout the night to sit up with the family, as was custom. Women stayed in the kitchen to prepare pots of coffee and to have readily available food brought in by friends and neighbors.

It was late in the afternoon by the time Charles and Albert returned with the undertaker, Morgan, following not far behind in his horse-drawn buggy. Morgan worked late into the evening to prepare the body for placement in the wooden coffin that the brothers had purchased from him.

Albert slept little that night. At times he would sit in the front parlor with an empty stare. He spoke only when spoken to and then in a monotone voice. In the early hours of the next morning, he finally retreated to his bed, as if that could somehow help him avoid the pain of his loss.

The next afternoon, the family and a group of neighbors and friends gathered around the coffin in the front living room for the funeral service. Primitive Baptist elders and Leonard spoke of the good life Nimrod had led as head of the family, as a church member at Rehobeth, and as a neighbor and friend. Following the service, Albert and his brothers placed their father's coffin in the same wagon Nimrod had used so many times for business or other outings. Old Blue, a mule Nimrod had purchased years ago, pulled the wagon out toward the main dirt path that ran in front of the house, the mourners walking behind. There, neighboring men who knew the family well had dug a grave and stood ready to lower the coffin into the ground with ropes.

Following the funeral and burial, Albert's brothers and sisters stayed close to home for several days in order to be of some comfort to their mother. Even Charles, who had married Flossie Mae Stephenson in January of 1902 and had become a father to son Edward Berk later in the year, would come during the first few days following their father's death to be with the family. Later on, there would be business to attend to, and quite naturally much of that responsibility would fall on the shoulders of Charles and Albert, since they were the oldest sons.

After a few days, life gradually began to return to normal. There was spring planting to do, and Albert busied himself with getting the land prepared to plant cotton and corn. He decided to continue his father's tradition of preparing a vegetable garden that would provide the family with tomatoes, squash, cucumbers, snap beans, butter beans, and peas.

Albert's social life, which had been put on the back burner throughout his father's illness and the mourning that followed, resumed, as well. He had met Mary Frances "Fannie" Langdon one Sunday at nearby Fellowship Primitive Baptist Church. Fannie stood out to Albert not only because she was pretty, but also because he enjoyed their conversations outside on the church grounds following services. It got to the point that Albert would attend services at Fellowship just to spend time with Fannie. Finally, one Sunday he got up the nerve to ask Mr. James Monroe Langdon, Fannie's father, if he might be able to call on her at their home that afternoon after church. Albert supposed that her father would probably agree to that, since the Langdons knew his family rather well. Albert figured that both of them were certainly old enough to begin a courtship, seeing as both were twenty-one at the time.

Albert began the courtship by appearing regularly at the Langdon home, where he would be greeted by Fannie at the front door. She was thin, and though she was shorter than Albert, her presence stood tall in his mind. Her dark, somewhat wavy hair was usually brushed back away from her face. Her eyes held the look of innocence, and she had a quiet strength about her that made her especially attractive to Albert. She was generally dressed in a long-sleeved, full-length dress or long-sleeved blouse and long skirt. Albert and Fannie discovered that they were comfortable with each other and talked endlessly about their families, farm work, and newsworthy events. This was all done in the family front parlor, except when they would take the opportunity to walk up and down the dirt path leading up to the Langdon house so they could have a few moments alone. It wasn't long before Albert knew that Fannie was the woman he wanted to marry.

By the time the fall of 1903 arrived, Albert was so convinced that Fannie was the right girl for him that he hitched Toby to the wagon and headed down to Benson to buy her an engagement ring. J. W. Whittenton had opened the first jewelry store in the county back in 1895, and through word of mouth Albert knew him to be an honest man. Albert had chosen to go on a Saturday, and there were already other customers inside looking through the display cases when Albert walked in. Mr. Whittenton greeted Albert and let him know that he would be with him as soon as he could. Albert was glad, because that gave him time to look at the assortment of rings.

When Whittenton finished with the other customers, he approached Albert and handshakes and greetings were exchanged. Albert's overalls and long-sleeved blue shirt contrasted with the more formal attire of Mr. Whittenton, who wore a starched white shirt and gray wool pants held up by suspenders.

Albert explained that he had recently asked for a young woman's hand in marriage, and he wanted to get her an engagement ring. "Nothing too fancy. More along the line of plain and simple," he explained. Even though Albert had the money to pay for a nice ring, he didn't want to spend a big amount, because he knew he was going to need money to get started in a new location once they were married. He also knew that Fannie would not expect an expensive ring. She'd never presented herself as being one to go for costly things.

After seeing several possibilities, Albert finally selected a good-looking ring with a gold band and a diamond solitaire in the middle.

"What size, Mr. Stephenson, would you say?" asked Whittenton.

"Hmmm. I'll be John Brown, if I know." Albert hunched his shoulders and smiled. He realized that Fannie's ring size hadn't even crossed his mind.

Whittenton gave Albert a reassuring smile. "You're not the first young man who's come in here not knowing the size. Tell you what. Let's make a guess, and if it's not a good fit, you may bring it right back in and exchange it for something either bigger or smaller, as the need may be."

Albert exhaled with relief and followed Mr. Whittenton to his desk at the rear of the store, where he paid for the ring in cash and thanked him for his help. He then headed back outside where Toby waited, tied to a post near the front of the jewelry store.

On the way back home, Albert felt good about his purchase and confident that Fannie would like the ring. As good fortune would have it, a few days later when he officially proposed to Fannie in the front parlor of the Langdon home, he found that the ring was a perfect fit. As news traveled that the couple was engaged to be married, wherever they went both Albert and Fannie were met with congratulations and well wishes.

Albert saw his engagement to Fannie as one of many steps he was taking toward independence. Although he loved his family very much and had many fond memories of their all being together in his years of growing up, it was time to move on and start a family of his own.

CHAPTER SEVEN

A LAND DEAL

With the decision to marry in February of the coming year set in place, Albert began turning his attention to other important matters. Prior to the beginning of rural farm delivery, several small post offices had served the needs of citizens in Pleasant Grove. One of them was known as the Caudill Post Office, which was located in the northwest corner of the township. Mathias Caudill had been one of the postmasters there, and by word of mouth Albert had learned that he had some land for sale.

After inquiring the whereabouts of the Caudill farm, Albert hitched up Old Blue to the wagon. It was a cold and cloudy December morning, the kind of day that usually brought folks to say that it looked like it was going to snow. The air was so chilly that Albert could see what looked like a steamy mist coming from Old Blue's nostrils as the mule pulled the wagon out onto the dirt path. Fannie had given him a solid brown scarf that he now used to cover the lower part of his own face and his neck.

As Albert rode along, he noted the cotton fields. Where there had been rows of cotton plants with lush green leaves producing countless bolls of soft white cotton, now all he saw were dried-up, brittle plants that would need to be plowed up before spring planting began anew. Not far from where he had been told to take a turn that would lead him down to the Caudill residence, he met a large brown milk cow coming from the opposite direction. As soon as the cow sensed the wagon's approach, Albert saw it veer off the path into an open field. It stood watching from a few yards away as he passed.

Albert had no idea what to expect as the wagon made a slight descent down the road to a two-story white house standing on the other side of the intersection of two dirt roads. He pulled back on the reins to slow Old Blue down so that he could take in the scene. The house appeared to Albert as well-constructed, and the area around it was not entirely unkempt. However, he observed that the home was in need of a fresh coat of paint. To the right of the house stood a small wooden shelter that Albert figured must have been built for whatever livestock the family might have, although he saw no animals underneath.

Albert guided Old Blue to the front of the house, where he got down and tied the mule to a tree, stepped up on the wraparound porch, and knocked on the door. After the cold ride in the wagon, he would welcome a fire to warm himself before talking any business.

A man with thinning hair and streaks of gray opened the door. Albert's first impression was that the man must be somewhere in his fifties, and though he was bundled up in a thick brown winter coat and a pair of tall, lace-up calfskin boots, he appeared to Albert to be a bit stockier than he. Albert explained that he had come to inquire about the land the man had for sale, upon which Mathias Caudill invited him inside. "Come in outta the cold," Mathias said without hesitation. "We got a fire going here, so you can warm up while we talk."

As Albert entered the front parlor, he could hear voices coming from another part of the house. He stepped up to the fireplace, where a robust fire provided him immediate relief from the near-freezing temperature outside.

"I was just reading about that new flying machine they tested right off the coast here. You heard about it?" Mathias pointed to a small article in a recent copy of the *News and Observer* that lay on the floor next to a rocking chair close to the fireplace. Albert saw that the headline was "They Flew Miles: Ohio Men at Kitty Hawk Have an Air Ship that Goes." Albert and Mathias talked for several minutes about how it was hard to believe that such a thing had been accomplished right there in North Carolina, and that there would be no way either one would ever want to get on one of those things. "It's a sign of the changing times we living in,"

Mathias said as he picked up a couple pieces of firewood piled next to the hearth. He used one to poke the fire to stir it up, and then tossed both in to be surrounded by the flames.

"Yep, I heard from some folks over near where I live that you want to sell some land," Albert told him, taking care not to sound overly interested.

Albert thought he could detect a hint of sadness in Mathias's face as he replied, "Yeah, I come here a while back from out in the western part of the state in Alleghany County. My brother Tyrell came down and stayed for a while, and we built that house down the road." He pointed with his right index finger to indicate the house Albert had seen earlier on the east side of the property. "We tried doing a little farming, but he went on back home. Things just hadn't worked out as good as I thought they would. Just been thinking about moving on." He looked down, as if he were still looking at the news article about the airplane flight.

Albert wondered why Mathias wanted to sell the land, but decided not to ask. He knew that some people had run into difficulty in keeping up with paying their taxes, but there was no way to know this short of asking him outright, and Albert felt it not proper to do so. "How many acres you got?" Albert asked.

"They's about two hundred and four, more or less. Besides the houses and the land, they's that shelter out there that the livestock can get under." Mathias went on to talk about how he had tried growing some corn and cotton, and that he'd had a few pigs and a cow.

Albert wondered if the milk cow he had seen earlier belonged to Mathias, but he decided to leave that alone. Instead, he shared how his father had raised cotton and livestock, and that he had learned a lot from working since he was a boy. Finally, Albert got around to asking his price.

"Well, seeing as how I'd be selling not just the land, but the house with it, I'm asking twenty-eight hundred," Mathias said without looking over at Albert. Albert would learn later that Mathias had paid twenty-five hundred for the land to W. A.

Ogburn and his wife, Delia, back in 1889. Their land bordered the property on the western side.

"Umm," uttered Albert as he considered what Mathias had told him. This was not the price he had hoped to hear. He turned toward Mathias and asked if it would be possible to look over the house and the land.

"Why, I'd be more than happy to show you around. You able to come and look now?" Mathias asked.

After following Mathias into the kitchen, Albert was introduced to his son, Andrew, and daughter-in-law, Callie, along with his daughters Margaret and Mary. "My wife, Margaret, she passed on a while back, so it's just us now," Mathias explained, looking down at the floor as he spoke. After a brief exchange of polite greetings, Mathias led Albert through the house. "It took us a good while to build this house when we come here, but it's solid," Mathias told him.

Albert saw that there was plenty of space, including the kitchen, adjacent dining area, a sizable front living room, and three bedrooms all on the bottom floor. Many of the rooms contained fireplaces, and because of the cold temperature outside, there was the pleasant smell of burning wood throughout the house.

After inspecting the bottom floor, Mathias led Albert up a set of creaky wooden stairs. Albert saw that there was another bedroom, with plenty of room for storage. The bed was piled high with quilts, because as Mathias told him, a boarder named Samuel slept there without the warmth of the fireplaces below. Albert looked out the window and saw the house to which Mathias had referred earlier. Mathias explained that his brother Tyrell had lived there briefly after the house was built, but at present the house was vacant.

After descending the stairs and bidding goodbye to the family as they finished their meal, Mathias told Albert that he would like to show him the shelter and as much of the land as he cared to see. The shelter was sizable enough, but was a very basic wooden structure; it had a roof, but no walls to enclose it. "It's just something for the milk cow, the mule, and a few pigs to get under if they's bad weather," Mathias explained.

As the two men walked around the barn and looked back at the house, though everything looked in need of loving care, Albert was suddenly struck by the possibilities that he saw. With some scraping, paint, and other needed touch-ups, he envisioned how the house—framed by two young evergreens in the front, some small elm trees to the left and right, and an oak on the west side—could be made to look rather handsome.

The men then proceeded back to the front of the house. Albert untied Old Blue, and he and Mathias climbed up on the wagon seat. Mathias first directed Albert to look at the expansive tract of land running in front of the house just across the dirt path that ran from east to west. He pointed to where the boundary line of the property approximately lay.

Then, they headed east down the path toward the vacant house. Just before the path took a deep turn down toward a small creek, Mathias signaled for Albert to stop. Albert saw that this part of the property, on the eastern boundary, was heavily wooded and would need some clearing, if he wanted to use the land for planting.

As the wagon rolled slowly along, Mathias continued to point out where the approximate lines of the property extended. They descended a small hill where the path flattened out. The men continued for about a half mile more until they came to another dirt path running from north to south. This, Mathias told Albert, was the western boundary of the property. Wherever he had seen land cleared, Albert noted that it looked as if no effort had been made to cultivate the land.

They were unable to see some of the land due to trees, mostly pines, blocking their view. Mathias told Albert to turn the buggy around, and as they turned back onto the pathway leading to the house, Mathias urged Albert to keep the mule going forward a bit. As they came around to the back, he pointed to the trees in the distance that formed the southern boundary of the property.

Albert marveled at the expansiveness he saw before him. Mathias then signaled for Albert to get down from the wagon and follow him for a bit toward the west, where he pointed out a large tract of flat land in the distance.

"You can see that some of that land yonder needs clearing, but I believe it'll be good for planting cotton. The land is flatter than it is down here closer to the house. I just hadn't been able to do much when it comes to planting. Was not able to buy mules for plowing, and seed for planting is costly, too," he added.

All Albert saw around him was infinite possibility. As the two walked back to the wagon, Albert felt convinced that with some plowing and proper care of the soil, he could bring this farm to life. Not wanting to sound too anxious, he said, "Well, I don't know. There's a lot of land here, but it needs a lot of work to get it ready for farming. House needs some work. Twenty-eight hundred is maybe too steep for me right now." As Albert climbed back up to the wagon seat, he said in a noncommittal way, "I'll have to study on it a spell. To tell you the truth, I was thinking more along the lines of about two thousand."

Albert tried to move his eyes toward Mathias without turning his face to see what his facial expression might be. Albert could see that the man was considering what he had said, and after what seemed a long time, Mathias countered with, "I have to be honest, Mr. Albert. That's a little low for me, seeing as how I built the house and shelter here. What if we maybe could agree on something more like twenty-five hundred?"

At that point, Albert knew at least that Mathias was willing to bargain, so he countered, "I appreciate you coming down some, but truth is, I will need some time to think. That's a lot of money, and I need to be sure I'm doing the right thing. Maybe need to talk it over at home."

"Well now, I get that, but look at all you would be getting. They's a lot of land here, and I suppose if you got the means to farm it, you could do all right. Maybe no time before you make back up what you paid for it."

Albert knew Mathias was right about this, but he felt like twenty-five hundred was too much, considering all he would need to do to get the place ready. "So, what if we could agree on, say, twenty-four hundred?" Albert said. "That would be more along the lines of what I could do, seeing as I'm just starting out and going to be married in February and all. It's a lot of money, but maybe if I can get a good start with planting in the spring, I could make a go of it."

Mathias Caudill stared off in the distance for a moment as he pondered Albert's offer. Albert had not worn gloves, and began rubbing his hands together to create a bit of warmth.

"Well . . . that's a bit less than what I wanted, but you look to be someone who could do right by this place," Mathias finally said. "I hate mighty bad to sell it for less than I paid for it, but . . . all right, I'll agree to twenty-four hundred."

Albert took in a deep breath and exhaled as he realized that he had just agreed to buy the rundown farm for twenty-four hundred dollars. At the same time that he felt a tinge of nervousness about the agreement, he also felt the power in his decision. This would be his land; he would be in charge, and he longed to see what he could do with it.

Albert told Mathias that if he would come to his house a few days later on the thirtieth, they would ride to Smithfield together to finalize the sale. After the two men shook hands, Albert got back in the wagon and began the journey home. As he rode along in the icy cold with the scarf wrapped around his mouth and nose, he thought about Mathias and the tough situation the man obviously must have found himself in that caused him to seek a buyer. He felt compassion for Mathias, and wondered what he would do once he and his family vacated the house.

As is often true when a man is alone and has time to think, ideas come from seemingly out of nowhere. A big idea came to Albert on that wagon—an idea that he would share with Mathias Caudill when he came to go with him to Smithfield.

CHAPTER EIGHT

THE FIRE

With Albert and Fannie's marriage less than two months away and with a verbal agreement to buy the land, Albert hitched Toby to the wagon to make the fourteen-mile trip southward into Benson. Albert knew that he would need to start looking at some farm equipment of his own, and Benson was as good a place as any to start looking. Fortunately, there had been no rain in the past several days. This meant that Toby would have an easier job of pulling the wagon down the dirt road that led to the southern end of the county.

All along the way, Albert encountered livestock wandering freely, sometimes crossing the road directly in front of the wagon. By making the trip alone, Albert was able to pass the time by thinking about what all he would need to do in the spring to get his land ready for planting cotton. At the very least, he thought to himself, he was going to need a plow and a good mule to break the land.

As Albert approached the outskirts of town, his mind wandered back to the time when he and his brothers had encountered the drunk man on Main Street, and he hoped that nothing of the sort would happen this time. Yet, sure enough, Albert soon spotted a saloon. Though it was midday, there already appeared to be a few patrons inside. Alcohol was frowned upon by many folks in the county where the Primitive and Free Will Baptists were entrenched. From what Albert had seen, alcohol drove men to act in peculiar ways, and thus far he had seen no need to find out what it might do to him.

Albert pulled on the reins to slow Toby down so that he could see the various places of business on Main Street, specifically looking for a place selling buggies and carriages. After spotting such a store, Albert brought the mule to a halt and climbed down from the wagon seat to speak to the owner about his inventory and prices. A tall man by the last name of Parker with a dark, close-clipped beard came out to shake Albert's hand. Albert introduced himself and explained his upcoming marriage and the purchase of the land.

The man, who spoke in a very slow, soft tone, smiled and seemed to display a genuine interest in what Albert had to say. "So, what brings you to my store today, Mr. Stephenson?" Parker asked.

"Well, mostly I'm just looking to see what you got. Been thinking about maybe getting either a buggy or a carriage. Not sure yet which one."

"Well now, as you can imagine, a carriage with a roof will offer you and your family some shelter from bad weather, but they're a bit more costly. I can probably give you a good deal on a nice carriage, though, if you're interested."

Albert followed Parker around the store and out back, looking at the different sizes of buggies and carriages. He reiterated again that he was only looking, but would most likely be back later to make a purchase.

After thanking Parker and leaving the store, Albert spied a blacksmith shop down the street. With Toby still tied to the post in front of Parker's store, Albert walked down to the shop and saw a rather portly man sitting on a wooden barrel and smoking a pipe. During an exchange of pleasantries, Albert learned that the man's last name was Barefoot. Barefoot pointed to a nearby barrel and invited Albert to sit for a spell and talk.

"Had a breakdown just outside of town," Barefoot began, "so's I had to come here to git my wagon fixed. What's bringing you in?"

Albert repeated what he had just told Mr. Parker. Barefoot wanted to know who Albert was marrying, who his daddy and mama were, and if Albert was kin to another man by the last name of Stephenson that Barefoot knew in Benson. He told Albert that he lived south of town in an area folks called Broadslab. Albert said he hadn't heard of it, but that maybe sometime when the weather was nice, he might ride down that way to see that part of the country.

Soon, Albert realized that it was getting late in the day and he would need to head back home before long, so he shook hands with the man, got back up on the wagon seat, and headed back toward the main road leading north from town. As the wagon rolled along, it felt to Albert that the temperature had begun to drop, and the wind seemed to have kicked up a notch or two. As Albert passed the jewelry store, he saw Mr. Whittenton inside helping a young man. Albert smiled as he imagined the young man buying his girl a ring, just as he had done a short while ago for Fannie.

As Albert neared the edge of town, his thoughts were interrupted by the sound of men yelling and women screaming in the direction from which he had come. Albert pulled Toby to a halt and turned around to see a cloud of smoke billowing high above the buildings, perhaps close to the blacksmith's shop or Mr. Parker's store. Simultaneously, people began to pour out of the homes and businesses along Main Street. A woman came up behind Albert's wagon and yelled, "Not again!" Benson had already suffered from two fires, the most recent in April of that year, when several businesses and homes had burned rapidly to the ground in a horrific blaze.

Five or six men came out of the saloon that Albert had seen earlier, a couple of them apparently so drunk they could barely stand. Albert saw their eyes widen, and they seemed to sober quickly as they gazed at the looming danger.

By this time, Albert could see flames shooting out from the windows and doors of some of the buildings and homes in the distance. Albert knew that the scene was real, but at the same time he felt that it could not possibly be happening. He knew there was no way the townspeople could fight such a blaze, and that all they would be able to do is get as far from it as possible. Most everyone who had been on Main Street had by now moved back closer to where Albert sat transfixed on the wagon seat. Though Toby faced the opposite direction, he sensed that something was terribly wrong and began braying like a donkey. Several times Albert had to pull on the reins to keep him from taking off out of town.

Albert sat in silence as he watched the flames destroy one building after another, until he realized that it was now dark. Because the fire had so lit up the sky, he was unable to detect whether there would be any light by the moon. He'd had the foresight to bring a kerosene lantern in the wagon, so he knew he would be able to have some light on the way back. He contemplated finding a room in town to spend the night, but he knew his family would worry if he did not return.

Finally, he slapped the reins on Toby's back, and the mule began to pull the wagon out of town toward home. Not long after he left the outskirts of the town, through the dim light of the lantern he saw two men on horses coming toward his wagon. The two men, dressed in heavy coats and wide-brimmed hats, pulled their horses to the right and stopped alongside Albert. As the men got closer, Albert could see that the two men were young, perhaps a bit younger than he. They told him that they had seen the big light in the sky and were headed into town to see what had happened. Albert briefly explained what he had witnessed. The young men seemed anxious to get into town to see at least some of the fire before it died down. They thanked Albert for the information and galloped off toward the blaze.

Now that Albert was alone with only the light of the lantern to help keep him on the road, it seemed to him that the cold was more biting. He pulled his scarf up and over his nose and mouth, all the while wondering if he would be able to complete the trip home. After about a half hour had passed, he spotted a light in the window of a small farmhouse to his left. Albert considered asking whoever lived there for a place to sleep by the fire until the morning, and almost pulled on the reins to direct Toby toward the house. But no, he thought that maybe, just maybe, he could make it to his own bed. He imagined that by now everyone at home had begun to wonder where he was.

After Albert passed the house, he did not see any more signs of life for what seemed like an eternity. His hands and feet began feeling numb, and he scolded himself for not either staying in town or going to the house where he had seen the light. He tried thinking more pleasant thoughts—thoughts of Fannie and of his family.

Finally, when hope had begun to fade, he saw the turnoff that would take him eastward. After traveling a good distance more, he made it to the path leading up to the house. Albert had not checked his pocket watch, but imagined it must be close to midnight, if not later. Someone had placed a lighted kerosene lamp in one of the front windows.

After unhitching Toby, leading him to his stall in the barn, and giving him a small bucket of oats, Albert opened the back door to find practically everyone in the house awake and awaiting his arrival. Albert immediately went to the fireplace and took off his boots to warm his feet and rub his hands over the fire. As his mother prepared him a plate of leftovers from the evening meal, his brothers and sisters all gathered around the table to listen to his telling of the fire's destruction and the ride home in the freezing cold.

"I've never been as worried," Mandy told him, drawing her eyebrows together and clutching the top of her nightgown. Albert reassured her that he had learned a big lesson, and next time he would find a place to stay instead of trying to come all the way back in the cold.

After Albert finished the leftovers, he dismissed himself quickly to his bed. Instead of falling asleep from the exhaustion he felt, he began to toss and turn thinking about the leaping flames and the smell of smoke. Finally, just before light appeared on the horizon, he fell asleep and did not wake up until almost noon.

It would be a good while before Albert was able to get past thinking about the fire.

CHAPTER NINE

SEALING THE DEAL

Christmas day of 1903 was a happy one at the Stephenson home. Callie came back to visit with her new husband, David Alvin Austin, whom she had married in November of that year. Charles and Flossie Mae were there, as well, but Albert noted the sadness in their eyes from the recent death of their infant son, Edward Berk. Of course, his brothers Leonard, Vasper, and Irving were there, along with sisters Kittie, Mary, and Hettie.

Albert had taken the mule and buggy early to the Langdon home to pick up Fannie. This was the first time she had spent a special day like Christmas with the Stephenson family. Mandy cooked a meal fit for a king that included a big hen, boiled ham, chicken stew, collard greens, corn pudding, baked sweet potatoes, and of course, biscuits—the kind that made Albert's mouth water just by smelling them. This spread was topped off with sweet potato pie for dessert.

After everyone was satiated from the huge meal Mandy had prepared, the family retired to the front living room, where they shared personal news and talked a little about other things going on in the area and beyond. Most already knew about Albert's plans to purchase land. With Fannie by his side, he told everyone about how he had managed to bargain a reasonable price, and that maybe sometime in the near future the family could all come there to celebrate Christmas.

Alonzo spoke up cheerily, "And now we know that Fannie will be there, too." He winked at Albert, and Fannie's face slightly reddened.

"Well, I 'spect so," Albert said with a grin. At that point, the conversation changed to the weather and other local news and gossip.

Later that afternoon, as Fannie snuggled into Albert to keep warm as they rode in the buggy back to her house, they talked more about the new farm. It just seemed like everything was coming together. They would be married soon and able to start their lives together in a house of their own. The substantial amount of land would provide the potential for good crops and, in time, good income.

When they arrived at the Langdon home, Albert took a few moments to accompany Fannie inside, where he wished her family a merry Christmas and a happy and prosperous new year. As the couple walked back out onto the front porch, Albert held Fannie and kissed her as he had not done before. He told her that he would be back just as soon as he had made the trip to Smithfield with Mathias Caudill to get everything settled. After saying their good-byes, Albert pulled his scarf over his face and began the bone-chilling ride back home. Even in the penetrating cold, he had a feeling of warmth in his heart that almost anything was possible. He was in love!

The next to the last day of December dawned with cloudy skies. There was a hint that maybe snow might begin to fall at any moment, but if it did come, Albert thought that maybe it would at least hold off until Mathias and he had taken care of their important business. Mathias had told Albert that he would try to be at his house very early, and sure enough, at a little past eight o'clock, Albert looked out the window to see him coming up the dirt path in his mule-drawn wagon.

Albert offered to take Toby so that Mathias's mule could rest until they got back from Smithfield. Talk along the way mostly centered around how the Caudill Post Office would soon close. Mathias said he was sad to see it close, but he expected a change in how people received their mail would be coming.

"Do you have any plans now that you are selling the land to me?" Albert asked.

"Not sure what I'll do," Mathias replied, "but I need to figure it out, because I gotta have some more money coming from somewhere."

Albert thought back to the idea that had come to him on his

return home after agreeing to buy the land. He nudged Mathias with his right arm and said, "What would you think about staying on at the farm and helping me out for a while?"

A brief moment passed before Mathias spoke. "Well, I'd have to think on it, but right off hand, I don't see why I couldn't. We could move in the empty house you saw when you was over until I decide what I'll do. Maybe I could work out a deal with you for us to stay there in exchange for helping you out some."

"Well, I'll be owing you for the farm, so I'm sure we can work out something that'll be satisfactory for the both of us." Albert looked at Mathias, who nodded his approval. The men spent most of the trip talking about the farm and the possibilities that lay ahead, as well as Albert and Fannie's upcoming marriage. Albert knew that with taking on the responsibility of having that much land to tend, he was going to need some help, and he was glad to see Mathias considering it.

Sometime close to noon, the men arrived at the courthouse in Smithfield, where they went to the Register of Deeds. Mathias was directed to write out the boundaries of the land that was to be sold and the terms of the sale. A man by the last name of Edgerton spoke to the pair regarding the details of the land boundaries, the number of acres, and how Albert would pay for the property. Albert needed to go heavily into debt to get Mathias paid for the transaction, and the two agreed on an arrangement satisfactory to both.

By early afternoon, all had been settled. Albert was a land-owner. In a way, it was hard for him to believe that he had been fortunate enough to even think about such a substantial purchase. On the other hand, Albert had envisioned for the past several years that he would come to buy some land and have a place of his own.

Conversation was sparse on the way back home. The air grew colder as they rode along. Albert guessed that, just as he had been doing, Mathias must be thinking a lot about what had transpired and what the future might be like.

About two or three miles from home, it began to snow—lightly at first, and then it started coming down with a fury. When they arrived at the house, Albert invited Mathias to come in and spend the evening with the family, because it would be very hard on him to try to get all the way back home in the cold and snow. Mathias confessed that even though his family would be worried, it would probably be best to stay over rather than attempt to get home in the rapidly falling snow. Later, after sitting with the family for a while in the front parlor, he gladly accepted the offer of a warm bed for the night.

Though it snowed a few inches during the evening, thankfully no ice formed. Mathias rose with the first rays of sunlight, and without disturbing those who were still in bed, he went to the barn to lead his mule back outside to hitch to his wagon. Shortly, he was on his way out to the main path, where he would make a right turn and head back to the farm that would soon be taken over by Albert.

CHAPTER TEN

THE WEDDING

Albert and Fannie set their wedding date for February 7. In January, Albert began spending his days at the house that Mathias Caudill and his family had vacated not long after the land settlement had taken place.

Albert's first task was to fill in the cracks between the boards in the walls with newspapers to act as insulation. In an attempt to keep the newspaper strips in place, he purchased a paste at the general store in nearby Woodsboro. As Albert and Mathias unfolded the old newspapers to tear into smaller pieces, Albert paused from time to time to share articles about cotton prices and advertisements for the sale of mules or horses. Mathias was fascinated by the many ads for substances claiming to be cures for a variety of ailments: Rheumacide, which claimed to have cured a helpless cripple; Orrine, said to be a cure for a whiskey or beer habit; then there was Dr. Greene's Nervura, supposedly praised by women as a cure for a variety of aches and pains.

Albert knew that he and Fannie needed some basic furniture items, such as a bed, a kitchen table and chairs, and something to sit on in the living room. Some of Fannie's family had already said they would like to give the couple some things to use in the kitchen. Getting everything together that the couple would need proved to be both challenging and exciting at the same time. The couple also decided that following the wedding, they would stay in Albert's bedroom at the Stephenson homeplace until the house on the newly purchased farm was ready.

Albert realized that with his impending marriage to Fannie, he needed to go ahead and purchase his own means of transportation. Returning to Benson with Mathias, he went to the business of J. D. Parrish and Son to look at mules and wagons. After looking over the mules held out back in an enclosure and speaking to Parrish's son, Alonzo, who was immaculately dressed in a dark suit and tie, Albert decided to buy two mules he determined to be the healthiest looking in the group.

Then, he turned his attention to the wagons on display. Albert's eyes were drawn to a wagon that Alonzo described as being made of pine. The wagon had been left in its natural color, rather than the red or green colors that some of the other wagons were painted. A wooden seat sat on top of two metal springs at the front of the wagon. The seat had a back and arm rests on the left and right that measured about ten inches in height. The four wheels, as Alonzo explained, were four feet in height, while the wagon box measured ten feet in length with a depth of nearly two feet.

Albert took plenty of time to walk all around the wagon, touching the wheels, flooring, and sides. He climbed up into the wagon and sat down on the seat, resting his feet on top of the box and imagining himself holding the reins as one of the mules he had just agreed to buy pulled the wagon along.

Alonzo told him that the wagon sold for thirty dollars, but he could give Albert a good deal of twenty-five dollars since he had bought the mules. Reasoning that this was a fair offer, Albert followed the younger Parrish into the store, where he added a single-strap harness to his purchase. After settling the business part, Alonzo followed Albert back outside, where he assisted Albert and Mathias in attaching the bridle, breast collar, traces, and side and hip straps to one of the mules. Alonzo produced a rope from inside the store, which he said Albert could use to tie the other mule behind the wagon to make the trip back home.

After thanking Alonzo, Albert climbed back up on the wagon seat. Mathias, meanwhile, followed Albert in the wagon that they had taken to Benson as they made their way out of town toward home. It would take them most of the remainder of the day to arrive, but Albert rode satisfied that he had managed to make a good deal. Though he was proud that now he had both his own mules and a wagon, it was the wagon that gave him the greatest feeling of satisfaction.

***

The morning of Sunday, February 7, came with clouds and periodic rainfall. However, it was Albert's wedding day, and no clouds or rain could suppress his sentiments of happiness and well-being.

Weeks ago, Fannie had invited a few young couples to attend the wedding ceremony at the Langdon home and an early-afternoon meal prepared by her mother, Eliza Jane. Mandy had let the wedding party know that they were also invited to come over to the Stephenson house for another celebratory meal that evening.

The invited guests had been asked to arrive at the Langdon home around nine thirty. Albert was to arrive just before the scheduled time of the wedding at a few minutes before ten. Although Albert did not want to admit to others that he was nervous, he found it hard to hide his anxiousness as he went about the business of preparing to leave. He spent considerable time in front of the mirror in his bedroom making sure that every hair was combed into place, even though he was going to make the trip in the buggy, which would not shield him entirely from the wind and rain.

Albert put on his new white shirt with a stand-up collar that he had purchased some time ago. He had selected a black suit and a black bow tie to give it a finishing touch. His mother and most of his family were not to attend the wedding, but were instead busy preparing for the feast that would come later that evening when the couple returned from their celebration at the Langdon home.

When Albert finally came out of the bedroom and into the kitchen, where his mother and sisters were busy preparing food, everyone stopped and turned toward him. A broad smile came over Mandy's face. She wiped her hands on her apron and said, "Lord, have mercy. I don't think I ever seen a finer-looking man.

Now, I'm not gonna hug you, because I don't want to get anything on that purdy suit, but I do want to give my son a kiss." She walked over and kissed Albert on the cheek, and this was followed by kisses and well-wishes from all the sisters.

Leonard hitched the mule to the buggy and brought it around front. Amid a flurry of pats on the back and winks from some of his brothers, Albert put on his long overcoat and black derby-style hat. Vasper handed him an umbrella. "Maybe this'll keep at least some of the rain off," he said with a grin. Amid a light sprinkle of rain, Albert stepped up and took his seat in the buggy, slapped the reins on Toby's back, and off he went.

Alonzo and his soon-to-be bride, Georgianna, along with his sister Kittie and Cleveland Langdon, had departed about forty-five minutes ahead of him for the ceremony. Though the Langdon home was not that far away, the rain had made the dirt paths muddy, and traveling was slower than normal. Fannie had instructed Albert to arrive at a rear entrance to their house, where he was to join Primitive Baptist Elder Johnson in the kitchen for a brief moment of prayer before heading to the front parlor, where the wedding ceremony was to be performed.

By the time Albert arrived just outside the house, the rain had stopped. He tied Toby to a tree not far from the kitchen door. Elder Johnson, dressed in a dark suit and holding a Bible, held out his hand to Albert as he entered the kitchen. He asked Albert about his trip over, and Albert told him that he had made it better than expected.

Albert began running his hand over his hair to make sure that the rough weather had not mussed his combing up too much. Scanning the kitchen, he noticed that much preparation had gone into getting a wonderful meal prepared for them that would be shared later. Because Albert had been so nervous and excited that morning, he had only managed to wolf down a biscuit with some molasses, so he knew that by the time the meal was served, he would be ready to eat.

Elder Johnson explained that everyone had arrived, Fannie

was ready, and he would pray with Albert before walking down to the front parlor, where everyone had assembled. The men closed their eyes, and the preacher took Albert's hands. He then asked for God's blessing and guidance as Albert entered into the sacred bond of marriage. As was customary, he implored the Holy Spirit to enable Albert to be a strong family leader and to use his faith as the guiding principle of everything that he was to do. All during the prayer, Albert could feel his heart beating rapidly.

After the prayer, Elder Johnson looked at Albert and, in a serious tone, asked, "Are you ready?"

Am I ready? thought Albert. *How does anyone feel ready for the big moments in life?*

The preacher turned, and Albert followed him down the hallway to the front parlor.

Fannie's mother stood at the door to greet the men as they entered the parlor filled with several young couples all dressed in their finery. The men mostly wore dark-colored suits, white shirts, and bow ties, as Albert did, while the women were mostly dressed in long dresses with big, puffy sleeves. They had donned big hats in all kinds of shapes: mushroom, sailor, turban. All had flowers, such as roses or daises, stitched on or around the crown. The attendees soon parted to create a pathway of sorts for Fannie, accompanied by her father, to approach where Albert stood next to Elder Johnson.

To Albert, Fannie appeared angelic. Her dark, wavy hair was perfectly coiffed, and her eyes seemed to sparkle as she approached. She had chosen a long, dark-blue satin dress that enveloped her physicality perfectly. Though he felt as jittery as the time he and his brothers had climbed on board the boxcar to coast to the bottom of that hill outside Four Oaks, Albert had no doubt as his eyes met hers that he had made the right decision in asking Fannie to be his wife.

He took his place by her side, and they faced the preacher to recite the vows. This was followed rather quickly by the exchange of rings—Albert had returned to Whittenton's just before the wedding to buy hers—more prayer, and the pronouncement that they were indeed now husband and wife.

Everyone who had come as witnesses to the occasion took a few moments to congratulate the newly wedded couple. This was accompanied by many handshakes, kisses, and pats on the back. Knowing that they were to be at Fellowship Primitive Baptist Church for the morning service, everyone got into either a carriage or buggy, and headed off in the direction of the church. Although the muddied road slowed them down some, the rain thankfully stayed away as the wedding party made its short journey.

Fellowship, a small, white wood-framed church, had been in existence prior to the Civil War. Albert had attended services there several times with the family during his growing-up years, and Fannie had been attending for some time, as well. Upon arriving at the church, the congregants stood and offered their congratulations to the young couple. As was the custom, the men took their places on one side while the women sat on the other. When the service began, Albert found that he was unable to concentrate much on what was said from the pulpit as his mind wandered, thinking about the remainder of the day and what lay ahead in the coming months.

Following the church service, the wedding party returned to the Langdon home in the early afternoon. Fannie's mother instructed the men to stay in the front parlor until everything had been arranged and ready for the wedding meal. Albert engaged in small talk with the other men about what he had accomplished so far and what his immediate plans were. When the men were finally invited in, everyone sat down to one of the most bountiful meals Albert had ever seen. There was beef, pork, and chicken, as well as vegetables in abundance. There were homemade biscuits and gravy. There was plenty of coffee, tea, and water to drink.

Everyone who had attended the wedding ceremony, including Elder Johnson and his wife, had been invited. Several members of Fannie's immediate family were also present, so some people had to fill up their plates and eat in the kitchen or in the front parlor. Conversation was lively, and Albert found himself repeating to the women the same plans he had already relayed to the men in the front parlor. Knowing that another feast would be held at the Stephenson home later in the evening, Albert tried not to overindulge in the food, but it was so delicious that he found it difficult to restrain himself.

Albert and Fannie stayed at the Langdon home talking with the guests, her parents, and her siblings until late in the afternoon. Finally, it became imperative that they leave and head to the Stephenson home so that they could arrive before dark. After thanking the Langdons for everything, including the wonderful meal, Fannie and Albert climbed into the buggy, and the mule began plodding through the mud.

Albert relished his short time alone with Fannie as they rode along with the light of the sun barely visible on the horizon. Finally, the skies had cleared somewhat. Holding the reins with his left hand and Fannie's hand with his right, Albert felt a surge of contentment come over him. It had finally happened. So much had transpired in a short period of time: the land purchase, Mathias's decision to stay on and help him, the fire in Benson, the preparations at the new farmhouse, the engagement, and the wedding. Even though there had been challenges, Albert felt that everything was coming together as it should.

When the newlyweds arrived at the Stephenson house, Albert pulled on the reins to guide Toby to the front porch, where some of his brothers had gathered to help them out and take care of the mule and buggy. The couple then entered the front parlor, where they were greeted by all of Albert's brothers and sisters. Alonzo, Georgianna, Kittie, and Cleveland had departed the Langdon house ahead of Albert and Fannie, and were among the happy faces, as well.

After embracing his mother, Albert leaned down and whispered, "We're still full from eating a big meal at the Langdons'. Can we wait a little while before we eat again?"

Mandy assured him that there was no hurry, so the couple sat down to tell all those who had not been present about the wedding, the church service, and the earlier meal they had enjoyed. After about an hour, Mandy came in from the kitchen and announced that dinner was ready.

Sometime after the death of his father, Albert had accompanied his mother to a furniture store in Smithfield, where she had picked out a solid oak dining table and eight oak dining chairs with genuine leather seats. The furniture was finished in a high gloss that accentuated the attractiveness. They'd also purchased a golden-oak sideboard with a French bevel plate mirror that had richly decorated carvings around it. There were drawers for the flatware, and it had a linen cupboard at the bottom. In preparation for the meal, Mandy and some of Albert's sisters had placed a white tablecloth on the extended table and set the table with fine china pieces adorned with scalloped edges and clusters of pink roses.

Huge platters of meats, vegetables, and fresh-baked biscuits now sat in the middle of the table. Although Albert couldn't imagine how he could have eaten another bite when they had arrived, as he looked over the table loaded with delicious smelling food, he suddenly felt hungry again. After Leonard said a brief blessing, Mandy indicated that Albert and Fannie would sit at the main dining table, pointing out that six others could join them, and everyone else would need to eat in the kitchen. Mandy handed out plates from the sideboard, and those eating in the kitchen piled their plates high. Then Albert and Fannie, Charles and Flossie Mae, Alonzo and Georgianna, and Kittie and Cleveland all took their places at the big oak table.

As the dinner conversation progressed, Albert ate slowly so as not to fill up too quickly. He realized the time and preparation that had gone into getting the meal prepared, so he did not want to disappoint his mother by not eating a fair amount.

After the main meal, Mandy pointed toward the sideboard, where she had placed a chocolate layered cake and a pound cake for dessert, and began asking everyone to make a selection. Albert and Fannie both chose slices of the pound cake, and while the guests made their selections, Albert's sisters Mary and Callie came in from the kitchen to pour cups of coffee all around. Finally, Fannie announced that she had eaten so much that she probably didn't need to eat for the next three days.

Albert put his right arm around her, his left hand on his stomach, and said, "That makes two of us."

Everyone laughed, and Alonzo spoke up, "It's a sin to eat that much."

This elicited more laughter from the stuffed guests. Albert thought to himself that it couldn't have been too much of a sin, because they would most likely do it again and soon, if given the chance.

One by one, those who needed to travel rose from the table or came out of the kitchen to say their good-byes to Albert and Fannie and to express their thanks to Mandy for a most glorious meal. The previously cloudy skies had cleared, and an almost-full moon offered the travelers some needed light as they traveled in the dark back to their respective homes.

Those who remained began helping to clear the table and wash the dishes, except for the newly married couple, who finally, after a day filled with ceremony and celebration, retired to Albert's bedroom for their first night together as man and wife.

CHAPTER ELEVEN

THE BEGINNING OF A NEW LIFE

Over the course of the following weeks, Fannie often accompanied Albert to their new home, where she spent her days on her knees scrubbing the wooden floors with water and lye soap, cleaning windows, and putting up curtains to give them some privacy. After cleaning the house as best they could, and after having moved in a few basic furnishings, Albert and Fannie took up residence at their home in mid-March, just a few days shy of the arrival of spring.

One cool, windy morning, Fannie heard a knock at one of the side doors on the right side of the house. Through the window she could see a thin, middle-aged woman in a light-blue bonnet. The man accompanying her, dressed in overalls and a wide-brimmed brown hat, stood behind her and to the right. Fannie opened the door, upon which the woman said, "Morning. I'm Lillie, and this here's my husband T. R. Mathias, the one that sold you all this house and land, is his brother." She nodded her head back toward her husband.

"Oh. Y'all come in," Fannie said, opening the door wider for them to pass through.

"We know you're busy, but we just wanted to come by a minute to get acquainted and let you know if there's anything we can do to help y'all, just let us know," Lillie said. "We live away in the western part of the state in Alleghany County—that's where Mathias come from—and we come to stay a few days with the family. Our boy, Talmadge, is down at the house with the family."

"I 'spect Albert's about the plan'ation somewhere," Fannie told T. R., "but I'm not exactly sure where. You're welcome to walk about, and look for him and Mathias, if you want."

T. R. appeared to welcome the opportunity to get outside with the menfolk and leave the women to themselves.

Fannie talked about their recent marriage, how she and Albert had a lot to do to get the house ready, and that Albert had a lot of planning to make so he could get started in farming. Lillie chatted about the rather large Caudill family back home, what a long trip it was to get to Pleasant Grove from Alleghany County, and about their four-year-old son. Before the women realized it, an hour had gone by. T. R. came back to the house, upon which the Caudills said their good-byes and walked back down the dirt road.

A few days later, Albert and Fannie learned through Mathias of the tragic death of T. R. and Lillie's son, Talmadge. Mathias explained that the boy had gotten sick, and that they had tried everything they knew to do, but by the time a doctor could be summoned to the house, the child had breathed his last. They were not sure what had ailed Talmadge, but Mathias guessed it must have been something like diphtheria from the description that he gave of the last days of the boy's life. Upon hearing of the death, Fannie and Albert took the wagon and rode the short distance down to the house to pay their respects.

As Fannie sat with Lillie and the other women of the house in the living room to offer her condolences, Mathias asked Albert to step back into the kitchen, where his brother T. R. sat at the table with Mathias's son, Andrew. Albert placed his hand on T. R.'s shoulder and then sat down with the men. For a few moments, no one spoke. Then, Mathias looked at Albert. "We need to bury the boy somewhere . . . and we was thinking . . ."

Albert did not wait for him to complete the question. "You absolutely can lay the boy to rest here. No need to worry about that." Albert could almost feel the collective sigh of relief.

Mathias went on, "A while back, my daughter Melissa, who you ain't met yet, lost her baby. We buried the infant up yon' in the flat area. There's even a little tombstone there. Says, 'Infant Burgess,' because her husband's name is Luther Burgess."

T. R. and Mathias constructed a small wooden coffin for

Talmadge, and before the lid was nailed shut, everyone gathered around the coffin to take a last look. As the family wept, Albert wondered how he would have felt under similar circumstances, and hoped that when he and Fannie had children, no such fate would befall one of theirs.

After the coffin was fastened shut, T. R. and Mathias carried it to a mule-drawn wagon just outside the back door. Then the men climbed up on the wagon seat and began the short journey to the graveyard in the flat land where Albert had been told the infant Burgess was buried. Mathias had instructed everyone to wait for a while until they had time to dig a grave before coming for the burial. So, Fannie and Albert continued to sit with the family to provide support. After an hour, everyone loaded up in either a wagon or a buggy to join the men at the grave.

Amidst a cold temperature and a northerly wind, the mourners stood around the small grave. T. R. recited the twenty-third psalm, after which the men lowered the coffin into the grave with ropes. Because of the cold and wind, everyone departed the gravesite quickly thereafter, while T. R. and Mathias stayed behind to fill in the grave with dirt.

Albert and Fannie rode back to the house in silence. A few days later, T. R. and Lillie stopped by to say their good-byes, stating that they needed to get back home. Albert and Fannie would not see them again.

***

Much of March was spent breaking some of the land using the mules and plows that Albert had purchased. However, some days were so wet from rainfall that it was too muddy to plow. Many farmers were beginning to use commercial fertilizers such as guano, and Albert read as much as he could to try to understand what best to use for his first cotton crop on the farm. A lot of farmers relied on the natural fertilizer of manure. Only problem was, Albert had no manure, since the only animals he had were the mules, and they didn't produce enough manure to be of benefit.

"They's a farm I know of just over in Wake County that probly has a lot of manure because of the large number of cows and pigs the owner has," Mathias announced one morning as they hitched up the plows to the two mules.

In April, after the men had broken all the land that would be used for planting, Albert told Mathias that they'd take the wagon over to that farm to see if they could get some manure to bring back.

On a sunny, warm spring morning, with the leaves on the trees beginning to bud out, Albert and Mathias arrived at the farm. Albert noticed a few cows and pigs roaming in a grassy field next to the barn. A man by the last name of Adams greeted them while he worked out front. Adams was a short, stocky man who appeared to have a lot of upper-body strength. *Probably from years of using shovels and pitch forks*, Albert surmised. He noticed that Adams was missing a tooth, and wondered if he'd been kicked in the mouth or if the tooth had just rotted out. Meanwhile, a strong odor of manure came from inside the barn.

Albert had planned what he was going to say on the way over in the wagon. "I bought a farm not too far away over in Johnston County, and I'm looking to raise some cotton this year," he ventured. "I was hoping you might have some manure I could buy from you to help fertilize the land."

Adams looked at Albert and took a few seconds before answering. "Well, to tell you the truth, I'd be happy just to let y'all clean the manure from my stables, and you can have it for nothin'. Otherwise, I'd just have to shovel it out myself and put it in a pile behind the barn." He pointed to an area where Albert could see the edge of a manure pile from where he stood. "I'm not raising any cotton right now . . . just some corn and such to feed my hogs and cows, so you're welcome to take as much as you want. Saves me some shoveling."

This was exactly what Albert had hoped for. Mathias and he would do Adams a favor by cleaning out his stables, and they'd get the manure for free.

After thanking Adams, Albert and Mathias grabbed the two shovels they had tossed in the wagon before heading out, led Jack the mule and the wagon close to the front entrance of the barn, and began the task of shoveling the manure into the wagon. With both men shoveling quickly, they filled the wagon with as much manure as they thought Jack could pull. Upon finishing their task, Albert found Adams in a nearby wooded area where a sow had recently delivered a litter of about eight piglets. "If it's all right with you, we'll get this load put out and be back sometime tomorrow for some more," Albert said.

"Looky here," Adams said. "I won't shore if that sow would have much luck this time. Had her for a long time. But she done pretty good. Hope she'll keep them all. Sometimes there'll be a runt or two in the litter that won't make it, but they all looking purdy good right now." His lips widened into a grin that revealed the missing tooth. "You thought about raising hogs? You'll need some meat if you's planning on a family."

Albert told him that they'd had some pigs on his family farm, but that he wasn't sure yet what he'd do. At the moment, he told Adams, he just needed to concentrate on getting cotton planted to have some income. Adams nodded in agreement, and Albert turned back to where Mathias waited on the wagon seat.

On the trip back to the farm, Albert told Mathias that he needed a manure spreader so the manure could be spread quickly and evenly. Otherwise, they'd have to do it all by hand, which could be time-consuming, given the fact that they'd need to return for more manure. Mathias mentioned a man he knew just a couple of miles away whom he thought had a spreader that he might be willing to allow them to use.

After the two men arrived back with the manure, Albert went in the house to let Fannie know that they would be taking the buggy to a nearby farm to see about getting a manure spreader. He and Mathias then unhitched Jack from the wagon and subsequently hitched the mule to the buggy. Mathias went into the barn to lead the other gray mule, Maude, out, and tied her behind the buggy. This was in case they could get the spreader that day, and one mule could be used to pull the spreader back to the farm.

After the men arrived in the vicinity of the farm where Mathias thought the spreader might be, Albert spotted a path through a wooded area to the right. The men followed the path up to a large, two-story house flanked by a barn on the right and a smokehouse on the left. Albert immediately noticed that whoever lived there kept the grounds in immaculate condition.

Two young boys ran around from behind the house, and Albert heard one of them call out for his daddy. As Albert and Mathias pulled up a few feet from the front porch, a tall, lanky man with a black beard and thick black hair stepped out on the porch. The man immediately recognized Mathias, and told the men to come up and sit on the porch in the wooden chairs to the right and left of the front door. Mathias introduced Albert as they took their seats, and for the next several minutes he explained to the man, Cyrus Johnson, all about the sale of his farm to Albert, how they were preparing the land to plant some cotton, and that he was looking to borrow a manure spreader.

"I'd be mighty grateful and would be glad to pay you, sir, for the use of your spreader, if it's convenient and all," said Albert.

"Actually, I was thinking about selling that spreader," Cyrus told Albert. "I'm using more guano now and don't have as much need for it as I used to. I could sell it to you for half what I gave for it. Why don't you come take a look at it, and maybe we can work something out." Johnson stood, stepped off the porch, and began walking toward the nearby barn.

Albert and Mathias followed him inside, and Johnson opened the barn door widely so there would be enough light for Albert to examine the spreader. Albert's eyes immediately went to the side of the wagon, where it read BONANZA SPREADER, WORLD'S BEST WAGON BOX SPREADER in red letters. As Albert walked around the wagon, Cyrus pointed out the mechanism at the rear of the wagon that would disperse the manure. He assured Albert that all the parts were working fine, and told him the price that he'd be willing to accept for the wagon.

Without answering immediately, Albert walked around the wagon again and put his hands on the spreading mechanism. He rubbed the back of his head and finally said, "Uh huh."

As Albert began another walk around the wagon, Cyrus, perhaps sensing Albert's uncertainty, said, "Tell you what. I've been knowing Mathias a good while, and seeing as how you all will be working together, I would like to offer the spreader to you for twenty-five dollars less than what I already told you."

Albert appeared to think over the offer for a few seconds more. Finally, he looked at Johnson and said, "Well, it looks like a good spreader, and you've made a good offer. I ain't got the cash to pay you right now, but if it'd be all right with you, we could come back by in the next day or two and pay you for it."

Cyrus let him know that would be perfectly fine, and Albert and Mathias hitched Maude up to the spreader. Albert told Mathias to ride on the spreader while he took the buggy back to the farm. After thanking Johnson, the two men headed back down the wooded pathway toward the main road, Mathias in the lead with the spreader.

After several trips back and forth to the Adams farm to get more manure, Albert and Mathias managed to get all the suitable land fertilized. Despite Fannie's complaints about the smell, Albert felt good that he had been able to obtain the manure spreader at a good price. He was optimistic that a good cotton harvest would easily pay for what he had spent. His optimism would prove to serve him well, not only in that first year of farming, but in the years to follow.

CHAPTER TWELVE

MAYLON AND PERCY

Working together, Albert and Mathias managed to get several acres of cotton planted that first spring. After they thinned out the rows of young plants, it became a matter of keeping the weeds from taking over. At times Albert would hire a couple of other men to come and help with chopping or weeding. As the cotton plants began to grow in the heat of the summer, Albert often turned to *The Progressive Farmer* to read articles on raising crops and farm animals. Albert decided to pay the dollar subscription price so he could get a copy delivered each month to the nearby Stephenson Post Office that stood near the Harnett County line.

Confident that the cotton crop would bring in some much-needed income in the fall, he began thinking about raising some animals. After all, on his family farm they'd had pigs, cows, goats, and sheep. He had learned a great deal over the years about how to feed and take care of the livestock.

"Calves," Albert announced to Mathias one morning as the man arrived for work. Albert was finishing off a ham biscuit that Fannie had handed him on his way out the back door. Mathias gave Albert a puzzled look. After swallowing another bite of the biscuit, Albert explained, "I've been thinking a lot about getting into raising some calves for sale. I believe it'd be a good decision, based on everything I've read."

Mathias turned his head slightly to the right and squinted. "Well, where would you put them? I don't think they'd last wandering around all the time, and they ain't much room under that barn shelter." The shelter that Mathias had built a while back was not closed in, nor did it have any stalls or pens. It just amounted to something for the mules to get under during inclement weather.

"I thought I'd hire some men to build some walls to enclose the shelter so the wind and rain won't be able to get inside. Maybe build some stalls for livestock, too," Albert said. "I was thinking that I'd get them to build a smokehouse. We'll need somewhere to put fresh pork." Albert pointed to an area behind the house that he thought would be a good place for the smokehouse. "I'm a-thinking that the best time to build might be in the fall. You and me will be picking cotton while the building is going on. My brother Charles and me, we have to get my daddy's estate settled. Once that's done, then maybe I can get some things done here."

Fresh pork would not be the only source of food for Albert and Fannie. Albert and Mathias had planted a small vegetable garden in the late spring. During the summer months while the men tended the cotton crop, Fannie went up and down the garden rows picking peas, butterbeans, tomatoes, squash, and gathering roasting-ear corn.

In addition to the vegetable garden, Alonzo had given the couple four hens and a rooster when they'd moved in the house. The chickens had roamed freely in the yard and under the house—that was, until a fox showed up and killed two of the hens. After that, Albert and Mathias built a small lean-to shelter and enclosed it with some wire mesh fencing Albert had found in nearby Angier, a community in neighboring Harnett County that had sprung up in the latter part of the 1800s. The fencing proved to be good enough to keep foxes and other varmints away from the hens, who began laying eggs. Whenever Albert went into Woodsboro, he would pick up a small bag of grain to feed the chickens. Fannie also threw vegetable scraps from the table over the fence for them.

In a short while, young chicks began to hatch. As the young chickens reached maturity, Fannie could occasionally be seen grabbing one, wringing its neck, or chopping the head off with a hatchet. She prepared meals of fried chicken and chicken stew for the hungry men when they came in midday. Albert often remarked that when the windows were open, he could tell what she was cooking before he set foot in the kitchen.

Additionally, Albert built a couple of rabbit boxes that he

placed next to the woods behind the house. On occasion, he would bait the rabbits with vegetable scraps or pieces of apple. Later, if he saw a rabbit trapped inside, he would raise the trap door of the box, and as the rabbit attempted to escape, he would grab it, place his thumb on one side of its neck and his forefinger on the other, and snap its neck. After skinning the rabbit, Albert would take the carcass inside to Fannie, who would use the meat along with potatoes and carrots to cook a tasty rabbit stew.

Albert would also sometimes kill a squirrel or two with his rifle. Both Albert and Fannie highly regarded squirrel meat. Fannie learned that the meat tasted less gamey if she soaked it in buttermilk for a while, after which she would coat the meat in flour and fry it in the bacon fat that she had saved in a tin can on a corner of the wood stove.

***

One morning in the early fall, Albert hitched Jack to the wagon and headed toward Woodsboro to check on the availability and price of some lumber for the improvements to the barn and for building a smokehouse. At a sawmill there, Albert told the man charged with helping him that he was looking for some carpenters.

"They's a couple of brothers that lives near here that does good carpenter work," the man said. "They may, if they don't have nothin' else to do right now, be able to help you out."

After the man explained to Albert how to get to the brothers' house, in a matter of about ten minutes the men found themselves standing on the front porch of a small white house that looked as if it has been repainted recently. Albert knocked on the door, and a man around thirty years old opened the screen door. About Albert's height, the man ran his hand over his unkempt, dark, wavy hair. Albert thought that he must not have shaved in several days, judging by the thick black stubble on his face.

The man wiped his hand on his overalls before extending it to Albert for a shake. Albert introduced himself along with Mathias. "We looking for Mr. Byrd. Would that be you?"

"That depends. I'm Maylon Byrd, and my brother Percy lives here, too. Which one you looking for?"

"Well, to tell you the truth, we're looking for you both. Man up yonder at the sawmill says you boys are good carpenters."

Maylon stepped out onto the porch and closed the screen door. He ran his hand over his hair again. "Percy's the real carpenter here. I just do what he tells me. Percy!"

From around the corner of the house a slightly younger, perhaps wirier version of Maylon appeared.

"These here fellers is looking to get some carpentry work done," Maylon said. "This here's Albert, and I believe you said Mathias, right?"

Mathias nodded, and Percy stepped up on the porch to shake hands with the two men. Albert noticed the roughness of his hands, a product no doubt of frequent manual labor. Where Maylon's appearance was unkempt, Percy sported a clean-shaven face, and his hair, though wavy like his brother's, was well-groomed.

"What you looking to do?" Percy asked, looking up at Albert, who stood about six inches taller.

Albert explained what he needed done at the barn and went on to talk about the possibility of building a smokehouse. As Albert talked about his plans, Percy alternated glances between the wagon parked near the porch and Albert's face. Maylon stepped down on the ground and took a seat on the porch, letting Percy do the talking.

When Albert had finished describing the work he could offer the brothers, Percy said, "I see you done bought some lumber. You looking to use that for your barn?"

Albert said that although the planks that he and Mathias had picked up at the sawmill would not be nearly enough to complete the work at the barn, he thought they could at least use them to get a start. Albert explained that it would be time to start picking cotton soon, so he would be depending on them to work at the barn on their own, and he could make arrangements for them to go back and forth to the sawmill to pick up more lumber, as needed.

"Let me see . . ." Percy paused and looked toward his brother, who had taken out his pocketknife to whittle a small stick he had picked up off the ground. Maylon continued whittling without looking up. "Well, seeing as how we ain't got another job we're bound to do right now, we might can help you out," Percy said. "'Course that depends on what you can offer us for our work." At this, Maylon stopped whittling and looked toward the men.

"What do you normally get for a week's worth of carpentry?" Albert asked.

"Hmmm . . ." Percy paused again and looked toward his brother. "On our last job we got twenty dollars apiece each week."

Out of the corner of his eye Albert saw Maylon's face turn away. He sensed that Percy was not telling the truth, and he knew of no one paying twenty dollars a week. He realized he had to come up with a counteroffer that might entice them to do the work, yet would be more in line with what he could afford to pay. "Well, sir, I believe that's a bit too steep for me, seeing as how I'm just starting out and all," Albert said. "Now my wife, Fannie, is a good cook—a very good cook. What if we feed y'all twice a day, and I offer you ten dollars each for the week?" Albert watched for a reaction from both brothers, but Maylon had once again turned his attention to his whittling. Percy looked off in the distance as if pondering his next move.

"Well now, I think we can maybe come down some, but ten apiece sounds mighty low to me for all we'll be doing. If you can feed us twice a day, that'd be good, but we need to live just like everybody else. They's a piece of land we been thinking about buying, and—"

Albert stopped him. "I tell you what. The man up at the sawmill says you all do good work. I'm willing to give you twelve dollars a week apiece and feed you two meals every day you work." Albert tightened his lips. "That's about the best I can afford to do right now."

Percy took a minute before he spoke. He looked over at Maylon. "Maylon, what you think? Twelve dollars apiece for a week of work and two meals a day?"

Maylon put down his knife on the porch, looked at his brother, and gave a slight nod of agreement.

"Well, Mr. Albert, I think you done got a deal here." Percy reached out his hand to Albert to confirm the deal with a handshake. Albert, glad to have the business dealings out of the way, told the brothers that he would send Mathias back the next day with the wagon to get more lumber, and that the brothers could meet him at the sawmill and follow him back to his house. With that, Albert and Mathias climbed back up on the wagon seat and headed back toward the sawmill to make arrangements for the purchase of more lumber, and then back home.

The next morning, under cloudy skies and with slightly cooler weather, Mathias set out early for the sawmill. Meanwhile, Albert walked about in the cotton field to see how much longer it might be before they could begin picking their crop. Then he turned his attention to the barn and tried to envision what the brothers would need to do once they arrived.

About midmorning, Albert looked up the dirt road to see Mathias returning with a load of lumber on the wagon, followed by the Byrd brothers in their wagon carrying a load, as well. Albert pointed toward the shelter as the two wagons approached the house. The Byrd brothers jumped down from their wagon seat and followed Albert under the shelter, where he explained what needed to be done. Percy told him that the first order of business would be to enclose the shelter on all sides except for a wide opening at the front and the back. There would be an open area in the middle, with the stalls constructed on each side.

Albert liked how Percy explained step by step what the brothers planned to do. "I know it'll take y'all a good while on the barn, but at some point, as I mentioned, I want to get a smokehouse built," Albert told the Byrd brothers. He indicated that the brothers were to follow him to the back of the house to an area Albert thought would be good for the construction of the smokehouse. Percy agreed that it would be a good location and that once the barn was finished, he felt sure they could get the smokehouse built.

Maylon, who'd remained mostly quiet while the men discussed the plans, sniffed and said, "Something shore smells good." The men were standing close enough to the kitchen to catch the aroma of Fannie's cooking.

"My wife's been cooking all morning. Smells to me like it's getting to be about dinner time," said Albert. "I'll bring a pan of water and soap, and y'all can get washed up and ready to eat." Albert couldn't help but notice that Maylon's expression had changed from serious to childlike delight. Albert supposed that the two men weren't accustomed to good homecooked meals like Fannie prepared.

Mathias took the time to walk down to the house for the midday meal. Albert, meanwhile, went inside to find Fannie, wearing a long white apron, hovering over the coal-and-wood stove that Albert had gotten secondhand from Charles, who'd recently bought his wife, Flossie Mae, a new Acme steel range that had six holes for cooking. After Maylon and Percy followed Albert into the kitchen, Albert explained that they would be working on the barn for the next several weeks and that they would be joining them for meals each day they worked.

Fannie opened the oven door and removed a pan of freshly baked biscuits. "Everything's about done," she told Albert. "Why don't you draw up a bucket of water from the well?"

Albert picked up a water basin and headed back outside to lower the bucket into the well. Albert drew up a bucket, poured the water into the basin, and took it back inside, where he filled four cups with the cool water. Then, he picked up a cake of lye soap from the sink and brought it on the porch for the Byrd brothers to use in washing up.

After Fannie put plates and flatware on the kitchen table, she dipped up a mixture of tomatoes and okra in one bowl and a bowl of corn in another. She had fried a whole chicken, and now arranged the pieces on a platter. Then she placed the biscuits on a plate and put a small jar of molasses alongside it on the table.

Albert called for the brothers to come in the kitchen.

"I declare, Miss Fannie, I don't think I've seen a finer meal," said Maylon, who seemed ready to dive headfirst into the meal.

"I hope y'all find it to be fitting," said Fannie. They all took their seats at the table, and Fannie said, "Now first, let me say a blessing."

The men lowered their eyes and Fannie offered up a quick prayer of thanks for the food they were about to eat. As soon as the prayer was over, Maylon, wide-eyed in wonder at the meal before him, continued, "I ain't et no fried chicken in a coon's age. And fresh biscuits and molasses . . . why, Miss Fannie, you done spoiled us already."

The others laughed as they passed around the chicken, vegetables, and biscuits. Albert could not help but notice that the Byrd brothers did not hold back from piling their plates high.

During the meal, conversation centered around getting to know each other's families. Albert and Fannie each talked about the big families they had come from, while Percy described how both their mother and daddy had died at a young age. He explained that there had been two older sisters who had their own families somewhere in Pleasant Grove, and that he and Maylon had practically raised themselves after the loss of their parents.

Albert felt compassion for the two men, now understanding why getting a good meal like the one before them was probably a rare occurrence. He watched as Maylon quickly devoured every-thing on his plate and then poured a small puddle of molasses in the middle. He began sopping a biscuit with the molasses. "Better'n a cake," he said in between bites.

Fannie couldn't help but grin as she watched Maylon wolf down three biscuits in rapid fashion.

After the meal was over and the Byrd brothers had expressed their thanks several times, the men retired to the living room to sit for a few minutes before heading out to start their work. Fannie could be heard clearing the table and washing the plates, pots, and pans. At the same time, the men talked further about how to begin the work on the barn.

Over the course of the next few days, Maylon and Percy showed up early each morning to savor Fannie's breakfasts, which often included either sausage or ham, eggs, biscuits, and grits. As soon as they finished one meal, Fannie would begin preparing the next.

Cotton-picking time soon came and occupied most of the working hours for Albert and Mathias. Albert managed to find and hire a couple of men to help with the picking. Seeing that he could trust the Byrd brothers to work steadily, Albert and the other men worked up and down the cotton rows planted directly behind the house.

One cool, cloudy morning in late October, Albert was at the far end of the cotton patch when he heard the ringing of the farm bell. Mathias and he had fastened the bell to a rectangular wooden frame they had built just feet away from the back door to the kitchen. Fifty pounds in weight and sixteen inches in diameter at the bottom, the bell could be heard all the way over in the flat land, where Albert and Mathias worked. Fannie would sometimes ring the bell to let them know it was time to eat, but on this morning, Albert knew that it wasn't mealtime.

Looking toward the house, he saw Fannie waving for him to come. Albert dropped his sack and practically ran toward the house. As he got closer to the backyard, Fannie began pointing toward the barn.

Maylon and Percy had brought their own tools when they had begun work weeks earlier, including handsaws, hammers, nails, a wooden ruler, wood planes, and a wooden extension ladder that could reach twenty-three feet in height. Albert had indicated to the men that in addition to the stalls and outside walls that needed to be built, he wanted an area above the stalls that could be used as a loft to store cotton or hay.

Out of breath and without taking the time to ask Fannie why she had rung the bell, Albert ran to the barn, where he saw that the extension ladder had fallen and Maylon was sprawled out on the ground next to it.

"He was working up on the ladder, and I was inside the barn, so I didn't see him fall," Percy said, his eyes flicking back and forth from his brother on the ground to Albert. Percy breathed shakily and began running a trembling hand through his hair.

Albert stooped down next to Maylon, who was lying on his stomach with his head turned to the left. Albert intuitively felt that something wasn't right, and without voicing it to Percy, he thought that perhaps Maylon had hit the ground so hard that the impact had killed him. He felt for the jugular vein in Maylon's throat. "I feel a heartbeat," Albert said, and looked up to see the worry in Percy's eyes. To Albert, it looked as if Percy's mind had already jumped to the possibility that his brother was gone. Albert tried to speak calmly. "Let's turn him over, and see if you and me can carry him to the house."

Percy squatted down next to Albert, and the two men slowly turned Maylon over. Other than the faint pulse Albert had felt, Maylon showed no other signs of life. Albert picked up the upper part of Maylon's body while Percy lifted his legs and feet. Awkwardly, the two men carried Maylon to the back of the house, where Fannie waited to open the back door. She instructed them to take Maylon to their bed.

Albert and Percy first laid the upper part of Maylon's body on the metal-framed bed, followed by his legs and feet. Percy continued to hover over his brother, rubbing his forehead and calling, "Maylon, can you hear me?"

Albert looked at Fannie and shook his head from side to side, beginning to fear that even though Maylon was alive, some permanent damage may have been done. Just how extensive that damage might be remained to be seen.

Fannie went into the kitchen and returned with a basin of water and a cloth. Wetting the cloth, she began patting Maylon's face. "Percy, I wonder if he broke any bones," Fannie said. "Why don't you and Albert run your hands over him to see if you can feel any that might be?"

Albert felt Maylon's arms, chest, and shoulders while Percy softly went up and down his legs and ankles. "I ain't no doctor, but I can't feel no broken bones," said Percy.

"Me neither," added Albert. "Let's just give him a little while, and he may come to."

At that, Fannie returned to the kitchen to continue preparing the midday meal. Albert and Percy each got a chair from the kitchen table and pulled it up next to the side of the bed. Percy continued to wet the cloth that Fannie had brought, and every few minutes he would speak to his brother in the hope it would elicit a response.

After about an hour had passed, Albert tapped Percy on the shoulder. There was movement in the fingers of Maylon's right hand. Then, the man lifted his hand and placed it on his chest.

"Maylon, can you hear me?" Percy asked with a tinge of excitement. He repeated, "Maylon, can you hear me?" Maylon's eyes slowly began to open. Percy stood up from his chair. "Maylon, you fell from the ladder. Can you understand me? Are you all right?"

Maylon let out a low-pitched groan. His head moved up and down as a sign that he could understand his brother.

"Now, don't you worry, Maylon," Percy said. You took a hard fall, and it must've knocked the breath out of you. You just lie here and rest now. You'll be all right."

Albert wasn't sure if Percy's last statement was more to reassure himself or his brother. At any rate, he was glad at least that Maylon was conscious and able to communicate a little. Albert stood and motioned for Percy to follow him into the kitchen. "You reckon we might better summon a doctor?" he asked.

"Well, I thought about that, but I know my brother to be a tough feller, so I think maybe we can just wait a little while to see if he don't get some better," Percy answered.

Albert nodded in agreement and decided that he would leave it up to Percy to make that decision.

Fannie brought in a cup of broth from the chicken she had boiled that morning. Albert and Percy propped up Maylon's head with the two feather pillows on the bed, and Percy began feeding him spoonfuls of the warm broth. Then Fannie brought in small plates of boiled chicken and baked sweet potatoes for Percy and Maylon, and Albert ate in the kitchen.

Gradually, the paleness in Maylon's face was replaced by a more natural, fleshy color, and he began talking more. After the meal was over and Albert had come back in to check on him, Maylon told them how he had probably set the ladder on some uneven ground and had carelessly climbed up without checking to see if it was firmly anchored. He barely remembered falling, he told Percy and Albert, and he had no recollection of them bringing him into the house. Albert insisted that he remain in the house until it was time to go home and that he need not worry; he would be paid for his time anyway.

"Tell you what," Albert said. "I'll have Mathias help Percy with the sawing and hammering for the rest of the day. I want you to stay in the bed for as long as you need to. Then, if you feel like it, maybe you can get up and walk about a little to try to get your strength back."

Percy expressed his agreement that this was the best thing for Maylon to do, and so the men left Fannie to wait on Maylon as needed while they returned to their work.

As Albert began moving up and down the rows of cotton, he thought about how the morning's outcome could have been different. What if Maylon had been severely injured? What if he had been killed? These were things that he had not contemplated prior to taking up farming, but he had learned a lesson that day. He would need to be more keenly aware of safety when hiring others to do work. By the end of the afternoon, Maylon seemed to have returned to normal, and he let Albert know that he'd be ready to work the following day.

It was several more weeks before the Byrd brothers completed the work on the barn. Albert admired the brothers' workmanship and understood why they had been recommended to him. The barn now had six stalls, a new floor above the stalls for storage, and a new roof. The entire barn, except for the middle hallway area, was now enclosed with wooden planks.

Now mid-November, some days felt as if they were in the middle of winter. Albert wanted the smokehouse built, but he also knew that with winter approaching, the availability of good working days could be few. It was decided among the three men that they would begin building the following March.

As Albert watched the Byrd brothers' wagon heading up the dirt road back toward their home, he stood for a moment reflecting on how fortunate he had been to get the two carpenters, how relieved he had been that Maylon had not been badly hurt or killed, and how he had managed to make a little money off his first cotton crop, which would see them through the winter months. Now that the barn was complete, he hoped to start raising calves soon.

During the cold, long nights of winter, he would have much to think about as he looked toward the coming year.

CHAPTER THIRTEEN

EXCITING NEWS

The Byrd brothers returned as planned in March to begin work on the smokehouse. Albert pointed out again where he wanted it to be built. "When it's cold," he told Maylon and Percy, "we won't have far to walk."

As the brothers began sawing the boards they would need to get started, Albert and Mathias turned their attention to getting the land ready for growing cotton and corn again. Albert planned to sow some oats, wheat, and grass of some sort, since he was thinking ahead to bringing in a few cows. He scanned advertisements in newspapers and in *The Progressive Farmer*, and in April set out with Mathias in the wagon to two different farms in Wake County.

At one location, Albert bought a young Holstein bull, mostly black except for white on the lower legs and underbelly. He and Mathias tied the bull with a rope to the back of the wagon and made a two-mile trip to another farm, where he managed to get a good price for three Holstein cows. All three of the young cows sported stylish black-and-white color patterns. The men tied the three cows together, one behind the other. With the bull fastened to the left rear of the wagon and the three cows to the right, Albert and Mathias made the slow trip back to the farm. When they came within sight of the house, they saw that Maylon and Percy had stopped work long enough to watch the men lead the animals out toward the barn. Even Fannie, who most likely had heard the mooing of the cows, stopped whatever she had been doing to come out on the porch to watch.

Knowing that he had no fencing, Albert told Mathias that the cattle could roam freely in the grassy area that extended from the right side of the barn down to a wooded area with a creek the animals could drink from. After talking with the farmer who sold him the cows, Albert decided that the bull and cows would need to be kept separated for a while. "If them cows get pregnant now, the calves will be born in the dead of winter. Be better they'd be born in the spring," Albert told Mathias.

Thus, the plan was to keep the bull and cows apart until July. At night, the cattle were housed in separate stables inside the barn. During the morning hours, the cows were allowed to roam. In the afternoon, the cows were brought back in the barn while the bull was turned outside. Albert talked to Maylon and Percy about building some gates that could be put at each end of the open hallway area in the barn where the animals could stay during the daytime when they were not outside grazing.

Albert and Mathias made a short trip to Woodsboro a few days after the arrival of the bull and cows to purchase cowbells. Albert explained that the cowbells would keep any harmful animals away from the cattle and also let the men know where the cows were when it was time to drive them to the barn at the end of the day.

Despite the periodic interruption of spring rains, Maylon and Percy were able to complete the smokehouse and the gates for the barn by the end of April. Inside the smokehouse they had nailed some long poles that ran from the front to the back. Later, when sausage was made, Albert would be able to hang the sausage up on the poles to dry out. The men also suspended thin wires from the ceiling with hooks at the end on which to hang hams or shoulders. The Byrd brothers also built a big wooden box that they placed at the rear of the interior, where cuts of salted meat could be stored.

After the brothers completed all their work, Albert gave them a few dollars extra in addition to the pay they had coming to them. He also thanked them repeatedly for having done such a good job and promised that if he needed any more building, he would most certainly send for them to come back.

Now that Albert had the responsibility of growing and

harvesting his crops along with taking care of the bull and cows, he found himself beginning most every day before the sun appeared on the horizon. Likewise, he often came in long after sunset. The only respite from field work came on Sundays, and even then he had to make sure the bull and cows were turned out to graze.

"You're working yourself into an early grave," Fannie often told him with a hint of a smile on her face. She had to coax him into taking a few hours on Sunday to accompany her to church or to take some time to visit with family.

Changes had been taking place in Albert's family as he busied himself more and more on the farm. His brother Alonzo had married his girlfriend Georgianna, and his sister Callie had given birth to a daughter named Verona. Charles and Flossie Mae had also welcomed the arrival of a new baby. In November, Albert and Fannie witnessed the wedding of Mathias to his new wife Mary, whom he had been courting for a while.

As Albert had expected upon Mathias remarrying, an evening came when he approached Albert before Christmas to let him know that he and Mary had decided to move. Pretending to be somewhat surprised, Albert asked, "Where y'all thinking about going?"

"Well, some of my family is over around the Smithfield area, so we got the chance to get us a place in Selma," he said. Selma was another one of those towns that, like Benson, had sprung up along the railroad line. "Some of the children is coming to help us get our stuff moved, and we ought to be out sometime after Christmas and before the first of the year."

"Hmmm . . ." Albert began, searching for the words he wanted to stay. "Of course, you know y'all are welcome to stay on as long as you'd like . . . but I understand. This will be a new start for you."

"Plus, I ain't as young as I used to be," Mathias offered as further explanation. Albert knew that Mathias was in his sixties and that doing hard farm labor was probably getting more challenging. The men then took some time to reminisce about the land transaction and all that Mathias had done to help Albert get started on the farm, for which, as Albert explained, he would be eternally grateful.

A few days after Christmas, Albert spotted two wagons in front of the house in which the Caudills had been living, and watched from afar as they loaded the furnishings that Mathias and Mary would be taking to Smithfield. Fannie cooked a big meal and invited them all to come and eat before heading out on the long journey to Selma.

Before the family left, Mathias spoke privately to Albert about being able to continue using the cemetery for family burials. "Since we done got two young'uns buried up there, we thought it'd be nice if they's any of us that wants to be buried alongside them babies, we can."

Albert assured him that there would be no problem, and that the Caudills were welcome to come back anytime they wanted to visit the graves.

***

In the spring of 1906, with the weather turning warmer and the birth of spring calves imminent, Albert heard about a meeting of the Southern Cotton Association in Smithfield that he decided he would attend. Following the departure of Mathias, Albert had managed to take in a boarder by the name of Samuel who had lived for a while with Mathias before he'd sold the land to Albert. Samuel would now stay at the house vacated by the Caudills so that he could help Albert with the livestock and farming. Samuel, in his forties and single, was a soft-spoken but hardworking man with muscular arms. Not one to care much for his appearance, he was hardly ever clean shaven and always seemed to be wearing the same old overalls and pair of lace-up boots no matter where he went.

On the morning of the meeting, Albert hitched Maude to the wagon and gave Samuel instructions on what was to be done on the farm during his absence. Then, he headed east for the approx-imately eighteen-mile trip to Smithfield. He had left as soon as the sun came up that morning so that he could arrive in time for the meeting.

After crossing the Neuse River into town, he was struck by the busy activity in Smithfield. It seemed to have grown even more since Mathias and he had traveled there at the end of December 1903 to finalize his sale of the land. The streets were filled with men riding horses and mule-drawn wagons or buggies. Albert passed the brick courthouse and the building housing the Register of Deeds, where he and Mathias had come that December day. He passed the Tuscarora Inn at the corner of Market and Second Streets. It was a large, four-story building with lodgers on the upper floors and offices on the ground floor.

Then he passed by Hood's Drug Store, where the words PEPSI COLA had been painted on the side. Albert had heard of Pepsi, but had never tasted it. He thought it might be nice to visit Hood's later, but he needed to get to the meeting first.

Albert arrived at the meeting site just as the main speaker was about to begin. The room was crowded with farmers from around Johnston County, and he ended up having to stand near the back. The speaker was introduced as Dr. Winston, the president of the State Agricultural and Mechanical College in Raleigh. Albert was impressed with Dr. Winston's address as he talked about the current best practices in cotton growing and what they could expect in the coming year in terms of prices. After the meeting, which included questions and answers following Dr. Winston's speech, Albert spoke briefly with a couple of other farmers about fertilizers they were using and how they were faring in terms of yield and profit.

After chatting for about a half hour, he decided he would ride back by Hood's Drug Store. As Albert walked in, he looked up to see the words SANITARY FOUNTAIN painted above the main entrance. Then his eyes immediately went to a counter where a young blonde woman dressed in a fancy blue apron was busy waiting on the customers seated on stools at the counter. Albert took a seat on one of the stools, and after a couple of minutes, the young lady, who couldn't have been more than twenty years old, came up to Albert and asked in a cheerful tone, "Can I help you, sir?"

"I want to try some of that Pepsi Cola. How much is it?"

"Fountain drinks are a nickel, sir. If you've never had it before, it's real good. Not like anything else. I can tell you that." All of this was delivered with a smile and the friendliness typical of most folks who worked in town.

"I'll have one then. Thought I'd give it a try before heading back home."

The young lady went to something that looked like a big box, and pulled a handle. A dark liquid began flowing into the glass in which she had placed a few cubes of ice. There was a sign on the wall that read DRINK PEPSI COLA/THE BEST FOUNTAIN DRINK. The young lady came back to where Albert sat and placed the glass filled with the brown-looking drink before him. "Here's your Pepsi, sir. I hope you like it." Then she turned and scurried down to the other end of the counter to wait on another customer.

Albert was not sure what he expected, but what he got was a sweet, almost syrupy taste that he found quite pleasing. He didn't want to drink it too fast in order to savor the experience, so he sat there for a few minutes just taking in the sights, sounds, and smells of Hood's Drug Store. After finishing the last swallow, he thanked the nice young lady, paid her a nickel, and headed back out to the mule and wagon. When he finally arrived at the house late in the afternoon, he was excited to tell Fannie all about the cotton growers' meeting and drinking his first Pepsi Cola.

Fannie chuckled and said, "Sounds like drinking molasses to me."

"No, it ain't quite the same as that. Not as thick. More like drinking flavored water," Albert explained.

Fannie said she'd be all right if she didn't get any of that Pepsi stuff. As Albert talked about what he'd learned at the meeting, he noticed that Fannie seemed to be preoccupied with something. She'd nod her head or answer with one or two syllables, but not much more.

As the couple finished their supper, Fannie turned to Albert. "I think we might be going to have a baby," she said, fixing her eyes on Albert to watch his reaction.

"Well, I'll be . . ."Albert's lips spread into a big smile. "Here I've been telling all about my trip to Smithfield, and you had this news! Why didn't you tell me first thing?"

"Well, I don't know that I can be for sure," she started, "but there's been some signs that I've heard other women talk about before that makes me think that I might be expecting. Let's give it a few more days, and I think I'll be able to be more sure."

A few days later, the morning sickness came. Some mornings Albert was awakened by the sound of Fannie retching into the chamber pot that she kept next to the bed. Seeing as there was little doubt that a new baby must be on the way, Albert couldn't withhold the news. In a short while, all the Stephensons and Langdons knew. Whenever Albert and Fannie went to services at the church or the home of someone in their family for Sunday dinner, Fannie was surrounded by women offering congratulations and advice of all sorts.

Not long after learning that Fannie was expecting, Albert and Samuel oversaw the birth of three black-and-white calves in the barn stables. Though Albert had been worried that something might go awry in the birthing process, all three of the Holstein cows had delivered with little problem. The calves would be kept in the barn until they were large enough to roam outside. Albert's plans to get started in the cattle business were off to a good start.

CHAPTER FOURTEEN

A JOYFUL BIRTH AND A SAD LOSS

Albert and Samuel, along with a few other hired hands, managed to get all the cotton picked by the beginning of November. Albert hauled the big sheets of cotton to a nearby gin for baling and sold it for a rather nice profit. "It'll be enough to see us through the winter," he told Fannie one chilly evening as they sat by the fireplace.

"I imagine so," acknowledged Fannie. Her mind, however, was clearly on the anticipated birth of their first child. "I don't think it'll be much longer," she said, rubbing her belly.

Albert had come to the house frequently to check on her while the cotton was being picked, and the closer it got to when they thought she would deliver, the more against he was leaving her alone out of concern that she could go into labor with no one around. Fortunately, before he left for Selma, Mathias had told them of a midwife, a middle-aged woman by the name of Annie Mae, who lived with her husband in a small house just a couple of miles away. The plan was that when Fannie felt the baby coming, Samuel would take the wagon to summon Annie Mae to the house to help deliver the baby.

One morning before the sunlight peeped through the curtains, Albert awoke to find his wife sitting on the edge of the bed. Reaching over to rub her back, he asked, "Is everything all right?"

Fannie turned toward him. "I ain't sure, but I think it might be starting," she uttered.

Albert drew back the two quilts, put his feet on the floor, and pulled on his pants and shirt. He could see by the grimace on Fannie's face that she was in some discomfort. "Well, I'm not waiting around. I'll go let Samuel know he needs to go get Annie Mae. You stay in the bed 'til I get back. It won't take me but just a few minutes."

Albert sat down on the edge of the bed alongside Fannie to put on his socks and boots. Grabbing his coat and hat, he disappeared through the kitchen and out the back door to make the short walk to tell Samuel what he needed to do.

After Albert banged on the front door several times, Samuel opened the door, sleep still showing in his eyes. Yawning, he invited Albert inside. Out of breath, Albert declined and asked Samuel if he could hitch one of the mules to the wagon and go get Annie Mae. "I think the baby might be coming, and I need to get on back to the house," Albert said as he turned to step back off the porch.

In less than five minutes, after Albert got back to find Fannie holding her belly and moaning, he saw Samuel through the window getting Maude out of the barn and hitching her to the wagon. As soon as Albert saw Samuel climb on the wagon seat, he opened the side door and went out to speak to him. "Try to hurry. She's acting like that baby might be born soon."

Samuel laughed. "Now, don't you worry. She ain't having that baby this quick. That's not the way it works. It'll be a good while before that child's born." Samuel then made a clucking sound with his tongue signaling Maude to move forward, and he headed out.

Returning inside, Albert hardly knew what to do with himself. He'd always managed to stay out of the house when his brothers and sisters had been born, and he knew next to nothing about the birthing process. Pacing back and forth between the kitchen and sitting room, he kept looking through the window to see if he could catch a glimpse of the wagon approaching from down the path. It seemed to Albert that it took an eternity for Samuel to return. Finally, he saw the wagon emerge from the trees lining the dirt road. As the wagon drew a little closer, he could make out the two figures seated on the wagon seat. "He's got Annie Mae with him," he said to himself, and immediately felt a flood of relief sweep through his body.

Once Annie Mae entered the kitchen with her black bag, Albert could see that she clearly knew how to take charge. Annie Mae was a short, thin woman who appeared to be in her fifties. She pulled off her hat to reveal straight, gray-streaked auburn hair that she had gathered and pinned in the back. Following a quick introduction by Samuel, Annie Mae told Albert to fire up the cookstove and put some water on in a pot. Then Albert led her to the bedroom, where Fannie was once again on the edge of the bed, moaning in anguish.

Annie Mae motioned for Albert to go back to the kitchen, placed her bag on the floor, and began asking Fannie some questions to determine how far along she might be. She next instructed Fannie to lie on her back while she ran her hands over her belly to locate the position of the baby's head. After completing her initial examination, Annie Mae left Fannie for a moment to speak to Albert in the kitchen. "If you could make some hot tea, that would be good," Annie Mae said with authority, "but if you ain't got none, just go draw up a little more water from the well and bring me a pitcher of that."

Since there was no tea in the house, Albert went out to draw up some more fresh water in a bucket. After pouring some of the water into a small pitcher and taking it to Annie Mae, Albert went out to the smokehouse to pull down some sausage given by a neighbor when he'd helped with a hog killing. He figured that with Fannie in labor and Annie Mae needing to attend to her, he was on his own when it came to fixing breakfast. Returning to the kitchen, he sliced off a few pieces of sausage and found a couple of eggs in a basket that Fannie had left in the pantry. He told himself that he could make do under the circumstances. After eating his breakfast, Albert joined Samuel outside to work on a fence they had been constructing around the barn area.

When the noon hour came, Albert and Samuel came in through the back door to find that Annie Mae, in spite of having to keep a check on Fannie, had managed to put together a simple meal of potatoes and spareribs for the men. Albert imagined that Fannie, in between labor pains, had managed to tell her where to find what she needed. While the men ate, Annie Mae stepped into the kitchen to let Albert know that she thought the baby might be born within a few hours, and to just leave everything to her. "I'll call you if I need you," she said, and then went back to Fannie's bedside.

All through the afternoon, Albert found it difficult to concentrate as he and Samuel prepared the farm for the winter months ahead. Several times he slipped in the back door only to witness continual sounds of discomfort coming from the bedroom. Late in the afternoon, in spite of Samuel's efforts to reassure him that everything would be all right, Albert found himself plagued by thoughts of *What if? What if there is something wrong with the baby? What if the labor goes on way into the night? What if something happens to Fannie?*

Finally, just as the last rays of sunlight disappeared in the western horizon and Albert stepped up on the porch to head back inside for the night, he heard Annie Mae command Fannie to push. Albert entered the kitchen, and suddenly the unmistakable cry of a newborn filled his ears.

Annie Mae called to Albert, "Come see your new son!"

A boy! he thought. Of course, Albert would have been happy to have a girl, too, but he was especially happy that their first was a boy.

Annie Mae was using a rag and some warm water from a basin to wash the infant as Albert marched into the bedroom beaming with joy. Fannie, spent from hours of labor and the final act of delivery, lay quietly under the covers. With a weak voice, Fannie said, "He's precious, Albert. He's just precious."

Albert could not stop grinning as he leaned over to kiss Fannie on the cheek.

"You want to hold him, Mr. Albert?" Annie Mae had finished washing the baby and was now wrapping him in a small blanket given as a gift to Fannie weeks earlier.

Albert reached out his arms to receive his son. It was hard to describe the feeling he had at that moment as he looked upon the baby's face, seeing that his head was covered in dark hair like his own. Speechless at first, Albert finally broke his silence. "This boy here will be a fine farmer one of these days," he proclaimed.

"I forgot to ask you, Miss Fannie," Annie Mae said, "what you was planning to name him."

"Well," Fannie said, her voice still rather weak, "Albert and me talked about that if it was a boy, we'd name him Jasper. Jasper Syrus . . . so I think that's what we'll call him."

"Well then, Jasper Syrus," Annie Mae said as she looked at the baby nestled in Albert's arms, "I'm sure glad you got here safe and sound. I haint never lost one," she said with an air of confidence. "If you folks ever needs me again, don't hate to call me. But if you think you can get by, I'd be mighty obliged to Mr. Samuel if he'd see me back home. I don't see no sign of trouble with this baby, so I think everything will be all right." Annie Mae went on to give some post-delivery care instructions to the couple.

Albert left out the back door with the key to the smokehouse, where he pulled down one of the hams to give to Annie Mae as payment for her midwife services. Then, he hitched Maude back to the wagon and rode down to ask Samuel to take Annie Mae back home. Samuel had walked home before the baby was born and was unaware until Albert arrived that Fannie had delivered at last.

Thanks to Annie Mae's instructions, Fannie and the new arrival got along just fine in the days following the birth. As word spread to the Stephenson and Langdon families, some began to pay visits to welcome Jasper into the family and to help as needed. With the cotton all harvested, Albert's main responsibility was keeping watch over the young calves, and he found more time to stay inside with Fannie and Jasper through the cold winter months.

Then, sometime in February of 1907, as Albert sat by the fire rocking Jasper, Fannie informed him that she felt certain she was pregnant again.

In that year, Teddy Roosevelt was president of the United

States. Martin F. Ansel was governor of North Carolina. The women's suffrage movement was well under way, and thousands of immigrants were streaming through Ellis Island in search of a new life in America. On the home front, Albert kept abreast of the news through reading the newspapers. With the advent of rural farm delivery, he could get mail delivered straight to the house. He paid to get subscriptions of *The Smithfield Herald*, the *News and Observer*, and *The Progressive Farmer* so that not only could he keep up with the news, but continue to remain informed on the best farming practices.

Each year since he had begun farming on his own, Albert had reinvested his profits into creating a larger, more lucrative operation. With the help of Samuel, he continued to clear land that could be used for planting cotton, corn, or other grains. He also continued to add cows to his stock so that, in turn, he could raise more calves. With the wheel of fortune landing in Albert's favor, in between caring for Jasper and taking care of the household duties, Fannie was able to track their profit.

After another successful cotton season, Albert and Fannie looked forward to the birth of their second child toward the end of October or beginning of November. Fannie let Albert know that since Annie Mae had been so good with the delivery of Jasper, she wanted no one else other than the midwife to bring their next child into the world.

On the last day of October, Albert came to the house in the middle of the day to find that Fannie had gone into labor. As he had done before, he quickly got Samuel, who had started walking home for his midday meal, to go get Annie Mae.

After Annie Mae arrived to take control, she spoke to Albert about getting someone to come and help with Jasper. "That way," she explained, "you and Mr. Samuel can go on about your work."

Leaving Annie Mae in charge in the house and Samuel working outside, Albert hitched Jack to the wagon and headed toward the Langdons to see if he could get Fannie's sister Victoria—or "Vic," as they called her—to come and stay with Fannie for a few days.

Albert thought as he rode along that Fannie would need another woman with her day and night for a while not only to help with Jasper, but also to cook and keep the house clean.

Upon arriving at the Langdon home, he was greeted at the front door by Vic, who had not yet married and still lived with her parents. Albert had always thought a lot of Vic. She kept her straight black hair pulled back off her face, as Fannie did, and they seemed to dress a lot alike in long dresses or skirts and blouses with long sleeves. Fannie's mother, Eliza Jane, appeared behind Vic, and listened as Albert gave a quick accounting of how it would be most appreciated if Vic could come back with him to stay with Fannie for a few days, being that she was in labor and would probably deliver sometime during the night. Both women agreed that it would be a good idea for her to stay for a few days. While Vic disappeared to her bedroom to begin gathering things together, Albert provided more details to Eliza Jane.

"I'm mighty glad you got that Annie Mae," she said. "Sounds like that woman knows what to do. I'll be looking forward to seeing another grandchild. Make sure you get word to us as soon as you can after it's born."

When Vic returned, she carried a small leather bag and had put on a long coat. Although the air was not yet chilly, it was cool enough that most people were wearing coats, especially when outside working or riding in a buggy or wagon. After hugging her mother, Vic allowed Albert to help her up into the wagon seat, and off they went. On the way, Albert took the opportunity to catch up on all the news from the Langdons. For Albert, the time seemed to pass quickly, and in no time at all, he was back home heading up the porch with Vic following closely behind.

Albert left Annie Mae to continue watching over Fannie while Vic took over the responsibility of looking after Jasper, who was now just shy of a year old.

When Albert and Samuel called it a day a little before sunset, he came back in to hear the same sort of moaning that Fannie had exhibited prior to Jasper's delivery. Vic had taken control of the kitchen while still keeping an eye on Jasper. Albert had built him a cradle out of pine wood a couple of months after his birth, and Vic had brought the cradle inside the kitchen while she worked at the stove.

After supper, Albert picked Jasper up from the cradle and held him in his lap as Vic cleaned up in the kitchen. In spite of Albert's best efforts to focus on the articles in the paper, he found it nearly impossible since he was so close to the bedroom. It seemed to Albert that Fannie's moaning through the closed door would never end.

Vic soon disappeared into the bedroom to be with Fannie and Annie Mae, and emerged late in the evening to find Albert with his eyes closed and Jasper sound asleep in his arms. She nudged Albert to wake him, and picked up Jasper to put him back in the cradle. "We'll be sitting up as long as we need to, Albert," she told him. "But I'll get some quilts and one of the pillows off the bed, and maybe you can at least lie down on the floor to try to get some rest."

Albert knew that if he expected to get anything done the next day, he had to try to get some rest, even though he imagined it would be almost impossible. After spreading out a pallet of quilts, Albert lay down on the floor next to Jasper's cradle. Perhaps from sheer exhaustion, he drifted off to sleep a little before midnight.

Sometime around two in the morning, he was awakened by loud voices coming from the bedroom. At first, he thought that Fannie must be delivering the baby and he would hear the newborn cry at any moment. As he sat up from his pallet and listened, however, what he heard seemed frantic. He kept hearing the word "breech," but he had no idea what they were talking about. He could hear Annie Mae telling Fannie to push and giving Vic sharp commands.

After several minutes, silence descended except for the sound of crying—crying that Albert felt sure was coming from Fannie. He stood and opened the bedroom door. There, on the bed in between Fannie's legs, lay a bluish-colored, lifeless infant. Fannie sobbed as Annie Mae picked up the baby and wrapped it in a blanket, much as she had done when Jasper was born, but this time there was no rejoicing on the part of those gathered in the bedroom.

Annie Mae did not make eye contact, but spoke quietly to Albert. "We done all we could, Mr. Albert, but he was born breech, and we had a hard time getting him out. Poor fellow didn't have a chance."

Vic could see that Albert was both shocked and puzzled by what he had just heard. "Normally, Albert, when a baby is born, the head comes first. But this time, the feet came first, and then when it got to the shoulders, we just couldn't get the rest of him out. We finally had to pull as hard as we could, but the cord must of got pressed up in there somehow. His head was trapped up inside too long. I'm so sorry." Vic placed her arm around Albert's waist in an attempt to comfort him.

Albert alternated between looking down at his sobbing wife and looking at the tiny bundle Annie Mae held in her arms. "Don't cry, Fannie," he said, his eyes growing misty. "You did the best you could, and you had the best help you could have had. Sometimes we just don't understand why something like this happens." He leaned over to wrap his arms around Fannie, who seemed at the moment to be inconsolable. He turned toward Annie Mae, who still could not bring herself to look up at Albert. "Miss Annie Mae, it won't be too long 'til morning. You're welcome to lie down on the bed there in the front room. I can help Vic get everything cleaned up. We'll put the baby in the other empty room 'til I can figure out what we'll do."

Taking the lifeless infant from Annie Mae, Albert went out on the back porch, where he found a wooden crate. Placing the baby in the crate, he brought it back inside to the unheated and unfurnished room at the front of the house. Albert hoped that the low temperature would keep the body cool long enough for him to make arrangements to get a tiny coffin.

Returning to the bedroom, Albert assisted Vic in gathering the soiled bedsheets and rags to take out on the back porch to be washed later. Vic insisted that after they got the bed changed, he should spend the remaining hours until dawn lying with Fannie. "If ever she needed you, it's now," Vic said. Vic then lay down on the pallet next to Jasper to try to rest a little before facing the sad day ahead.

***

As soon as Samuel showed up to begin the day, Albert got dressed and walked out to the barn to let him know about the loss of the baby. When Samuel was finished feeding the animals, Albert told him to hitch Jack to the wagon. They would take Annie Mae home and then go on a little further into Angier to see if they could find someone who made and sold coffins. Once again, Albert opened up the smokehouse and appeared in the kitchen to hand Annie Mae a long strand of stuffed sausage and a Tom thumb that Charles had given them last January. At first, Annie Mae refused the payment, saying that she felt guilty that the boy hadn't survived. Yet Albert insisted, saying that no matter what, she had spent a lot of time and done a lot of hard work, not to mention that she'd also had little to no sleep.

After delivering Annie Mae to her house, the two men continued on to make the five-mile trip into town. After stopping at a general store and making inquiries, Albert and Samuel located a business on the north side of town where they might be able to get a coffin for the baby. As it turned out, they were able to purchase a small, plain, pine coffin with a lid that could be lifted off and put back into place once the body was ready for burial.

Back at home, Albert sent Vic in the wagon to inform Fannie's parents of the loss of the child. Realizing that there was not enough time to get word to everyone, Albert and Fannie agreed that they needed to bury the baby as soon as they could. So, Albert and Samuel, with the baby in the coffin, left for the Stephenson family cemetery to begin digging the grave where Albert's father had been laid to rest years earlier.

As soon as Albert arrived at his mother's house to let her know what had happened, he sent his younger brother Irving to bring over Fannie and Jasper. Vic also arrived with Fannie's parents by the time that everything had been made ready. As the small gathering encircled the gravesite, Fannie's father asked if a name had been given to the deceased infant.

"We were going to name him after his daddy," Fannie said with a vacant look on her face. "Willis Chester."

Fannie's father delivered a prayer for all to be comforted in their sadness. Following the prayer, Samuel and Albert lowered the coffin into the grave with ropes while the others turned to walk back toward the house. Albert privately wondered how such things as the loss of an innocent child could happen. It was a questioning that he would revisit again and again in the months and years to come.

CHAPTER FIFTEEN

A SUNDAY-AFTERNOON VISIT AND AN EERIE DISCOVERY

Following the death of Willis Chester, family members on both the Langdon and Stephenson sides came to offer their condolences and help to Fannie as she tried to get some semblance of normalcy back into her everyday life. After all, Jasper still had to be taken care of, and there was always plenty of washing and other housework to be done.

Always thinking ahead, Albert turned around and bought two more cows to add to his small herd. He had been reading about a fatal disease affecting cattle exposed to the cattle tick. Some counties in North Carolina would eventually be placed under quarantine that prevented shipment of cows in order to try to thwart the spread of the disease. Albert kept a watchful eye on all his cows for any sign of infestation.

One Sunday in the spring, with planting in full swing on the farm, Albert dropped Fannie and Jasper off at his mother's house to visit. While there, he found his brother Leonard sitting on the front porch of his nearby house, dressed in a dark-blue suit, white shirt, and light-blue bowtie. Leonard shared how he had felt called to preach one day while out plowing. In fact, earlier that day, he had delivered the sermon at Rehobeth.

Albert thought a great deal about how Leonard had felt the call to preach and how Fannie had felt called to become a member at Fellowship, but thus far he'd felt no such calling. Surrounded by family and neighbors who were members of the Primitive Baptist Church, Albert often wondered how they perceived his lack of membership in the church. He told himself that he knew right from wrong, so he didn't really need the preacher to tell him what he already knew. Still, Albert respected Leonard's decision and always looked forward to hearing him preach when he could.

Following their visit, Albert and Fannie returned home in the late afternoon to find a man approaching the house in a wagon pulled by a black mare with a small patch of white between the eyes. After helping Fannie down with Jasper, Albert watched the man pull on the reins to bring the mare to a stop in the yard. Fannie and Jasper entered the house through the side doorway to the sitting room, but the man did not get down from his seat. Albert observed the man's belly protruding between his suspenders holding up his brown pants. He wore an old, brown, faded-out hat similar to the black hats that Albert usually wore. The man had a black moustache that curled up slightly at both ends, and he appeared to have something on the inside of his lower lip. *Probably snuff*, Albert thought.

"How you doing, sir? What brings you in this part of the country today?" asked Albert.

The man leaned over to the other side of the wagon and spat on the ground. A small amount of brown liquid ran down from his mouth, and he reached up to wipe it off. "I'm Lubie—Lubie Ray," he said, and extended his hand down to Albert.

"I'm Albert Stephenson. How do you do?"

Lubie spat again. "Doing fair to middlin', I suppose. Just out riding today to speak to a few farmers over this way. I live not far over in Harnett County."

"Un huh," Albert muttered.

The man continued in a slow drawl, "Well, I'm shore you been a-hearing about some unspeakable acts that's been a-happening to our fine young girls and women. I represent a group of like-minded men that's been a-getting together for a while now, and I know you're probly like me . . . you want to make sure that them that respects our women and girls and our Christian way of life is being protected when maybe the gov'ment won't do its part. Them brutes that don't value the innocence and purity of our women ought not to go unpunished . . . and in a way that is befitting their crimes." By now, another trail of brown spit was running down the left corner of his mouth.

Albert was pretty sure he knew the brutes whom this man was talking about, but he allowed him to keep on talking.

"Need I remind you, sir, of the poor little white girl who was violated not too far from here?"

Albert did recall an assault that had taken place not too long ago. Fannie and he had talked about the awful crime and wished swift justice on whomever was found to be guilty of it. As the man brought up other cases locally or in other parts of the country, Albert began to realize what this man was part of and why he had come.

"So, you see, Mr. Albert," Lubie continued, "we got ourselves a darky problem, and I believe—"

Albert stopped him before he could say more. "Well . . . I thank you for stopping by, but we ain't never had much problem with the colored around here. Now, I know they got their place and we've got ours, but my daddy, when he was living, and now me too . . . we ain't never had no trouble."

Albert, being an avid reader of the newspapers, had read articles about lynchings and how mobs were taking the law into their own hands. He recalled how colored men suspected of crimes were referred to as "brutes" in the papers. He understood well the segregation that was accepted as normal, but he'd never thought he could be part of any violent act.

Not willing to give in quite yet, Lubie continued, "Now, sir, I would beg you to reconsider. What if someone in your own family was brutally attacked? The darky can't be trusted, I tell you." By now, his face was beginning to turn a little red. "Before we know it, they'll be taking over in the gov'ment, and then you'll be wishing you had stood up against that sort of nonsense."

Albert looked up at Lubie. "Well, you present a good case, but the truth is, I ain't really got the time to be part of anything much other than taking care of this farm. I thank you again for stopping by, but my wife is waiting on me to come in for supper." Albert had no idea if Fannie had supper ready or not, but he was anxious to get rid of this man. Though Lubie had never used the word "Klan," Albert figured him to be part of the clandestine organization he had read about.

"All right then, sir. Thank you for your time." Lubie turned and spat, pulled on the reins to turn around the mare, and headed back in the direction from which he had come. Albert stood watching him for a few moments in deep thought. For some reason, his mind flashed back to his childhood when his parents were talking about an article they'd read in *The Smithfield Herald* about a prominent white man, a member of the Methodist church, who had been arrested with a colored woman for adultery and fornication.

"What's adultery and fornication?" he remembered asking his brother Charles. Charles had said that he didn't know, but that it must have been something pretty bad for the man and woman to be arrested and locked up in the jail.

Albert knew that there were lines that folks were expected not to cross, but he'd never felt that anyone other than the law should deal with criminal activity. He had been hiring colored folks to help with picking cotton, as his father had done, and other than dealing with someone trying to steal cotton off another worker's sheet in order to add more weight to his own, he'd never had a problem.

Albert went inside to find Jasper sitting on the kitchen floor while Fannie warmed up leftovers from the midday meal. Albert told her about Lubie and that the man had wanted Albert to join the Klan's cause, but that he'd sent him on his way. Fannie agreed that it was best not to get tied up in something like that since there was no way to tell where it might lead.

***

In February of 1908, after discussing his plan with Fannie, Albert deeded thirty acres of land he had inherited from his father's estate back to his mother for $325. His mother gave him part of the money at the time they made the transaction and signed a note confirming that she owed Albert $175. Now that he was debt free, Albert could focus on getting even more of a profit off his cotton and calves. Albert looked forward to investing more of his money into the farm in order to do just that.

In May of that year, with much of the spring planting already completed, Albert picked up a copy of the *News and Observer* and saw a headline that grabbed his attention. Prohibition had gone into effect in North Carolina. Back in 1903, the North Carolina General Assembly had made it illegal for distilleries to operate in Johnston County, and in 1908 voters in North Carolina passed a resolution to ban the manufacture or sale of alcohol. Despite the passage of the resolution, Albert was well aware that unlawful activity continued in the county.

One morning in June, with the sun shining through a cloudless sky, Albert and Samuel worked along the edge of the woods separating the farm from another on the opposite side of the creek that ran behind one of the cotton patches. The men had been working for some time trying to clear a little more land of vegetation and tree stumps so that Albert could increase his cotton acreage. A neighbor had graciously allowed Albert to borrow his stump puller. The work was slow and tedious as the men attached the hook and steel cable to each stump while the two mules strained and slowly pulled the stumps from the ground.

Samuel paused for a moment, reached up to his brow, and wiped away the sweat with the sleeve of his shirt. His eyes moved above the line of trees to the right that ran along the perimeter of the cleared land. All of a sudden, he pointed with his left index finger and said, "Look over yonder, Albert. I think they's some smoke coming through them trees."

The trees appeared to be within Albert's property. "Wonder what in the world . . ." Albert's voice trailed off. He peered at the line of smoke, which looked as if it could be coming from a chimney, except there was no house in the woods there. "I 'spect we better go over there and see what's going on."

Leaving the two mules to rest, the two men strode off toward the rising smoke. Picking their way through the undergrowth, they arrived at a clearing next to a small stream, where they encountered the source of the smoke. A big fire had been set underneath a large metal cooker. A spiral-shaped coil extended out from the cap of the cooker leading to two other barrels sitting nearby. In fact, there were several wooden barrels around.

Albert immediately recognized it as a liquor still, since he and his brothers had run across one while out playing down near Middle Creek years earlier. It was obvious to both men that whoever had fired up the still had been there not long before, and could even be hidden somewhere nearby.

Albert kept his voice low. "Samuel, we don't know who put this thing here or where they might be. What we can do, though, is put out this fire and knock over that cooker. Then we can dump whatever's in these barrels out on the ground. Maybe that'll be enough to keep them from coming back, if they see somebody's on to them."

"I'll get some water in that bucket." Samuel pointed to a bucket among the other barrels possibly full of moonshine.

As quickly as they could, Albert and Samuel doused the fire with water, removed the tops from the barrels, and dumped the clear liquid on the ground. Not wanting to touch the cooker with bare hands, Albert located a couple of fallen limbs, which the two men then used to push the cooker off its blocks.

As they stood looking at the toppled cooker and empty barrels on their sides, Albert said, "We'll keep this spot watched the best we can for the next few days to see if they's any sign of anybody coming back around. If they try to start it up again, I'll find out who's the best man to get in touch with and see if they can't get rid of whoever put that still down here. I tell you what, Samuel. Folks that does such as that is about as useless as teats on a boar hog."

Samuel chuckled. "They're mighty slick, though. Something tells me they'll be back, but maybe when they see what we done, they'll think twice before starting it up again."

The two men turned and headed back to continue pulling stumps. As they walked, Albert made a mental note to be more diligent in keeping an eye out, especially in the distant boundaries of the property, for any sort of illegal activity.

CHAPTER SIXTEEN

THE HORSELESS CARRIAGE

A few days after destroying the still, Albert announced to Samuel that they would be taking another wagon ride to Smithfield to look for a disc harrow that Albert was interested in buying. Albert had been interested in buying a harrow that could be used in cultivating the land, and he had heard he could probably get a good price in Smithfield. This time, Albert decided to hitch both Jack and Maude to the wagon in order to have plenty of power to haul the disc back on the long trip.

Just before light, Albert and Samuel climbed up once again onto the wagon seat to make the eighteen-mile trip to Smithfield. "Don't look for us to be back 'til after dark," Albert told Fannie, who had wrapped up a few ham biscuits and filled a jar of water to hold the men over until they could get to Smithfield.

The trip to town was uneventful. Occasionally, they met a farmer in a wagon or a family in a buggy. Since there had been no rain for the past few days, navigating the dirt road leading eastward into town was fairly easy. Here and there, a cow or group of pigs crossed in front of them, and the men paused to allow the animals passage.

Arriving around noon, the two men went to Holt's Hardware House, where Albert purchased a Kenwood reversible disc harrow for $14.55. The disc harrow had a seat attached to a metal post that elevated the seat to a high level above the harrow. From that point, the person operating it would be able to maneuver the two levers standing up vertically from the middle. With the help of store employees, the men lifted the harrow into the bed of Albert's wagon. Because of the width of the harrow, a part of it hung out of the back of the wagon. One of the store workers helped them tie a rope to the harrow near the front of the wagon to prevent it from sliding or falling out.

109

Before getting back up on the wagon seat, Albert and Samuel took a few minutes to eat the ham biscuits and drink the water that Fannie had provided them earlier that morning.

"While we're here," Albert told Samuel, "let's stop in and look around in Woodall's. I've been wanting a new suit, if I can find one, and maybe a new hat."

Samuel, who had never been in Woodall's, readily agreed that they should make the trip even more worthwhile by looking around some while they were there.

Impeccable in his taste for nice clothing that could be worn to weddings, church, or any other event that called for more than a pair of overalls, Albert had a special affinity for dark, often black-colored suits, white shirts with standup collars, bowties, and black, stiff hats. At Woodall's, he found a handsome black suit and a black hat to match, while Samuel ended up buying a brown golf-style hat for himself. The men then took the wagon over to Allen Lee's, a prescription druggist who had candies and baskets of fruits and nuts of different sizes and prices. There, Albert bought three pounds of candy at nine cents per pound, as well as a basket of fruit and nuts for two dollars. Samuel bought some candy and fruit, too, and both men agreed that the candy, fruit, and nuts would be a nice surprise for their wives.

As the men left Allen Lee's to return to the wagon and head home, they suddenly heard a loud racket coming from the east side of town. Their eyes widened and mouths agape in astonishment, they saw a noisy black contraption coming right down through the middle of town. Albert could hear dogs barking and pigs squealing. Horses and mules reared on their hind legs as the horseless buggy moved forward amidst what seemed to be a series of explosions. There was a man sitting high up in the machine, and he appeared to be working some knobs on the strange contraption as it progressed in spurts. Once the machine got right in front of Albert and Samuel, the man working the knobs squeezed what looked like a small black balloon, and a honking sound came out. By now, people had poured out from all the shops and businesses on both sides of Market Street. The man on the machine had a huge grin on his face, but Albert wondered how anybody could be enjoying a ride on something that made that much noise and sent the animals into such a frenzy.

Eyebrows raised, Albert looked at Samuel.

"What in the Lord's name was that thing?" Samuel asked, leaning forward to watch as the horseless buggy made a turn and went out of sight.

"I've read and heard about those things," Albert said. "They call them 'horseless carriages.' It's a new invention, but I'm telling you, with all the noise it makes, I wouldn't want one of them."

"Anybody that would want such as that would be a fool," added Samuel.

"I can't see," began Albert, "how that thing could be of any use to me. It makes so much noise, it would scare the cows and mules to death—not to mention women and small children." Albert shook his head back and forth.

Samuel nodded in agreement, and the men climbed back onto the wagon seat and began heading out of town. The sight of the horseless carriage gave them much to talk about on the way home, and of course Albert couldn't wait to tell Fannie about it.

It was dark by the time the mules pulled the wagon out by the barn. After unloading the disc harrow and unhitching the mules, Samuel left to walk back home while Albert grabbed his sack of goodies and the boxes containing his new suit and hat. After showing off his new clothes to Fannie, Albert described the day's events over a supper of fried Tom thumb and fresh vegetables while Fannie cut up small bits of an orange for Jasper.

"You oughta seen that machine sputtering down Market Street." Albert, who usually spoke in a calm, even tone, couldn't contain his excitement over having seen the horseless carriage. "I heard some people in the street saying them things would replace horses and mules pretty soon." He cut a piece of the Tom thumb and savored the spicy taste in his mouth a moment before continuing. "I don't see how such a thing as that can be counted on, though. Too much racket, and that thing looked like it might stop working any minute. Mules and horses will be more dependable."

Sitting at the table, Fannie wanted to know all about the stores Albert and Samuel had been to. After hearing all about the nice clothes in Woodall's, Fannie looked up from feeding Jasper. "I have some news myself," she said. Her smile let Albert know it was not bad news that she was about to deliver. "I'm pretty sure I'm expecting again."

"Well, I will be . . . here I was running on about that horseless carriage, and you had news like that to tell me?" Albert rose from his chair with a big grin on his face and picked up Jasper from Fannie's lap. "You hear that? You're gonna have a baby brother or sister." He kissed the boy on the cheek and rubbed his head. He looked down at Fannie. "When do you think it might be born?"

"Well, I can't say exactly, but I'm thinking sometime in the spring." Fannie went on to express that she hoped that Jasper would soon have a playmate. "It don't matter to me if it's a boy or a girl," she said, "as long as it's born healthy."

For a moment, neither she nor Albert said anything. Ever since the death of Willis Chester, Albert had worried about Fannie having another child. He wondered how it would affect Fannie if she delivered another lifeless child. He did not voice this concern to Fannie on what was otherwise a happy evening, but he knew that it had to be on her mind, as well.

CHAPTER SEVENTEEN

HOG-KILLING TIME

What constitutes a prosperous life? Some will say that one's prosperity depends upon the wealth one is able to acquire. Others will say that a prosperous life must be defined in broader terms and measured not only by one's material wealth, but also by the blessings that come from good health, having loving support from family and friends, and having work that brings a sense of joy and fulfillment.

By all of these measures, in 1909 Albert was a prosperous man. In April, he and Fannie were joyful that the complications that had surrounded the sudden death of Willis Chester had not paid another visit during and following the birth of their baby boy James Myatt. Under supervision, Jasper was old enough to hold the baby, and once he got baby Myatt in his arms, it was hard to get him to let go.

With spring planting in full swing and an ever-increasing herd of cows and calves to deal with, Albert left it up to the women in both the Stephenson and Langdon families to take turns spending a few nights with them to help care for the two children, cook, and clean.

Since the smokehouse had been built, Albert and Fannie had relied on fresh meat obtained from family members or neighbors. Sometimes Albert would be given a ham or shoulder, or perhaps some stuffed sausage in return for helping during a hog killing in the colder months. He would then bring the meat back home, salt it down, and store it in the large wooden box in the smokehouse or, in the case of sausage, hang it up on one of the poles to dry it out for later use.

By the end of 1910 and into the winter of 1911, Albert had not yet made any plans for how he might expand his cattle dealing into dealing with swine. However, with the help of Samuel, he had built a few pens adjacent to the barn that could be used for the shoats that he would occasionally buy from a neighboring farm. He would set about feeding the shoats well in preparation for slaughter when the weather turned cold enough.

One cold, cloudy day, Albert announced to Fannie that he planned on killing the eight pigs that he had been fattening up. He had already put the word out that any who could come and help would be welcomed, and that each family would be given some meat to take home. "Now, don't you worry too much about trying to help out," Albert told Fannie. "You don't need to be doing nothing to strain yourself too much. They'll probably be enough women that'll come anyway."

Albert shuffled back and forth in front of the fireplace in the sitting room to warm himself. Fannie, meanwhile, sat on the recently purchased davenport. Jasper, now five, and Myatt, who had turned two back in April, were engaged in some sort of imaginary play on the floor. Just a short while ago, Fannie had shared with Albert that she thought she was pregnant yet again. Still unable to forget the lifeless body of Willis Chester, Albert knew that Fannie already had her hands full with their two small children, and privately worried that any additional stress or strain might endanger the new baby's chances of survival.

"Well, if I had somebody who could watch the children, maybe I could help some . . ." Fannie paused. "But I don't know of anybody that I could get on short notice."

Albert insisted that she not concern herself with trying to help, and Fannie had to admit that it would probably be all she could do to take care of the boys and do some of the cooking for the big hog-killing crowd, even though some of the women would bring some food, as well.

Albert and Samuel spent most of the day preparing. First, they had to dig out a spot next to the smokehouse where they would place a big scalding vat. Back in the fall, the men had constructed the wooden vat from some leftover lumber and had sealed it with pine-tree resin. They also needed to place some big iron kettles beside the vat. Later, they drew up bucket after bucket of water from the well to put into the kettles, where the water would be heated and transferred to the vat when the first pigs were killed. They also drew up water to be placed in buckets for use in cleaning the intestines. Another huge kettle was placed in a spot several yards away from the smokehouse, where the cut-up skins would be cooked later to make lard.

Several days prior, the pair had dug holes next to the smokehouse and placed inside two large tree limbs that had been sawed off evenly at one end that went into the ground. They carved the other end of each limb into a V shape. Then they took another tree branch, somewhat smaller in diameter but greater in length, and placed one end into the V-shaped end of each wooden post. Several much smaller branches were sawed to about two feet and sharpened at each end. These would be used to hang the carcasses up on the wooden pole once the hair of the pigs had been removed. As Samuel prepared the wooden hangers, Albert sat on the seat to his grindstone and worked the pedals with his feet to turn the wheel to sharpen butcher knives.

Next, the men set up two big wooden tables in front of the smokehouse, where they would cut up each carcass into smaller pieces. Albert had acquired a meat grinder, which they fixed to one side of the table with a clamp. He'd also gotten an eight-quart sausage stuffer that, up until then, had been stored in the smokehouse. Albert used the big metal key to unlock the door to the smokehouse, then brought the stuffer out to place on the table with the meat grinder. Finally, the pair brought out a few wooden tubs from the smokehouse and set them next to the spot where the carcasses would be hung to catch the intestines once the hogs had been cut open.

Even though both men were exhausted after completing all of the preparations, they still needed to feed the livestock before calling it a day. Afterward, Samuel walked home with a promise to be back before sunrise while Albert walked in the house to partake in a supper of chicken and dumplings, along with some hoe cakes. After spending a few minutes with the boys, he fell asleep by the fireplace in his rocking chair. Finally, Fannie had to wake him up so that he could get to bed and rest before the big day.

Early the following morning, it seemed to Albert that he had just gotten into bed when he felt Fannie nudging him on the shoulder, urging him to get up. Just as the sun inched over the horizon, neighbors began to appear in either a buggy or wagon. Shortly, Albert's brothers Charles and Alonzo each came separately, while his sister Hettie came with his youngest brother, Irving. Fannie's brother Cleveland left Kittie at home to care for their three young children while he came to help. All together, there were about twenty who showed up to assist.

Albert, who prided himself on being organized, quickly let each one know what jobs needed to be done and selected the ones who could best perform them. Samuel was instructed to hitch one of the mules to the wagon. As each pig was stunned and bled out, the carcass would be loaded onto the wagon and hauled from the barn area to the scalding vat. Charles and Alonzo were to take turns hitting each pig just above the eyes with an ax, then stick the pig in the jugular to begin the bleeding-out process. After the pig was loaded into the back of the wagon, Samuel would make the short trip to the scalding vat, where Cleveland and three other neighbors would lift the pig out and place it in the heated water on top of two chains used to move the pig back and forth. Albert had learned that the water had to be just the right temperature: hot enough to cause the hair bristles to be easily scraped off, yet not so hot that the skin would be cooked. To ensure the right temperature, he submerged thermometers in the kettles to determine when the water was ready to be poured in the vat for scalding. When the men determined, under Albert's supervision, that the carcass was ready, the hog would be rolled out of the vat onto a large wooden pallet, where they would use round metal scrapers with wooden handles to scrape off the hair.

The scraping process needed to be done quickly, and as each carcass was readied, Albert cut slits in the back of each hind leg just above the hoof to find the tendon. Then, taking one of the wooden sticks that had been sharpened at each end, he slid the sharp end behind the tendon. A group of men then lifted the hog up to hang it on the horizontal pole that rose about eight feet parallel to the ground. It was just high enough that the snout did not touch the ground. As the pig was lifted up to hang, the men slipped the other end of the sharpened stick behind the tendon in the other hind leg.

As the process was repeated again and again in the background, the men who had been charged with disemboweling the carcass set to work. First, a long incision had to be cut down the middle of the pig's underside from the hind legs to the head. Further cuts were made to cause the insides to fall into a wooden tub placed below the carcass.

The intestines were separated and taken to a group of women waiting to clean them. Using the water drawn up from the well, the women cut the intestines into sections before emptying the undigested food into wooden tubs on the ground. With one person holding the intestine, another poured water into it. The one holding the intestine would then move her arms back and forth to slosh the water around inside to clean out any remaining particles.

Once an intestine was cleaned, it would be transferred to another basin for later use. It was a smelly process that one became accustomed to when working in a hog killing, but many of the women and men looked forward to seeing the intestines stuffed with sausage or fried later for a good chitlin supper. "Nothing like a good mess of chitlins," some folks would say. Other pig innards such as the liver, kidneys, and brain were separated out, some of which would be given to the many helpers to take home to cook immediately.

After the insides had been removed from each hog, some men took down the carcass to begin cutting the meat into pieces. The ears, feet, and snout would be used by some for pickling. Then there were the jowls, which some liked to slice up and fry or use later for seasoning vegetables. A more tedious process was cutting out the ribs, parts that could be cut into pork chops, and the inner sections of fat used to make lard. Leaner scraps and cuts would be used for making sausage.

Around noon, Fannie came out the back door to announce that if everyone would wash up, they could come in and get a plate of food. By then, all the pigs had been killed and their insides removed. Hettie had been with Fannie all morning helping with the children and the preparation of the food. Together with the dishes that had been brought in by some of the neighbors and family, a spread awaited the hungry folks as they entered the kitchen through the back door. There were collards, snap beans, stewed tomatoes, chicken stew, fried chicken, ham biscuits, and fried sausage. There were so many people that everyone had to fill a plate and eat wherever they could find a spot in the house. Many elected to eat as near to a fireplace as they could to warm themselves. Some of the women enjoyed spending time with Jasper and Myatt, who had been under Hettie's watchful eye. Once, Jasper had wanted to go outside to see what was going on, and she had taken him out on the porch for a few minutes. Though the boy had been curious, Fannie didn't want him to wander out among the workers out of concern that he would be in the way and might get hurt.

Fannie and Hettie scurried around inside the house refilling cups with water or hot coffee. Everyone who had been working outside, on the other hand, ate and engaged in lively conversation. Without taking much time to rest, the men soon headed back outside to continue cutting meat. The women stayed around to help wash the dishes and put away what was left of the food until it was time to head back outside to finish cleaning the chitlins.

Around the middle of the afternoon, Albert began turning the hand crank on the meat grinder. Charles and another man took the ground meat, seasoned it with black pepper and sage, and placed it in the black cast-iron sausage stuffer until it was full. A couple of the women who had brought over pans of casings—intestines that had been cleaned—helped by placing one end of each casing on the long tube that extended from the bottom of the stuffer while pinching the other end until the casing was full of sausage. Then they tied both ends of the casing with string and placed it in a big metal pan. To make Tom-thumb sausage, they added more sage and stuffed the lower part of the large intestine. Later on, when the Tom thumb had hung in the smokehouse for a while, it would be taken down, sliced, and fried. Many considered it to be a delicacy.

As the men cut the fat, it was handed over to Samuel, who had built a roaring fire under the large black kettle that sat nearby in which he had put a small amount of water. As the fat cooked, a clear, brownish liquid appeared in the kettle. When deemed ready, one man was charged with dipping up a bucket of liquid at a time. Another two men stood by to skim the cracklings off the top of the liquid and add a small amount of baking soda to turn the lard white. Next, a bucket was used to dip up the liquid and strain it through a piece of cloth held over a storage can. As the liquid fat solidified, it turned into the creamy lard that the women would use in cooking, mostly frying. Some folks would later take some of the cracklings home to use in making cornbread or corn mush.

It took everyone working at a feverish pace to get almost everything done by dusk. Women who lived nearby wanted to get home before dark, and Vasper and Hettie needed to get back to their mother's house before she became worried. A few of the men stayed late to cook the remaining fat and fill the storage cans. Albert gave everyone who had helped some cut meat and stuffed sausage to take home after promising to help them during their own hog-killing times. Samuel, of course, stayed until the last man had departed in his buggy.

Fannie insisted that he come sit with Albert and have a plate of brains and eggs. "Don't come early tomorrow morning," Albert told him between bites. "You've earned some rest. I'll handle the feeding in the morning so you can stay in and rest." Samuel didn't argue with the offer and decided to wait until the next day to get some of the meat to take home.

The temperature had dropped significantly with the setting of the sun, and the fireplace was again a welcomed respite from the hustle and bustle of the day's activities. Albert was too tired to talk or play with the boys, and he fell asleep in front of the fire. Later, after Fannie woke him and he climbed into bed, Albert reflected on how well everything had gone during the hog killing. He was glad that tomorrow would be a day of getting back to normal.

CHAPTER EIGHTEEN

MARY IVA

In August of 1911, Fannie and Albert were overjoyed when new baby Iva was born. After having given birth to the boys, Fannie was especially glad that it was a girl this time. As had been the case following the birth of their other children, women on both sides of the family took turns staying for a spell and helping with the new baby, Jasper, and Myatt. Because of the August heat, Fannie allowed the boys to play outside underneath the shade of the oak tree as long as someone was available to watch over them. Sometimes she would bring the baby out on the porch and sit for a while in a rocker, but she often ended up spending quite a bit of time fanning away the ever-present flies due to the nearby barn and pig pens.

Because Albert had met with such success in raising cotton, corn, and calves, he and Fannie were able to add some nicer furnishings inside the house. They replaced their metal-framed bed with a rather handsome three-piece mahogany bedroom set. The headboard rose high and was rounded on each corner. The footboard matched the design of the headboard except that it was lower in height. A dresser with two smaller drawers at the top and two larger ones at the bottom was accentuated by a French bevel-plate mirror at the top held in place by two wooden arms rising up from the top of the dresser. A tall chiffonier with five drawers and a mirror completed the set and provided plenty of storage space for clothing. Albert moved their metal-framed bed for Jasper and Myatt to share to an adjacent bedroom, and Iva slept in their bedroom in a new white-maple cradle padded with either a small blanket or quilt.

The couple had also finally been able to afford some furniture for a rather nice dining room next to the kitchen. Coupled with the kitchen table, they now had more room for guests to sit. There was a rectangular oak dining table that had an extension when needed, and there were eight oak chairs with hand-carved claw feet. A six-feet-tall china cabinet rounded out the set with carved feet to match the chairs. Two carved columns in the front separated the glass plates in the cabinet door from those on the sides. There were four shelves altogether, on which Fannie placed a display of their best china. Each piece was decorated with a pink floral spray, green leaves, and vines.

Albert and Fannie talked about fixing up the front part of the house with a more formal living room. However, they decided to wait for a while since, as Albert put forth, they needed a buggy or surrey for transportation in addition to the wagon.

So, Albert and Samuel returned to Parrish's in Benson, where Albert negotiated the purchase of a surrey. After looking over the selections, he decided on one with a front seat that folded down so that the back seat could be moved forward to make it a one-seat buggy. The top, which was lined with dark-green cloth on the inside, could be raised or lowered. Both the front and the back seats were upholstered in imitation black leather, and the hardwood body was painted black, as well.

After paying sixty dollars for the surrey, Albert unhitched Maude from the wagon and moved her to pull the surrey while Samuel used Jack to pull the wagon back home. The surrey would end up serving the family well over the next several years when they went to church or social gatherings.

Since the price of cotton went up in 1909 and 1910, Albert had made a handsome profit on the bales of cotton he had sold. In addition to that, he began lending cottonseed to friends and neighbors in the spring. In the fall when the cotton was ginned, they would return seed to Albert, who would turn around and sell it for a good price. Albert read *The Progressive Farmer* to gain insight on dealing in cottonseed. He found that some farmers fed cottonseed meal to their livestock, preserved the manure, and then returned the manure to the land to build up the quality of the soil. Others sold their cottonseed and reinvested their profits in fertilizing materials such as lime and potash, which they coupled with crop rotation to ensure healthy soils for growing. Albert leaned more toward the second alternative, since commercial fertilizers were becoming more available and a railroad spur line reached into the county from neighboring Harnett County that could bring fertilizers to nearby Woodsboro.

Wisely, he turned his profits from selling bales of cotton and cottonseed into investing further into his cattle herd and increasing his cotton and corn acreage. Those profits also would come in handy during the leaner years when the price of cotton would drop. After two good years in 1909 and 1910, cotton farmers suffered a drop in prices in 1911. Fortunately, prices rebounded in the next two years, and the economic prosperity that Albert and Fannie enjoyed was nothing short of glorious.

Social gatherings were rare for Albert and his growing family in those days. Except for church, a wedding, or a family meal, Albert kept his focus on his work. He always thought ahead to how he might improve his farming and livestock-raising methods, and he frequently shared what he learned with family members, who also profited from his experience and knowledge.

After a long, cold winter, Albert looked forward to getting back into the fields to ready the land for another season of growing cotton, corn, and whatever other grain he chose. With the leaves beginning to bud out on the trees and the fresh smell of spring in the air, Albert rose early each morning and found that as he went about the day's work, he did it with a heightened sense of possibility.

Meanwhile, with two small boys and a baby girl in the house, Fannie's days were consumed with taking care of the children, cooking, and washing clothes on a scrub board. Jasper's curiosity often led him to play outside or follow his father while he fed the livestock. Once, while climbing up on the wooden fence surrounding the pigs that Albert had once again bought to fatten up for use as meat later, Jasper tumbled over and landed in a big puddle of mud and manure.

Fortunately for him, Albert was working close by and saw him fall. He ran to the boy, who was covered in mud from head to toe and smelled to high heaven. Albert lifted his oldest son back over the fence before the pigs could get to him. "Don't you never do that again," Albert chastised. "What if I hadn't a-been here and you'd fell in with a boar hog or that bull?" He nodded his head in the direction of the bull, who was kept separated from the other livestock in a fenced-in area on the other side of the barn. "Now, run on back to the house and tell your mama what happened, and see if you can't get cleaned up."

Jasper looked as if he would burst into tears at any moment. Albert decided to say no more as the boy turned to walk toward the back side of the house.

Fannie sometimes allowed Myatt to play on the back porch, where she could watch him from the kitchen window. When she saw Jasper come up the back steps all muddied, she hurried out on the porch. She placed her hands on her hips, looked at Jasper, and asked, "What in this world . . . ?"

"Mama, Jap tink. Jap tink." Myatt scrunched the muscles around his nose.

"Yeah, I know he does, and he'll need to wash that mess off before he comes back in this house. What happened, son?" Fannie asked.

A few tears gathered in the corner of Jasper's eyes as he told his mother about standing high up on the hog-pen fence and falling into the mud.

"Well, I reckon you learned your lesson from that." Fannie figured that Albert had probably scolded Jasper pretty good, so she decided that further reprimand was unnecessary. "Let me warm up some water on the stove to pour into that tub." She looked toward the wooden tub that she kept on the back porch. "Myatt, you get on back in the house for now. Jasper's got to get cleaned up. Lord have mercy, I've never smelled such a scent!" Fannie turned and placed her hand on Myatt's back to guide him back into the house.

A while back, Albert and Samuel had installed a cast-iron water pump and sink in the kitchen so they wouldn't have to draw up water from the well every time they needed it. Fannie now moved the handle up and down until she was able to fill a white basin of water, which she then put into a large pot to heat up on the stove. When the water was deemed warm enough, she carried it outside and poured it in the wooden tub, then repeated the process once again to ensure that Jasper had enough water to get clean. She took a cake of lye soap from the kitchen and told her boy to take off all his clothes, get down in the tub, and scrub himself clean. When she determined that Jasper had washed himself to her satisfaction, she rinsed him off and told him to get inside and find some clean clothes. It would not be the last time that one of the boys would come to the house covered in mud and manure.

***

About the middle of April, Fannie and Albert talked about inviting some of the family over for a midday meal after church on Sunday. Because so many children had been added to both sides of the family over the past few years, they settled on inviting family from the Stephenson side. Later on, they agreed, they would host a meal for the Langdons.

On the Sunday morning of the meal, Samuel showed up early to assist with whatever feeding that needed to be done. Fannie, after taking care of the children, went about the business of cooking. Although she knew that everyone who came would bring some food to share, as well, she wanted to make sure there would be more than enough. Albert went to the hen house, caught two young chickens one by one, and used his hatchet to chop off their heads. After plucking off the feathers, he lit old newspapers to singe the remaining feathers off before taking them inside to Fannie, where she made stew with one and fried the other. Sweet potatoes that had been stored over the winter months were brought out, sliced, coated with sugar, and fried. Despite having the responsibility of caring for three young ones, Fannie had managed to put up many jars of canned vegetables the summer before, so she was able to open some of those for use, as well. Then, just before family began to arrive from church in the early afternoon, she baked a large pan of sweet-potato biscuits.

They arrived by buggy, surrey, and wagon, and before long the house, porch, and yard were filled with adults and children. It had been a while since most of the family had gathered together, and many had not yet seen the home improvements Albert and Fannie had made and everything Albert had invested in the farm.

All of Albert's brothers and sisters had married except for Vasper, Hettie, and Irving, who remained at home with their mother and arrived together for the gathering. After losing their first child a year after he had been born, Charles and his wife, Flossie Mae, had raised five more. Their children ranged in age from eight-year-old Alzula down to Ralston, who was just over a year old. In the middle of those two children were Ione, Onslow, and Palmon.

Alonzo and his wife, Georgianna, brought their two children: five-year-old Iola and David Nimrod, aged three. Georgianna was also pregnant and expected to deliver in June. Albert's sister Callie and her husband, Alvin Austin, arrived with their five children, too. The children ranged in age from one-year-old David to six-year-old Vernona.

Sadly, Leonard's first wife, Callie Ann, had passed away in 1910, and at the beginning of the year he had married again, this time to Alice Lassiter. From Leonard's first marriage, the couple brought three-year-old Ava. Kittie, who had married Fannie's brother Cleveland Langdon, had been busy raising four children. Rosa Carol, James Hector, Iris Jean, and Grover Nimrod were all about a year apart. Kittie had learned that she was also expecting a baby that would be born in November. Albert's sister Mary Valeria and her husband, Willie Lee, arrived with their one-year-old son, Denton Farmer. Mary was also expecting and would be delivering very soon, by the looks of the swelling under her dress.

Since most everyone had attended church services that morning, the men were dressed in dark-colored suits with either ties or bow ties. The women all wore dresses with long skirts in a variety of styles, and some wore large, stylish hats. The young girls were mostly attired in white or light-colored dresses with bows tied in their hair, while the boys either wore long pants or knee pants with long, dark socks.

With the help of the other women, Fannie got all the food out on the tables in the kitchen and dining room. Knowing that Fannie would not have enough plates and flatware for everyone, several families had brought their own. Albert asked Leonard to bless the food, and the women immediately set about helping the children fill their plates and find places to sit before taking their own seats in the kitchen and dining room. The men, after loading their plates with food, went out to eat and talk on the porch.

As Albert sat eating with the menfolk, the conversation, which started out with the usual banter about the upcoming growing season and livestock, suddenly took a different turn. Vasper, leaning against one of the support posts, asked, "Did y'all hear about that big ship that sunk out in the ocean?" Since Albert read *The Smithfield Herald* religiously, he had seen the articles about how the *Titanic* had struck an iceberg and had gone down in the Atlantic with tremendous loss of life.

Since some hadn't read about the disaster, Vasper eagerly took the lead in explaining how the huge ship had been ripped open by the big chunk of ice, and that within a short period of time the ship sank, taking with it over fifteen hundred people.

"Didn't they have lifeboats on that thing?" Alonzo wanted to know.

"From what I read," Irving chimed in, "they didn't have enough. They called for help, but the closest ship was hours away and couldn't get there in time. Most of the survivors were womenfolk and children, from what I understand."

Albert said, "To make it worse, it all happened at night. Can y'all imagine being on something like that and it sinking in the middle of the night?"

Everyone just shook their heads as they imagined the panic

and terror aboard the sinking ship. "God rest their souls," said Leonard.

Albert's brother-in-law Cleveland shook his head back and forth. "I'll tell y'all one thing. I won't be going on no ship like that in the middle of the ocean."

The others either nodded or muttered their agreement.

"I'm a-telling you," added Charles, "they'd have to put a gun to my head to get me on one of those ocean liners, and even then I don't think I could do it."

Albert privately thought about how he was quite content to be at work on the farm. *Too many bad things that can happen out there in the world*, he thought.

For a minute, they were silent before Charles, in an attempt to change the conversation, said, "I read in *The Herald* that Governor Aycock died while giving a speech in Alabama." The men turned their heads toward Charles as he continued, "Yep, I believe he was a good governor in some ways, especially education."

The truth was that Aycock had been North Carolina's governor from 1901 through 1905, and had been a strong supporter of building new schools and paying teachers more. On the other hand, he had also been a strong proponent of "keeping blacks in their place." It was his view that black people were not fit to rule, so therefore they should not have the right to vote.

As several of the men expressed their views about Aycock, Albert stayed out of the conversation. Not much one for politicking, he voted as he deemed necessary, but he rarely stepped into debate over the views of the various candidates for public office.

Irving and Vasper collected their plates to return them to the kitchen as the men finished eating. Cleveland wanted to see the livestock, so Albert led the men out to the barn and fenced-in area to see his growing herd of cows, calves, and the shoats he would keep until hog-killing time came around again. Afterward, they walked around the edge of the fields, where spring planting had begun. Albert talked about the upcoming cotton-growing season and gave the men some good cottonseed to take back home.

As the men walked about, some of the women washed dishes while others spilled out onto the porch to watch the children play. Some of the women stepped off the porch to play games with the children, including hopscotch, London Bridge, marbles, and jacks. The fact that the children were delighted was evidenced by their laughter and squeals of delight. Their fun was only slightly marred when Myatt and Palmon, almost the same age, got into a push-and-shove match over a brown teddy bear that someone had brought along as a toy for the children. Somehow Myatt had gotten the bear, and Palmon was trying to get it away from him. The three-year-olds wound up on the ground pulling at the bear and wailing. Fannie and Flossie Mae rushed off the porch to separate them. Fannie took the teddy bear and handed it to Hettie, who took it in the house and away from the crying boys. After Flossie Mae managed to get the boys separated and calmed down, the remainder of the afternoon was enjoyed by all.

When the men finally came back up to the house, each family began to gather together their belongings and thank Fannie and Albert for a most wonderful afternoon. With promises made to get together again soon, one by one the families loaded up and made their way home.

Albert took a seat in one of the rockers on the porch. Fannie rocked in the other while holding Iva, and Jasper and Myatt ran about in the yard. "You'd think they'd be tired by now," Fannie said to Albert with a grin.

Albert pulled out a red tin box of tobacco, filled his pipe, struck a match, and lit the tobacco. As he sat basking in the peacefulness of the waning afternoon light, reflecting on the day, he thought about how fortunate he was. He had been successful in getting a good start on his farm, and they had three wonderful children. In a way, he felt on top of the world.

*Willis Albert
Stephenson, circa 1904*

*Mary Frances (Fannie)
Langdon Stephenson,
circa 1904*

*Albert and Fannie's children:
(front center) Albert Hugh; (left
to right) Mary Iva, Jasper
Syrus, and James Myatt*

*Albert Hugh Stephenson,
circa 1930s*

Jasper S. Stephenson and wife,
Beulah McGee Stephenson,
circa late 1920s

Willis Albert Stephenson,
circa early 1900s

(Left to right) Flossie C. Stephenson,
Mary Iva Stephenson Sauls, James
Myatt Stephenson, Sherwood
Lassiter, Mary Ryals Stephenson,
Myra Stephenson Lassiter, and Albert
Hugh Stephenson, circa 1960s

Fannie Stephenson and
daughter Myra Stephenson
Lassiter. Myra was born
after Albert passed away in
1919.

Taken in 1954, this picture shows author Randy Stephenson in front of the house where he grew up that originally belonged to his grandparents Willis Albert and Fannie Stephenson. The house has undergone remodeling several times and has had other owners since the early 1990s. It is located on Landmark Road in western Johnston County.

This tombstone depicts the burial site of Mathias Caudill, who, along with other members of the Caudill family, is interred in a field off Landmark Road in western Johnston County. At present the small cemetery is in a dilapidated state.

The gravesite at Fellowship Primitive Baptist Church of Willis Albert and Fannie Langdon Stephenson and their two infants, Willis Chester and Mary Ann.

CHAPTER NINETEEN

A TRIP TO RALEIGH

After two good, solid years of cotton profit in 1912 and 1913, Albert found himself, along with other cotton farmers, facing another downturn in prices in 1914. One October evening, with the coolness of fall setting in, Albert placed some kindling in the fireplace in the sitting room. After lighting the kindling, he took a seat in his rocker and turned to Fannie, who sat nearby knitting a sweater for Iva.

Iva, now three, was getting around easily in the house. She sat on the floor next to her mother playing with a doll that Albert had brought back to her from a trip to Benson earlier in September. Jasper and Myatt, now seven and five years old respectively, were amusing themselves in another part of the house.

"I've been thinking," Albert began as he loaded his smoking pipe, "and I have some idea about maybe how we could turn the situation of low cotton prices into something to where we'll come out to the good in the end." Fannie turned toward Albert and raised her eyebrows. Albert continued, "What if, I was thinking, since bales are selling at no more than six cents a pound or so this year . . . what if I went around and offered to buy cotton bales from farmers around here, and held on to them 'til the price goes up again? Then, I could sell them and make some pretty good money." Albert looked for Fannie's reaction.

"Well . . . how can you be for sure prices will go up? What if you get stuck with all that cotton, and the price don't go up, and—"

Albert stopped Fannie before she could finish. "Well, I've been studying over it, and I've seen that the cotton market, since I've been farming here, has gone up and down. It'll go back up, I'm pretty sure. I just may need to hold on to it for a while." He took a puff on the pipe and blew the smoke toward the fireplace. "I believe I could probably get at least close to a hundred bales from folks around that'd be willing to sell." The confidence in his voice was unmistakable. "What I would want to do, though, is see if I can get a bank to lend me the money for now, so I won't have to go into what we've got saved. I'll need that for next year's crops and the livestock."

Fannie ended up agreeing that even though there was a risk to Albert's plan, his reasoning sounded logical. "Where you thinking about borrowing the money?" she asked.

Albert explained that he wanted to combine a trip to the state fair with a visit to a bank or two in Raleigh. "The fair starts up next week. Samuel could go with me, and we'll see about getting somebody to come stay with you and the children for a night, because we'd probably have to spend the night somewhere up there."

So, over the next few days, Albert arranged for his sister Hettie to come stay with Fannie and the children while he and Samuel made the trip. On the morning of the journey, Albert's youngest brother, Irving, brought Hettie over early in the morning by mule and buggy to stay until they returned the following day.

"We won't stay long at the fair," Albert told Samuel as Jack pulled the wagon northward on Old Stage Road. Albert was thankful that even though it was cloudy and cool, at least they'd be able to travel without freezing. "Mostly I want to see the hogs and cows. If we had more time, maybe we could take in a show or something, but I've got business at one of the banks in town. What we'll do," he added, "is ride out to the fairgrounds first, and then go back to the business section of town. Thought we'd find a room somewhere to spend the night. It'll be too late to ride back home tonight."

Albert had seen more and more automobiles on his trips into town since that first encounter with the horseless carriage years earlier. He'd also heard talk from people who had been to Raleigh about the electric lights, the streetcars powered by electricity, and the various styles and colors of automobiles they'd seen. Albert and Samuel each shared what they'd heard about electricity. Neither seemed able to comprehend how it worked or how it could light up a building, much less power a streetcar.

After exhausting their conversation about what they would witness once they arrived, the two rode in silence for several minutes. Then, from a good distance behind them, Albert thought he heard the sound of some kind of machine, but he couldn't tell what. Albert nudged Samuel with his right arm. "What's that I hear behind us? Can you hear anything?"

Samuel careened his neck to look back toward the sound. All at once and with excitement, Samuel said, "See if you can get the mule off to the side of the road. I see something coming, and it may be one of them horseless carriages."

Albert pulled on the reins to guide the mule to the right side, so that the wagon was about half on and half off the road. He turned around and could hardly believe what he saw. It was indeed another motor-powered carriage, but this one was a lot different from the contraption they'd first seen in Smithfield. Painted a bright red with what looked like brass trim in the front, the roadster came close up behind the wagon and then veered slightly to the left. Two young men dressed in dark suits and golf-style caps sat in the front seats. In the back sat two young women dressed in fashionable dresses and large hats with artificial flowers of various colors for adornment.

As the young people passed, all four waved. Jack became excited from the sound of the motor and began braying and moving nervously about. Albert pulled on the reins to keep the mule from bolting. As soon as the roadster had progressed well ahead of the wagon, the mule calmed down.

"Good that bridle's got them blinders on it, or I do believe that mule would've took off toward them woods and took us with him." Albert sounded relieved that the mule's first encounter with an automobile had gone as well as it had. "Thing about it is," he continued, "we're liable to run into several more of them things as we get nearer to town. Animal that's never been around something strange like that is bound to be nervous. Reminds me of something that happened in Raleigh a few years back."

Albert paused for a few seconds before continuing. "They was this woman. I don't know why I remember her last name, but it was a Mrs. King, I believe. She had come into town on her buggy with her two young boys. Well, from what I remember, they had stopped to watch a streetcar pass on Fayetteville Street, and when that streetcar got close to where they was, her horse that was pulling the buggy got startled, reared up on his hind legs, and took off running. She ended up jumping out of the buggy. Her two boys was found later in the buggy that had turned over on its side. The boys wa'n't hurt, but the woman got hurt up pretty bad, and they had to carry her to the hospital."

Samuel raised his eyebrows. "Well, I declare . . ."

Albert went on, "So, we'll have to be careful, especially in the beginning, about the mule getting scared. Sure don't want any such thing as that happening to us."

"It's a wonder she won't kilt," said Samuel, "or else her boys."

The men talked some more about the incident and then fell silent once again as they neared the outskirts of town. Just outside of the south side of Raleigh, after spotting a clearing in a small grove of trees, Albert guided the mule and wagon off the road and into the clearing. "Let's take a few minutes to eat what Fannie put in the bucket for us, and then we'll be on our way." Samuel agreed that it would be good to get off and stretch his legs for a few minutes, as well as eat some food.

While dining on the egg-and-ham biscuits and chasing them down with water, the men watched as an occasional buggy or wagon passed by. Once, another automobile approached from the southern direction. As the car passed in front of them, Albert pointed and said, "I think that must be one of them new Ford Model T's. I've seen pictures of them in the newspapers. They just started making them this year, according to what I read." Albert admired the all-black Model T as it passed and thought for a moment that maybe he might change his mind about getting an automobile sometime. "Problem for us," he told Samuel, "is that the roads is so bad, particularly in rainy weather, that I don't see how something like that would be worth the trouble." Albert went on to share that he and Fannie had once seen an automobile stranded in the mud on the side of the road. "Nobody was in it when we come up on it," he said, "so I imagine whoever was driving it had to go get some help to push it out. Just seems like too much of a problem to me to have such as that."

After they finished eating, they got back up on the wagon seat and continued the ride into town. The closer they got, the more activity they saw. Houses and other buildings became more numerous, as well as the number of wagons, buggies, and automobiles. Although the number of wagons and buggies outweighed the number of cars, Albert imagined that the country was on the verge of change. After passing by what looked like another Model T with the mule showing fewer signs of nervousness, Albert turned his head to Samuel and said with a chuckle, "I tell you what though. I think that it won't be long before there'll be automobiles as thick as ants crawling on the ground."

"I 'spect you might be about right on that. But they sure will have to do something to better the roads before that happens," Samuel offered.

As the men neared the business district, Albert reined the mule in front of a grocery shop to ask directions to the fairgrounds. Leaving Samuel in the wagon, Albert went inside and spoke to the butcher who, in his soiled white apron, explained that once they got farther up, they would need to locate Hillsboro* Street and head west toward the North Carolina A&M College; they'd find the fairgrounds across from there. Albert thanked the man, who only nodded and continued cutting meat. Joining Samuel back on the wagon seat, Albert relayed what the butcher had told him, and they continued forward into town.

Soon, Albert saw that Jack was getting increasingly agitated by the unaccustomed noises. The wagon passed by a well-dressed

---

* The spelling for Hillsboro would later be changed to Hillsborough.

man walking into town, and Albert pulled on the reins to bring the mule to a stop. He leaned forward to call out to the man, saying that they were looking to get to Hillsboro Street to go out to the fairgrounds, and could he please direct them to where they needed to go?

Much friendlier than the butcher at the grocery shop, the man told them that he would recommend they turn left on Lenoir Street and then right on Dawson. He added that they might want to consider finding a stable in that area to board the mule, and then walk up to Hillsboro to take the trolley west. "Trolley will take you right out by State College and the fairgrounds. Only will cost you a nickel apiece to ride it. If you keep going up Fayetteville Street, you'll come to a trolley that runs in that direction, and there's a lot more activity and noise on that street that you may want to avoid since you've got your mule with you here."

Albert thanked the man, grateful he had been so helpful. Advancing forward amidst the sights and sounds of the business district, Albert was able to locate the left turn that they needed to make on Lenoir Street. After a few blocks, they came to Dawson, where they took a right and spotted a sign advertising boarding stables. Albert thought to himself that he couldn't have planned it any better.

After making arrangements with the man on duty, the two men were shown a place where they could unhitch and leave the wagon until they returned the next morning. Leaving the mule to be led to a stable, Albert and Samuel walked up a few blocks more, where they came to the trolley tracks on Hillsboro. Seeing a small group of people gathered across the street apparently waiting on the trolley, Albert told Samuel that they would walk over and ask if that spot was where the trolley would stop. The two did obtain confirmation from an older gentleman smoking a pipe, and the men waited about ten minutes until they saw the trolley approaching from the east.

Carolina Power and Light had secured control of Raleigh's trolley system the year before. While some trolley cars were open on the sides, others were closed in. Not knowing passenger protocol, Albert told Samuel they would enter the car last so they could watch what everyone else did. As the trolley approached, Albert could hear a bell ringing. *Perhaps that's the signal that the streetcar is making a stop*, he thought to himself.

The small group of men and women assembled ahead of Albert and Samuel each handed the conductor the nickel fare and moved toward an empty seat. Following suit, the men were able to find a seat near the back of the trolley, and as soon as they had taken their seats, the bell rang again and they were off. After the car had gained full speed, Albert saw that the trolley was moving much faster than if they had taken the mule and wagon. Hillsboro Street was unpaved, and they passed by open fields of corn and grain as they moved along. As they passed St. Mary's School, Albert nudged Samuel with his arm and pointed to the school dedicated to the education of young women.

Everyone on board the trolley rose to get off when they arrived at the stop for the fair. "They all must be going to the fair, too," Albert told Samuel in a low voice.

After the two men stepped down from the trolley, Albert pointed out the State A&M College on one side of the road and the entrance to the fair on the other. Walking toward the entrance, Albert took in the sights and sounds around him. In front of the main entrance to the fairground was a mixture of horse- or mule-drawn buggies and a few automobiles. A white fence of about six feet in height had been erected along the perimeter of the fairgrounds, and he could hear the noise of the people inside and the music of a carousel. A tall building with a rounded roof and the North Carolina flag flying from the top stood behind the main-entrance gates.

After paying the fifty-cent admission price, the pair entered the midway, where a throng milled about. Children laughed and screamed on various rides, and men stood on platforms beckoning passersby to come in a tent to see a show. Albert was on a mission, though, and before long he and Samuel found the building where cows, bulls, and steers of a variety of types and colors were on exhibit. Since Albert was accustomed to the smells that came from keeping cattle in a confined space, he immediately felt at home when they entered the building.

They passed pens holding beef cows, such as the black Angus, red Herefords with their white faces, and the Red Polled, a breed that Albert was seeing for the first time. There was also a variety of dairy cows, including the black-and-white Holsteins, the brown-and-white Guernseys, and the fawn-colored Jerseys. He took particular notice of the young Holstein calves and remarked to Samuel that they didn't look any better to him than the ones he had been raising. "Maybe if it wa'n't so far to bring them up here, I could've brought a few of mine and won first prize." As he said this, he grinned and winked at Samuel.

After walking through the cow building, the men strolled over to another building nearby where the swine were on display. They paused for a moment to admire the handsome all-white Yorkshires and the black-colored Hampshires, who had a contrasting band of white running across the top and down the front shoulder and leg. Just after walking by the pens housing the Hampshires, they came to a row of pens with signs indicating that the breed was the Poland-China. Albert had seen reference to the Poland-China in *The Progressive Farmer*, but knew very little about them. Albert took note of black coloring over most of the Poland-China gilts' bodies, except for some white around the bottom of their legs and around the snout. As they passed other pens holding boars or sows, he noticed that some of the pigs had a band of white under their heads.

"I'm thinking before long I'll get into raising some pigs," he told Samuel. "I like the looks of these here Poland-Chinas, but I don't know anything about them. I'll need to read up on them and decide."

Samuel suggested that he might want to learn more about several of the breeds before getting started, because there would be a lot to consider. Albert pulled out his pocket watch, and seeing that it was already midafternoon, he told Samuel they would need to see about getting back into town before the banks closed.

After making their way back through the crowd, which seemed to Albert to have grown even more since their arrival, they found their way back to Hillsboro Street to catch the trolley as it headed back into the business district. They got off at Union Square and walked by the front of the state capitol building with its Doric columns and domed top. The pair then walked down Fayetteville Street and turned on Martin, on which they walked just a short distance to Wilmington Street, where the Commercial and Farmers Bank was located. The bank had been organized in 1891 and was housed in a modern four-story building with rows of paned windows on all four sides. The men arrived to find finely dressed men and women entering and leaving the bank, while others stood in front engaged in conversation.

Having no idea to whom he would need to speak or how long he would be, Albert told Samuel to take some time to browse around the area outside the bank, and he would wait for him at the front entrance when he finished. Albert then entered the bank and was struck by how, in his view, no expense had been spared in the construction and decoration of the interior. There were ornately decorated columns and cashiers' windows constructed of dark wood that rose to a height taller than he, but did not extend all the way to the ceiling.

With only one person speaking to a cashier, Albert walked up to the other window and was greeted by a Mr. Jerman, an affable man perhaps in his thirties dressed in a dark-blue suit, white shirt, and a gray-and-blue tie. Albert introduced himself and said, "I'd like to speak to someone about a loan."

Jerman replied with a smile, "Yes, sir, Mr. Stephenson. I'll be happy to help you get started with an application." The cashier turned, opened a drawer to a cabinet behind him, and returned with a two-page application. "If you'll take a seat over there"—he pointed to a row of dark-brown leather chairs—"and use this pen to fill in as much of the information as you can. When you're finished, please return the application to me."

Albert thanked Jerman, took the pen he was offered, and sat in the comfortable chair to begin filling in the information. Albert knew they would ask for collateral, and now that he had paid for his land in full, he would be able to use that to secure the loan.

After filling in all his personal information and the amount he wanted to borrow, Albert returned to the window and handed the application to the cashier. Jerman took a minute to read over the application before speaking. "I see here, Mr. Stephenson, that you have some land that you are offering as security for the loan. May I ask where this land is located and if you have any proof of ownership?"

Albert explained that his land was located in western Johnston County and that he had made arrangements for its purchase in 1903. He then produced a copy of the signed deed.

Once again, the cashier took a moment to read over the document before continuing. "Certainly. Everything looks good here, Mr. Stephenson, but I will need to hand this over to another gentleman here who supervises our loans. If you'll take a seat and give me just a few minutes to submit your application to him, we'll be back with you shortly."

Albert had expected this and was prepared to make a case as necessary for the money he needed. After about ten minutes, Jerman called Albert back to the window and told him to go to an open door to his left. Following the cashier's directive, Albert was subsequently introduced to a Mr. Jackson, who invited Albert to take a seat in the wooden chair facing his desk. Jerman took his leave to return to his cashier's window while Mr. Jackson took a few minutes to talk informally about Albert's background and current living situation. Like Jerman, Jackson was impeccably dressed in a suit, but with a black bowtie. Also like Jerman, he spoke in a friendly manner, and Albert immediately felt that if he could get a loan anywhere, it would be there.

Mr. Jackson took a look at the papers Albert had brought

showing land ownership, asked if there was a house on the property, and asked if Albert could describe it. "Could you give me a more detailed explanation of why you are seeking a loan with us today, Mr. Stephenson?" Jackson asked.

"Well, I've been successfully raising cotton for some time now, but as you may be aware, the price of cotton went way down this year. Some's been selling for five or six cents a pound."

Jackson nodded and said, "Yes, I follow the cotton market pretty closely. We have many farmers from around the area who bank with us."

"Well, I got to thinking about it, and the way I see it is that the price is bound to go back up at some point. I thought that what I could do is maybe make an offer to other farmers in my area . . . maybe pay them eight cents or so a pound to buy their bales off them. I would then hold the cotton at my place and sell it on the market when the price goes up." Albert watched Jackson's face for any sign of approval.

"Let me ask you this, Mr. Stephenson. What if the market does not go up, say, next year or even the next? The loan would need to be repaid, and perhaps you would not be able to fulfill your obligation to us." Jackson did not change his tone or expression as he said this. He just looked straight ahead into Albert's eyes to let his words sink in.

Albert was ready with his reply. "The thing is, I do have some money saved up in a bank in Benson. I just didn't want to use all my savings, because I have necessary farming expenses during the year. Plus, I'm thinking about getting into raising some pigs to bring in extra income and will need some of that money to buy a boar and some gilts. My land is worth quite a bit more than I'm asking for, and I understand the consequences if I default on the loan."

"Umm . . . yes, Mr. Stephenson, it is important that you understand that. Here's where I stand on this, sir," Jackson said. "Since you do not have an account with us and we do not know you, I feel that I can speak on behalf of our bank leadership that we would perhaps be able to lend you about half of what you are asking for. I agree that the price of cotton will most likely rise again, but things like that can be unpredictable. I would like to offer you a loan of three hundred dollars at six-percent interest. Now, I know that's not what you wanted, but I don't think our managers here would agree to more under risky circumstances."

Albert felt that he had no choice but to accept. After signing the necessary papers, Jackson told him that that the funds would be sent to his bank in Benson and would be available in two weeks. Albert had anticipated that he might run into an issue at the bank when asking for a sizable loan and had already thought of an alternate plan.

After leaving the bank, he found Samuel waiting on him just outside the main entrance. Albert explained that he would need to go to another nearby bank to see if he could get an additional loan. In a matter of minutes, the men found themselves in front of the Carolina Trust Company. Like the Commercial and Farmers Bank, the Carolina Trust Company was located in a new four-story building, though it was somewhat smaller in size.

Samuel once again waited outside while Albert entered and repeated the same request that he had done at the other bank. After listening to Albert's plans and his efforts to convince them that cotton prices would be on the rise, bank officials at Carolina Trust agreed to another three-hundred-dollar loan. Albert met Samuel back outside after signing the necessary papers.

While in the bank, Albert had inquired about a good place to stay the night, and was told that they shouldn't miss staying in nearby Yarborough House, a popular three-story hotel. The hotel had gained fame because two North Carolina governors, Jarvis and Scales, had resided there before the Governor's House was built in 1891, and also because it had been the hotel of choice for Presidents Andrew Johnson and Teddy Roosevelt. Albert had previously planned to rent a room for the night in a private home, but now that he was basking in his good fortune after securing the two loans, he was up for something a bit more appealing.

After making arrangements to get a room with two beds, Albert and Samuel dined on a delectable meal of beef stew and vegetables in the hotel's large dining room. The men slept soundly that night until the following morning, when they returned to the stables to hitch the mule to the wagon and head back to Pleasant Grove. Albert could hardly contain his excitement as they made their way back out of the city and down the Old Stage Road. He was confident that he had made a good decision.

***

Weeks later, Albert put out the word that he was willing to buy bales of cotton for eight cents a pound, which was above the market price. He went by wagon from farm to farm, accompanied by Samuel, to make the purchases and haul the baled cotton back to the house. Much of the cotton ended up being stored in the unfurnished front part of the house.

As it turned out, the cotton would be there for a while.

CHAPTER TWENTY

A SPRING SNOWFALL
AND ANOTHER LOSS

Around the time that Albert and Samuel returned from Raleigh, Fannie told Albert that she thought she was pregnant yet again. She expected that the baby might be born sometime next summer. Fannie expressed her hope for another girl. "That way," she said, "Iva will have someone to play with."

Winters could be cold in Pleasant Grove, and sometimes there would be snow. Albert's activities were confined to making sure the livestock were adequately fed, and any young calves were kept inside the barn away from the brunt of the cold and wind. Jasper had been attending school at nearby Ogburn Grove, and Myatt would be joining him as soon as he was old enough. Most days, Albert would take Jasper in the surrey or the wagon so he wouldn't have to walk to the one-room school during the four-month school term. When spring rolled around, children were expected to help out on the farm, so Jasper would stay at home until the next term began later in the year.

In March and April, as he had done in all the years that he'd farmed, Albert began plowing up the land once again to plant cotton and corn. By the time April came, Fannie's pregnancy was showing quite a bit, and the couple looked forward to when she would deliver once again.

One morning, with the leaves beginning to bud out on the trees and with springtime's renewal in the air, Jasper followed his daddy out to the barn to help feed the pigs and calves. Albert was giving more responsibility to Jasper so that one day, as he explained to the boy, he would be able to do everything on his own when he had his own place. Fannie was out scrubbing clothes in a wooden tub on the porch. little Iva tried to help by putting each piece of washed clothing in a large basket to be hung on the clothesline later.

Meanwhile Myatt, ever the curious one, walked around looking for anything that he might use to play or build something with. As he rounded the corner of the house into the backyard area, he came upon the rooster walking straight toward him. Earlier, Albert had let the chickens and rooster out to roam freely in the backyard. Perhaps because the rooster sensed danger from the boy, without warning he flew up into Myatt's face and began clawing at his overalls.

Fannie was alerted by Myatt's loud cries and came running down from the porch. Albert, who had been standing just outside the pig pen, also heard the commotion and ran toward Myatt. Fannie managed to reach him first and pulled the rooster off him. Myatt was by now crying uncontrollably. Fannie checked him for scratches before leading him inside, where she applied some liniment to the affected areas of his face and arms.

Albert, angered by the rooster's actions, grabbed the ax that he'd left lying on the back porch, chased the rooster down, pinned it to the ground with his feet, and chopped off its head with one swing. When Fannie reappeared on the porch, Albert called out, "I guess you know what we'll be having for supper!" He held up the headless rooster.

Fannie nodded and said, "Good enough for him. We can't have that mess around here. It's a wonder he didn't put out one of Myatt's eyes."

Encounters with animals, and not just farm animals, were common out in the country. There was always the possibility that a fox would appear in stealth to try to make off with one or more of the chickens. Occasionally an opossum or a raccoon would leave footprints around the smokehouse or barn. Once, a female cat had come out of nowhere and birthed kittens under the porch. When Albert had tried to get them out, the kittens hissed and scratched at his bare arms, so he ended up leaving them there.

One day they just weren't there anymore, and he never knew what happened to them.

A few days after Myatt's encounter with the rooster, Pleasant Grove residents were surprised by a snowstorm. While not uncommon to get a sizable snowfall in March, getting one in April, especially after the signs of spring were all around, was nothing short of freakish. The snow began with large flakes falling in the afternoon so rapidly that the ground was covered in no time. Albert and Samuel hurried to make sure all the calves had plenty of straw for bedding inside the barn. They put the mules in a stable together. The bull and the cows would be left out in the pasture, but Albert had seen them make it through the cold and snow before. Finally, Albert told Samuel to go home before the snow got too deep.

During the remainder of daylight and even into the early evening hours, Jasper, Myatt, and Iva spent much of their time at the windows watching the snow come down. Albert had made sure that they had plenty of firewood for the night, and Fannie had gone to the smokehouse to pull down some stuffed sausage from the last hog-killing. That night, she cooked a meal of sausage, baked sweet potatoes, and biscuits. After dinner, Fannie sat on the davenport reading the Bible while Albert read the newspaper and smoked his pipe.

The next morning, they awoke to see that the snow that had fallen was being covered by sleet. Fannie fried some ham slices and cooked eggs and grits, and they all gathered around the kitchen table to eat and stay warm. The children were beside themselves with excitement. As soon as there was enough light, they begged to go outside to play in the snow.

"Y'all need to wait a little. It's a-sleeting, and it's cold as ice out there," Fannie told them. "Your daddy's got to get out and look after the calves. Maybe when he's through, he can walk out with you. I'm not a-putting my foot out there, I'll tell you."

Some time ago, Albert had purchased a new pair of black lace-up boots. He now put them on along with a heavy coat, hat, and gloves.

The temperature had dropped during the night, and coupled with the sleet, conditions made for a treacherous walk. Several times Albert felt as if his feet were going out from under him.

He kept a supply of ground feed and hay in the barn during the winter months, because there was always the possibility of bad weather, but because it was April, he was getting low on supply. First, he looked in on the calves to make sure they were all right. In spite of the cold, all looked to be to Albert's satisfaction, so he made his way to the well to draw up a bucket of water. Albert slowly lowered the bucket into the well, watched it fill up, and drew it back up. When the bucket reached the top of the well, Albert leaned over slightly to grasp it, and just as he did, his feet flew out from under him and he landed on his backside, the water spilling all over his clothing.

Fannie was watching through the window and saw everything. She called to Jasper and Myatt, "Y'all come here quick! Your daddy fell out there trying to draw up some water. Put you on a coat and your boots, and see if you can make it out there to see if he's all right."

In a matter of seconds, the boys ran to grab their coats and lace up their boots. In the meantime, Fannie watched through the window as Albert attempted to stand up. As the boys made their way ever so carefully over the slick blanket of snow, Albert managed to hold on to the side of the well for support so that he could stand. Seeing the boys coming toward him, he decided to stay put until they reached him.

"Are you all right, Daddy?" asked Jasper when they finally got within a few feet of their father.

"Well, I ain't the best in the world, but at least I didn't break any bones." Albert attempted to smile to reassure his sons. "Listen here, you and Myatt go and get a bucket apiece from inside the barn over there. But mind and don't fall."

The boys carefully walked across the frozen snow to get the two buckets sitting inside the doorway to a stable unoccupied by calves. Then, carefully positioning himself against the well so that he wouldn't fall again, Albert drew up one bucket after another and poured it into the two buckets the boys had placed on the snow next to him. Their eagerness to help their daddy was endearing to Albert. As their father filled each bucket, Jasper and Myatt took turns taking the bucket of water to one of the stables to pour water into troughs for the calves and mules.

"What'll the cows and bull do?" Myatt asked after they had poured water into all the troughs.

"I 'spect they'll go down to the creek and drink," Albert said. "You don't have to worry about them. They'll find water."

With the snow-and-sleet mixture still coming down, Albert turned his attention to the shoats in a pen next to the barn. The pigs had huddled together under a small lean-to shelter. Albert drew up more water and poured it into the buckets. Then, with the boys' help, he took the buckets and lifted them over the wooden fence to pour into a trough. The pigs quickly drank all the water, prompting Albert and the boys to fill up the buckets again. After the second round of water had been poured, the boys followed Albert back inside the barn, where he filled a bucket with some ground feed that he had bought in Woodsboro. When they returned to the pen, Albert stepped over the fence and poured the feed into a wooden trough. In the pigs' eagerness to get to the feed, Albert almost found himself on the ground again as they crowded around him. Fortunately, he was close enough to the fence that he could grab it and hold himself steady until he could step back over.

"What a time we're a-having in this weather!" said Fannie when Albert and the boys finally got back inside to warm themselves at the fireplace. "It's a wonder you wa'n't hurt bad, Albert. Calves or no calves, pigs or no pigs, it won't be worth it if you break your arm or leg," Fannie said.

Albert did not answer, but he knew she was right. He'd have to think of a plan before next winter came so that watering and feeding the animals wouldn't be so risky.

The snow and sleet dwindled down to a few flakes here and

there by afternoon. Way before dark, Albert got the boys to go back with him to the barn to check on the livestock and make sure they all had plenty for the cold night ahead.

The next day, the temperature rebounded, and much of the snow and ice began melting. The springtime snow would become fodder for conversation around the dinner table for families in Pleasant Grove for several days. Although there would be cold snaps in the spring in the years to come, there was never again an April snowstorm like that one.

***

As spring blended into the summer, Fannie knew that she would deliver soon. One morning in June, she told Albert her prediction, so he spoke to Samuel about getting Annie Mae when the time came. He also decided to ride down to the Langdons to ask Vic if she could come again and stay with Fannie until the baby was born. Vic readily agreed to come, so the day after Albert had paid her a visit, her father accompanied her by horse and buggy to Albert and Fannie's house. Upon arriving, James Langdon and his daughter Vic entered into the sitting room. Even though it was the middle of the week, Mr. Langdon wore a dark-blue suit and white shirt, as if he were headed to church, while Vic was dressed in a long black skirt and white, lacy blouse. Albert had thought highly of the Langdons ever since he had begun courting Fannie years ago, and now felt glad that they had come as he had requested.

James went into the adjacent bedroom to speak to Fannie, who lay in the bed resting. "Now, don't you worry," he told Fannie. "You'll be in good hands with Vic here. She can manage the children and the cooking."

Fannie, still in her nightgown, squeezed her father's outstretched hand and thanked him for bringing her sister to stay with them. Although Fannie begged him to stay for a while, James told her that he needed to get back to get some things done. After taking his leave, he climbed in his buggy and headed eastward back home.

Vic took command of the house immediately by asking what

they wanted to eat. Albert took her out to the smokehouse to explain where she could find everything. Then, he gave strict instructions to the children to mind their aunt and to do whatever they could to help their mother.

The children enjoyed the change of pace that their aunt brought and seemed eager to please her. During the daytime, when the boys were not helping their father, they played outside while Iva either stayed inside with her aunt or played out on the porch. After a few days had gone by and the children were all occupied, Fannie called for Vic to come to the bedroom, where she lay on her back in obvious discomfort. "Vic, I feel like the baby might be coming, but I'm not sure."

Vic, not wanting to appear overly alarmed, replied, "Well, let's go ahead and get Annie Mae up here so if the baby does start coming, she'll be here to help. Now, don't you worry," she added, rubbing Fannie's head and moving her hand over her belly. "I'm sure everything is going to be all right. Let me see if I can find Albert or Samuel, and I'll have one of them go get Annie Mae."

Samuel took the mule and wagon to Annie Mae, who dropped everything she was doing and accompanied him with her black bag back to Fannie's bedside. In the meantime, Albert spoke to Vic. "If you'll kind of look after the children and so forth when Annie Mae gets here, she can sit with Fannie. If the baby starts coming, then she may need your help. I've been thinking that if it looks to you like the baby will be born pretty soon, I'll take the children over to Mama's and let them stay there until after it's born."

Vic acknowledged that Albert's idea would be best, and left Annie Mae to attend to Fannie while she went to work in the kitchen. Intermittently, Annie Mae would go to the kitchen to speak softly to Vic about whatever was transpiring. Late in the afternoon, she told Vic that she needed let Albert know that if he was going to take the children to his mother's to stay, they needed to make preparations now. "I think she's starting to go into labor," Annie Mae told Vic.

With the sun getting low in the sky, Albert loaded the three children into the surrey and headed toward his mother's house. Not long after, Fannie began to moan and turn back and forth in the bed in an effort to get comfortable. With no doubt that she was now in labor, Vic and Annie Mae went about making preparations for the birthing. Vic made sure there were plenty of clean cloths near the bed.

By the time Albert got back from taking the children to his mother's, Fannie's labor was in full swing. He came in and sat down at the kitchen table, and Vic filled him a plate of meat, fresh squash, and snap beans. Albert knew to stay out of the way when Fannie was being attended to by the women, so after supper he took his pipe and a kerosene lamp to the porch to smoke and read *The Progressive Farmer*. After a few minutes of attempting to read, Albert finally gave up, disturbed by the moaning and cries of discomfort coming from the bedroom. He sat for what seemed a long time in his rocker until Vic appeared on the porch. Even in the dim light, Albert could see the perspiration on her forehead.

"To be sure, it won't be much longer," she said, rubbing her hands down her skirt. "I'm mighty glad that Annie Mae was able to come, because she knows more than I do. Do you want to try to lie down and get some rest? We'll be up with her even if it's all night, but you'll need some rest before you start back to work tomorrow."

Albert had no idea if he'd be able to sleep, but agreed with Vic that he should at least try. After putting out his pipe, he picked up the lamp and took it back into the sitting room. He passed by the bed where Fannie lay moaning with her eyes closed, and opened the door to the boys' bedroom. Removing his shoes, he kept his pants and shirt on in case he needed to get up quickly. As expected, Albert was unable to sleep, partly because of the anticipation of the birth, but also because of Fannie's discomfort.

Sometime in the wee hours of the morning, he had almost drifted off when he heard Vic and Annie Mae loudly encouraging Fannie to push. Albert sat up on the edge of the bed. The women's voices suddenly changed to what sounded to Albert like alarm.

Albert stood up, opened the door to the bedroom, and saw that the baby had indeed been born. However, he'd heard no cry.

Vic, with a wearied look on her face, looked up at Albert. Annie Mae took the newborn and held her up to slap her on the backside. Still no cry. "Oh, my goodness, she's not breathing!" erupted Annie Mae. It was obvious to Albert by the look on Vic's face that the situation was grave.

"Oh, my lord, what's wrong?" Fannie managed to get out weakly.

Annie Mae placed the baby on the bed next to Fannie, opened the infant's mouth, and tried to breathe into her lungs. Nothing. She picked the baby up again and slapped her on the back. Still no response. Vic went around to where Albert stood as Annie Mae continued to work on the baby.

Vic placed her arm around Albert's back. "I'm so sorry. I'm so sorry." Tears began flowing down her cheeks.

Fannie squeezed her eyes shut, as if closing them would somehow mean that what she was witnessing was not really happening. Finally, Annie Mae appeared to give in to the fact that the baby was gone. She sat for a few moments with her head down, perhaps unaware of what words could bring any degree of comfort in a time like this.

Albert knew that Fannie needed him, and went around to take the chair next to the bed. Without speaking, he held Fannie's hand. As he sat there, it dawned on Albert that the baby was a girl—the girl that Fannie had especially wanted. Now, all the optimism that they had both shared prior to the delivery was shattered.

Annie Mae and Vic began cleaning up all the mess that came with giving birth. No one spoke. Albert knew that the pain Fannie was feeling upon losing a second child was far greater than the labor pains she had gone through.

***

The next day, the baby was wrapped in a blanket and placed

in a tiny coffin brought to the house by Albert's brother Charles. Charles and Flossie Mae could identify with the heartache that Albert and Fannie felt, since they, too, had lost a child.

Charles helped Albert hitch Maude to the wagon, and the two men placed the tiny coffin inside. Albert assisted Fannie into Charles' buggy, and the pair followed the wagon on another sad trip to the Stephenson family cemetery.

When they arrived, Mandy, Vasper, Irving, and Hettie all came out to witness the infant's burial. Mandy explained as best she could to Jasper, Myatt, and Iva that their sister had been born, but had already gone to heaven. It was a forlorn sight as they all stood in the cemetery while Charles and Albert lowered the coffin into a grave. Afterward, since neither felt like socializing, Fannie and Albert headed back home. Charles followed behind in the wagon with the children.

Over the course of the next few days and weeks, as family and neighbors learned of the death of the baby that they had decided to name Mary Ann, Albert would hear again and again the often-repeated words of "We don't know why such things happen, but God knows," or "It's all part of God's plan." Albert knew that people meant well, but he just couldn't understand why an innocent baby like theirs could be taken away so abruptly.

After the burial, Albert absorbed himself as much as he could in his work. Work, he thought to himself, would at least take his mind off the loss some. As he and Fannie went about their daily activities, Albert could tell that Fannie was just going through the motions. It would take a while and the expectation of another child before either was able to move beyond the loss they felt.

CHAPTER TWENTY-ONE

ANOTHER TRIP TO THE FAIR

In the fall of 1915, with most of the cotton picked and baled, Albert decided that he wanted to go back to the state fair in Raleigh. His visit would have two purposes: one, to take Jasper and Myatt with him to see the livestock and perhaps enjoy some of the midway; and two, he had plans to stop by a nearby farm in Wake County that had advertised Poland-China pigs for sale.

Knowing that there would always be lean years in which cotton would not bring a decent price, Albert looked to invest more in livestock to diversify his income. His cattle dealing had proven lucrative, and he saw no reason why he couldn't make some good money off raising swine. Albert had read and studied about several different breeds. Hampshires, Yorkshires, and Durocs all had their good points, but after careful consideration, he kept coming back to the Poland-China.

"I want to give them a try," he told Fannie of his plans one evening in mid-October. "Samuel will be around to look after everything. We'll find us a place to stay overnight and will be back the next day."

The next morning, as Fannie packed a lunch they could carry in a bucket, Albert and the boys set about hitching both mules to the wagon to get an early start toward Raleigh. Jasper and Myatt looked almost like twins in their overalls and long-sleeved blue shirts, while Albert had traded in his everyday farm attire for a nice pair of navy-blue serge pants, a white shirt, and his trademark black stiff hat. Because the weather had turned cooler in the past few days, both boys wore corduroy coats and Albert wore a long black overcoat.

When the wagon was ready and the bucket of food had been placed inside, Jasper and Myatt jumped into the bed of the wagon while Albert climbed up on the wagon seat to take the reins. With Fannie and Iva standing on the side porch waving good-bye, Albert and the boys turned eastward down the dirt road that passed in front of their house. As he had done before with Samuel, Albert planned to take the Old Stage Road into town.

The wagon rolled northward toward Raleigh, and the trio noticed a mixture of horse- or mule-powered transportation and automobiles. Jasper and Myatt had seen cars before when they'd accompanied their father into town in Benson or nearby Angier, but as they drew closer to the capital city, they were awestruck at the different types and colors of cars they encountered. They especially delighted in the roadsters, and one or both of the boys would call out to their father, "Can we get one of them?" Albert still was not ready to consider buying an automobile due to the condition of most of the dirt roads in Johnston County.

Just before reaching the outskirts of town, Albert pulled the wagon over to a small clearing to eat the biscuits that Fannie had packed for them in the bucket. She had put slices of ham in some and molasses in the others. After finishing the food, they got back in the wagon to continue into Raleigh.

Following the same plan as before, Albert left the mules at a stable in town, and he and the boys walked to Hillsboro Street to take the streetcar out toward the fairgrounds. Jasper was especially curious about how the streetcars operated by electricity. Albert found that explaining electricity was a challenge, since it wasn't something they could see. He just knew that it powered the streetcars along the tracks.

When they reached the gates outside the fairgrounds, Albert could tell that the size of the midway had grown even more since his previous visit. Throngs of people stood in line to pay for tickets. As they waited to pay their admission, they witnessed the arrival of Governor Craig and other important officials in automobiles decorated in red, white, and blue. The governor was slated to speak at the official opening since this was the first day of the fair.

When Albert, Jasper, and Myatt finally gained entrance through the main gate, they were immediately bombarded with the sounds, sights, and smells of the midway.

"Can we ride on that?" Jasper asked, pointing to the Ferris wheel.

"Maybe later," answered his father. "Let's see what the governor has to say first, and then I want to look at the hogs and cows. They have some shows going on today, too, so let's see what's happening."

Albert and the boys walked over to where a huge crowd had gathered around a platform to watch Governor Craig give his welcoming remarks. Just as he finished, a group of boys marched in. Albert overheard someone say that they were in the Corn Club, and that today was Corn Club Day at the fair. He told Jasper and Myatt to stick closely behind him as they walked past several booths where Corn Club products were on exhibit. Albert had looked at a schedule of events and had seen that at one o'clock, horse races were to be featured in the grandstand, followed by an airplane show. Knowing that the boys had never seen an airplane, he decided to put off looking at the livestock, and they headed toward the grandstand.

The grandstand had been constructed to accommodate up to three thousand spectators. The seats were mostly on the second floor, where Albert and the boys sat down to watch the races. Jasper and Myatt entertained themselves by picking out the horse they thought would win each race, cheering wildly as they ran around the track.

Following the horse races, a show billed as the "bombardment of forts" by a Captain Worden began. Before the plane appeared, Albert pointed out the direction of the sound of the plane as it approached the grandstand. Then, there it was. As the plane flew in front of the grandstand, something appeared to drop from the plane, as if a fort were being bombarded.

"Look at that!" Myatt jumped up from his seat and pointed at the plane. "How does that thing get in the air?"

Albert didn't understand much about how planes got in the air himself, but explained it by saying that the engine's propeller forced the plane into the air and kept it going. He went on to tell the boys about the first plane flights that had taken place right there in North Carolina at a place called Kitty Hawk. "Now, how would you like to ride in one of them things sometime?" Albert drew his head back, raised his eyebrows, and smiled.

"I don't know about that," replied Jasper. "It might fall out of the sky."

"Well, I'll tell you what I think," said Albert. "It may be that someday that's how people will get about."

Both boys just shook their heads dubiously.

After the plane passed the grandstand a few more times, Albert coaxed the boys out of their seats and back out into the midway, where they made their way to the livestock barns. First, they walked through the pens where calves, cows, and bulls were on exhibit. The boys were enthralled by the size of some of the cows and bulls.

"I didn't know a cow could get that big," Myatt remarked as they passed by milk cows with huge udders. Albert noted the boys' curiosity about the different breeds and took time to explain what he knew about each.

After seeing the cattle, they walked into another barn where swine were on exhibit. Once again, Albert paused to talk about the various breeds. When he came to some pens holding Poland-China gilts, sows, and boars, he explained that he wanted to get started raising the breed and that they'd be stopping by a farm on their way back home the next day to look into buying a few gilts.

Following their viewing of the pigs, they took a few minutes to pass through another area that had goats. Although Albert had never chosen to raise goats, he told the boys about how his family had raised goats when he was growing up.

Next, they walked back into the midway. Jasper and Myatt were wide-eyed with wonder as they passed by shows advertising oddities such as the "Fat Lady" and the "Alligator Boy."

Burlesque shows had begun making their appearance on the midway, and a crowd of young men stood in front of one of the so-called "hoochie-coochie" shows.

Jasper tugged on Albert's arm as they passed in front of the Ferris wheel. "Can we ride that?" he asked.

Albert looked at Myatt and saw that both were eager to ride the big wheel, so Albert paid the fare and they waited in line until it was their turn to enter one of the seats. The boys had never been up so high before, and they enjoyed pointing out the places they'd already visited and other things they wanted to do.

After the Ferris wheel, Albert bought them tickets to ride the carousel. Each climbed up on a hobby horse and rode around and around while music played in the background. The smiles on their faces were endearing to Albert, and he hoped that he would be able to bring them back to the fair in the years to come.

With the afternoon waning, Albert told the boys that they could all go to a nearby dining hall to get something to eat before leaving the fairgrounds. After waiting a few minutes to get three seats together, Albert went to the counter and ordered hot dogs and Pepsi-Colas for all of them. It was the first time that Jasper and Myatt had tasted a hot dog or a Pepsi. They seemed fascinated.

"I think I like this hot dog better than sausage," Myatt said in between bites.

Jasper let his father know that he agreed by nodding his head up and down, not wanting to interrupt his eating with talk.

After they had all savored the last of their delicious meal, Albert stood up and told them that they needed to get back on the streetcar and head back into town before dark.

Upon arriving back into the business district, Albert asked directions for how to get to the Raleigh Hotel. The hotel was located on West Martin close to the Raleigh *News and Observer* building. As they approached the hotel, young boys passed by on their bicycles and pedestrians walked along in front of the hotel and the residences nearby.

Albert spoke with the clerk on duty at the desk and paid for one room for a one-night stay. The boys had never stayed where there was indoor plumbing, and were intrigued by the bathroom facilities. The window in their second-floor room gave the youngsters ample opportunity to observe the comings and goings of passersby on the street. Albert finally ran them away from the window and told them they needed to get into bed, that it had been a long day, and they had another big day coming up. Myatt slept on a small fold-out bed while Jasper and Albert shared the larger metal-framed bed.

Not long after they lay down, all three drifted off to sleep. They were awakened the next morning only by the sound of the activity in the street and the light that crept through the drawn curtains.

CHAPTER TWENTY-TWO

A WAGON MISHAP

After getting the two mules from the stable where Albert had left them the day before, he and the boys rode at a steady pace through the south side of Raleigh back out to the Old Stage Road toward home. As they made their way out of town, trees and other vegetation replaced the buildings, houses, and activity of the capital city. A light dusting of frost covered the ground as a reminder that cold weather would be coming soon.

After leaving the outskirts of town, Albert turned his head to the right so the boys could hear him where they sat in the wagon bed. "How did y'all like your first time at the fair?"

"It was the most funnest day ever!" answered Jasper immediately.

"For me, too!" Myatt joined in. "I ain't never seen nothing like that man that was flying that plane. That was the best part for me."

Jasper agreed. "That was something, but I liked it all. Boy, I wish I had another hot dog right now . . . and a Pepsi drink, too."

"Well, now you'll have something to tell your mama about when we get home. Maybe if y'all are good, we might can come back to the fair next year." Albert figured that would give them something to look forward to, and perhaps he could use it as motivation to get them to complete their chores at home and to do well in school.

As the mules plodded along, there were few signs of life except for an occasional farmhouse or wagon. Only one car had passed them since they'd left town, a black Model T. Albert enjoyed riding past the tall pine trees interspersed with deciduous trees, such as red maples and sweetgums, in their colorful fall splendor.

After about an hour, Albert spotted the small wooden sign

advertising PIGS FOR SALE that he had been looking for. He pulled the reins to the right to guide the mules down a long pathway running deep into the woods. Through the leaves and branches, a small wood-framed farmhouse in need of a coat of paint appeared. As they drew nearer, he made out two barns not too far away from the right side of the house. Albert pulled the mules to a stop in front of the front entrance to the farmhouse.

"Now, remember to stay behind me and be quiet," he told the boys. Jasper and Myatt fell in behind their father as he went to the front door and knocked. A young, redhaired boy opened the door. "Your daddy at home, son?" asked Albert. "I want to talk to him about his pigs he's got for sale."

"He's in the barn," the boy answered without smiling. His eyes moved to try to see the two boys standing behind the strange man who had come to the door.

Albert motioned for Jasper and Myatt to follow him, and they began walking toward the first barn. The redhaired boy stepped out, closed the door behind him, and followed them. Without explanation, he started moving faster in order to get ahead of the visitors, leading them around to the south entrance to the barn. Seeing his father just inside the entrance, the redhaired boy called out, "Papa, a man's here to see you!"

The boy's father looked up from whatever he had been doing and said to Albert, "What can I do for you?" Even though the weather was cool, he had obviously been sweating—so much so that his hair was matted to his forehead.

"I heard from down where we live that you might have some Poland-Chinas for sale here," Albert said. "I been looking to get started in raising some pigs, and I been studying up about that kind of hog. I thought I'd see what you have."

"Henry, why don't you take them boys out in the yard and y'all can shoot some marbles or something 'til we get done talking," the redhaired boy's father said.

Henry nodded and motioned for Jasper and Myatt to follow him. Albert reasoned that the boy might be glad to have a couple of playmates for a while, since by the looks of things there was nobody except him and his father. He'd seen no sign of a wife or any other children.

When the boys left, Henry's father put his shovel down, pulled off his gloves, and held out his right hand. "I'm Wilbur Thomas. Nice to meet you. I've been raising Poland-Chinas and Hampshires for a while. I imagine if you been studying about them, then you know the Poland-China is a good breed. I've been able to sell quite a few to some that's looking to raise young pigs to sell and some that's just looking for a good meat hog."

Wilbur started walking toward the barn next door, where he indicated most of his younger pigs were. On one side of the barn, he pointed out two Hampshire sows. In a pen next to the two sows was a young Hampshire boar that Wilbur explained had been used in breeding the two sows. "Now, that's a good hog, too—the Hampshire. I've had pretty good luck with having good litters, and the sows have been gentle to work around."

On the opposite side was a row of four pens. Each held Poland-Chinas: one boar, a sow, and four young gilts. "What I'd recommend," Wilbur said, pointing out the gilts, "is you get some or all of these females to give you a start. I ain't got a boar for sale right now, but if you'll look around, you might find one at a good price. These gilts here ought to be about ready to breed in the spring."

Albert estimated that the pigs must have weighed around sixty or so pounds each. He and Wilbur talked for a few minutes about raising pigs until Albert finally decided to make an offer on all four of the young females. After settling on the price, Albert paid Wilbur in cash.

Wilbur explained to Albert that he would need to pull the wagon to the other end of the barn where a wooden chute had been constructed allowing the pigs to walk up to and in the wagon. Albert made a mental note that he would need to build something similar if he planned on raising pigs.

After getting the side of the wagon as close to the top of the chute as possible, Albert let down the back panel. Wilbur had already lured one of the pigs up the chute with some ground feed. When she got to the top of the chute, Wilbur closed a gate behind the gilt so that she could not back down. Wilbur then placed some short boards over the gap from the chute to the wagon, opened the outside gate, and handed the feed bucket to Albert so he could coax her into the wagon.

"Pays to load pigs when they're hungry," Wilbur told Albert. "That way, they'll go for the food better, and you'll have a much easier time loading."

The men repeated the same action for the other three pigs. At last, with all four gilts loaded, Albert went to find Jasper and Myatt, who were shooting marbles with Henry under a magnolia tree on the other side of the house. Now that the pigs were in the wagon, the boys climbed up on the wagon seat beside their father.

As the mules began pulling the wagon away from the farm-house, Wilbur called to Albert, "I hope you have good luck with them gilts!" Albert acknowledged with a wave while Jasper and Myatt waved to Henry, who stood with a rather forlorn look on the front porch. It was the same look Albert had seen when they first arrived.

With a pensive look on his face, Jasper said, "I wonder if he's got a mama. I didn't see nobody except his daddy. He looked sad, except for when we was shooting marbles."

"Maybe his mama died," Myatt offered.

"I'm glad you boys played with him," Albert remarked. "I imagine he don't have nobody much to play with. It would have been nice if he could have gone with us to the fair."

"Yeah," the boys responded in unison.

Unaccustomed to riding in a wagon, the four young pigs grunted and squealed as the wagon made its way out to the Old Stage Road. After turning southward once again, the boys fell silent, and all that Albert heard were the occasional grunts of the pigs. His thoughts began to wander, and he imagined the profit he could potentially make once he started raising pigs of his own. He thought about the good fortune he had experienced since buying the farm back in 1903. Sometimes he wondered if he had put too much emphasis on making money. He recalled a Bible verse that said something about the difficulty of a rich man getting into heaven. He decided that would be something he'd have to talk about sometime, perhaps with his brother Leonard.

As the afternoon wore along, Albert noticed that Jasper and Myatt had grown tired, and at times they appeared to be riding with their eyes closed. They had not seen another wagon, buggy, or car for a good while. Even the four pigs had ceased grunting and had lain down in the bed of the wagon.

Because the mules had blinders on their bridles, they did not see the huge buck that emerged from the trees to the left of the road. Out of the corner of his eye, Albert saw the animal with his huge, tree-branch-like antlers standing clear of the trees. He pulled on the reins to bring the mules to a stop and spoke softly to the boys. "Look. Have you boys ever seen a deer that big?"

Jasper and Myatt came to life and turned to see the buck still standing motionless just yards away from the wagon. Albert put his finger to his mouth to signal that they should keep their voices down.

"Wow!" Jasper whispered. "I hadn't ever seen one that size."

"Me neither," added Myatt, wide-eyed with wonder. The mules sensed the presence of a nearby animal and began first to whinny like a horse and then heehaw like a donkey. Albert grew worried that the buck might become aggressive.

"It's about rutting season," Albert whispered to the boys. "Let's wait for him to move on, if he will."

"What's rutting season?" Jasper wanted to know. His eyes darted between his father and the buck.

"That's when a buck's looking for a mate," Albert explained. Momentarily, the buck began to paw at the ground, and then a stream of strong-smelling urine began to pour onto the ground. "He's marking his territory," Albert went on. The mules continued to whimper. "Let's give him a little more time, and maybe he'll move on."

At that very moment, the buck turned and went back into the woods. The four pigs, who had been quiet up until then, began to stir around and grunt again. Albert clicked with his tongue, shook the reins, and once again the mules began their forward march.

"Boys, I'm glad that buck didn't come after the mules or the wagon. Don't have my rifle with me, so I would have had to deal with him another way," Albert said. He wasn't sure what other way he would have used, but was thankful he didn't have to find out.

Albert noticed Jasper and Myatt yawn and fidget as they continued moving down the road. This was understandable, he thought, because they had been at the fair the day before, and with the long wagon rides into town and back home, he knew they were getting tired. He had been so preoccupied with the buck's sudden appearance that he hadn't noticed the gathering of dark rain clouds, and it wasn't long before the first raindrops began to come down.

"Looks like we're gonna get wet," he told the boys. This was something he had not planned on. Although he was used to working outside sometimes in the rain, he knew that in the cooler fall weather, getting soaking wet would not be a pleasant experience for any of them.

The light rain eventually turned into a downpour. The pigs milled about in the wagon grunting and squealing. The heavy rainfall added further difficulty to their travel in that the mules now had to pull the loaded wagon through the mud. With the rain beating down on them, Albert said, "I wish I could find a spot where we could stop and get under something, but I can't see a thing."

Almost at that very moment, the right wheel of the wagon made a huge dip. Albert held on as best he could to Jasper and Myatt to keep them from tumbling out of the wagon seat. The mules stopped dead in their tracks and began heehawing again. Albert turned around just in time to see all four pigs jump out over the right rear side of the wagon.

"Oh, lord!" shouted Albert. "You boys try to jump down, and we'll see if we can round them up!"

Jasper jumped down first, mud splattering all over his shoes and overalls. Myatt followed by landing on his feet and then tumbling forward, falling on his hands and knees in the mud. Albert slid off the seat and onto the ground. With four Poland-China pigs scattered somewhere in the woods, Albert knew they had to act quickly. He saw that their calamity had been caused by the right-rear wheel that had fallen into a washed-out place in the road.

"Don't worry, Daddy, we'll find them!" yelled Myatt through the pouring rain.

With daylight gradually disappearing, both boys ran into the woods in the direction they had seen the pigs go. Albert dashed behind them. Just a few yards in, he spotted Jasper cornering two of the pigs in a small clearing.

"Hold your arms out!" Albert called to him. "Let's get behind them and see if we can get them back out to the road." Slowly, Albert and Jasper moved to get behind the two pigs.

"Let's go!" Jasper spoke to the pigs as if they would just suddenly obey him.

"Take it easy with them, son. They'll go. They're just scared." Albert looked as if someone had poured a bucket of water on his head. Trembling, the two pigs moved back through the trees toward the road. Fearful that they would run away again, as soon as they reached the wagon, Albert reached for a rope. He had not counted on having to use it, but now he was awfully glad he had thought to toss it in the wagon the day before. With Jasper standing guard with outstretched arms, Albert tied a loop around one of the hind legs of each pig and gave the ends of the rope to Jasper. "You stay here and hold them, if you can. I'm going to look for Myatt."

Running back into the woods, Albert thought he heard the grunting of one of the other pigs. Moving toward the sounds he heard, he saw that it had gotten caught up in some of the thick underbrush and was unable to get out. There were sharp briars all around, but Albert had no time to worry about himself. With his bare hands, he grabbed hold of the mesh of briars to pull them apart. He felt the sting of the briars sinking into his fingers and hands, and muttered, "Devilish mess!"

The pig, sensing there was nowhere else to go but out, ran forward. Albert let go of the briar netting, got behind the pig, and gradually urged her back to the road. Jasper was drenched, but held tightly to the two pigs his father had already tied with the rope. Albert took one end of the rope and tied another loop around the hind leg of the third pig. After telling Jasper to hang on just a little longer, he turned back to the woods, exasperated yet determined to find Myatt.

Just as he was about to head into the thicket once again, a sight appeared that would have been comical, except for the fact that they were in a dire situation. To keep the fourth pig from running away, Myatt had climbed on her back and was riding her, feet dragging, as if she were a tiny pony. He had leaned over and wrapped his arms around her neck to hold on, and it appeared that he was not about to let go.

When Jasper saw his brother on top of the pig, he erupted, "Hold on to her, Myatt!"

As if they were performing in a show, the pig, with Myatt holding on for all he was worth, ran straight to where Jasper stood holding the other three. Albert strode over through the mud to secure the pig with the rope.

"I got her, Daddy," Myatt declared, covered in mud from head to toe.

"Yes, you did, son. Yes, you did."

In all the excitement, Albert had not noticed that the rainfall had begun to subside. With the boys still holding on to the pigs with the rope, Albert went around in front of the mules, pulled on their harnesses, and coaxed them forward out of the hole. Then, he went back to the rear of the wagon, let down the back panel, and lifted each pig up into the wagon.

By the time Albert and the boys climbed back up on the wagon seat and the mules were plodding through the mud, the rain had come to a stop. Albert looked down to see his arms and hands scratched and bloodied. His pants, from the knees down, were totally covered in mud, as was the case with Jasper. It was Myatt, though, who looked as if he had fallen into a muddy pig pen this time.

Albert chuckled. "Well, look at us. I wonder what your mama is gonna say."

The three laughed and talked about the wild experience they just had. At last, they made the turn off the Old Stage Road that would take them back home. Albert was thankful that perhaps they would have just enough daylight to ensure they got back home before nightfall. He was even more grateful that the situation had not been any worse.

CHAPTER TWENTY-THREE

ASSOCIATION

Albert indeed found a fine Poland-China boar from a nearby farm in Harnett County. In March, when he saw that the four females he had purchased were in heat, he turned the boar and the young sows into the fenced-in area that he had constructed around the back side of the barn. He waited for nature to take its course, figuring he'd have some young pigs by sometime in July.

Meanwhile, Fannie announced one evening in the kitchen with the children out of earshot that she was expecting again. Fannie's excitement over the news was tempered by the memory of the loss of two babies, and she expressed her concerns to Albert. Truth be told, Albert was concerned himself, but knew that he needed to present an optimistic front to Fannie. He encouraged her to go ahead and decide on a name for both a boy or a girl, saying that this time they would seek a doctor who could give her a check-up to make sure everything was all right.

Still holding on to the cotton bales that he had bought from neighbors and friends, Albert went about the growing season as normal. In June, with Samuel's help, he built some lean-to shelters that the gilts could get under to farrow when the time came. As he had expected, one by one the sows began giving birth to litters in the middle of the summer. He fretted when one or more of the pigs were stillborn or got smothered underneath the weight of the mother. In general, however, those first litters of young pigs turned out fairly well. One sow had as many as ten that survived, while the others had around seven or eight.

Throughout the summer, the piglets suckled from their mother, and as fall approached, they were ready to be weaned. Albert fed the hogs in wooden troughs and noticed that as the pigs grew, they began to try to feed from the trough, as well. Albert put out word that he had Poland-China pigs for sale, and in no time he found himself bargaining with would-be buyers. He took pride in the profit he was making off both the young pigs and the calves.

***

Albert sometimes attended services at the Rehobeth Primitive Baptist Church, where his family went when he was growing up. After his marriage to Fannie, they generally attended Sunday services at Fellowship. Fellowship, Rehobeth, and other Primitive Baptist Churches were part of the Little River Association, and each year a different church hosted a weekend-long event that some pronounced as *sosayshun*. In the fall of 1916, it just so happened that it was Fellowship's turn to host the event.

For several days leading up to the association meeting, local families planning to attend began preparing for the arrival of relatives or friends who would stay with them throughout the weekend and attend the lineup of preaching and business meetings. Albert's mother, Mandy, sent word to Albert and Fannie that they were invited to come to her house on the Saturday evening of the special weekend for a meal, and that they should plan to stay overnight. Fannie was glad that she was not being expected to stay at home and cook, because she was expecting to deliver in about a month.

On the Thursday before the event, Albert took the children over in the wagon so that they could help his mother clean and get ready for any family who might come in addition to them. Iva was not yet old enough to do much cleaning, but she worked alongside Hettie to sweep the floors, dust, and wash the windows. Jasper and Myatt helped Irving take all the rugs outside to air out on the clothesline and to sweep the yard with brush brooms. Since Albert knew that the preaching could go on all day at the association meeting, he arranged for Samuel to take care of the feeding while he was away from the house.

On Saturday morning, Albert and his family all dressed up in their best. Albert wore a black suit and vest along with his black hat. Fannie wore a long black skirt with a long-sleeved white blouse. She chose her wide-brimmed black hat with a white band and red rose, and she secured it in place with a hat pin at the back. Jasper and Myatt were dressed in their blue suits with knee pants and long socks. Fannie dressed Iva in a blue gingham dress and tied a blue ribbon in her hair to match. When the mule pulled the surrey out into the dirt path to head east to the church, Albert thought to himself that they looked quite handsome.

Since Fellowship was not that far away, in a short while they were in sight of the church. There had been a scandal of sorts a few years back involving one of the church members who had shot, as he called them, "two fice dogs" that he said had attacked and killed some of his sheep. The problem was that one of the dogs belonged to the pastor, Moore Stephenson. From what Albert understood, the pastor and several church members turned against the one who had shot the dogs, and several withdrew their membership from the church. He remembered his mama and daddy talking about it.

As they got closer to the church, they saw a large number of mule- or horse-drawn buggies and wagons. There were even a few automobiles. There was also a pulpit set up several yards in front of the church. Although Fellowship was fine accommodating the people who attended regular Sunday services, the church was not big enough to hold the crowd that would gather for the association meeting. Rows of benches that had been placed facing the pulpit were already beginning to fill with association attendees. Others listened from their wagon or buggy, while some sat on quilt pallets on the ground.

Jasper and Myatt called out and waved to anyone they recognized, while Iva was so transfixed by the sights and sounds of the day that she just stared, trying to take it all in. Albert called to Jasper and Myatt to help him so that Fannie could manage Iva. First, he found a good place for the surrey under a tree that gave ample shade from the sun. Even though fall had just arrived,

Albert thought it best to keep the food Fannie had packed in a basket under the shade. The boys helped Albert unhitch the mule, and he tied him to a nearby tree away from the other mules. Albert had brought a bucket, and so sent Jasper and Myatt to the well where someone was standing to draw up water for anyone who needed it. Jasper brought back the bucket of water for the mule, and Albert poured out some oats for him to munch on during the preaching.

"Now, you boys listen to me good," Albert told them. "You are to stay with us on the bench until later on. They don't want children running around and making noise, and we sure don't want anything bad to happen."

"There ain't nothing bad going to happen," Myatt said, as if he were absolutely certain of it.

"Well, maybe not, but several years ago, this young girl was playing outside after services at the Juniper church down below Four Oaks, and she got her skirt caught in a fire and got burned real bad."

"What happened to her?" Jasper asked.

"Son, she was burned so bad that she died."

"Oh, lord," gasped Jasper.

Myatt just looked down, not wanting to even consider how such a terrible event had taken place. Finally, he spoke up and said, "Daddy, they ain't no fires here."

"That's not the point," Albert explained. "What I'm trying to tell you is that things can happen, fire or no fire, and I want you two to stay around where I can see you." Albert could see by the looks on their faces that what he had told them about the young Parker girl had made an impression.

With that, they joined Fannie and Iva on a bench about fifteen yards from the pulpit. Several family members were in attendance. Leonard, who had already started preaching at Rehobeth, came with his wife and child. Charles came, but since Flossie Mae had just had a baby back in September, she stayed home with the children. Albert's sister Kittie and her husband, Cleveland, were there, and his sister Hettie and her husband, Hildred, also attended. Hettie was eight months into another pregnancy. Albert's brother Vasper and his new wife, Vera, had just had a baby on the fifteenth of that month, so they decided to stay at home. In addition to Albert's brothers and sisters, several members of Fannie's family were in attendance, as well.

J. T. Coats had been chosen as the moderator for the association meeting, and the opening sermon was delivered by Elder Jones, who preached on the sixteenth chapter of Matthew. Visiting brethren from member congregations were welcomed and recognized.

After conducting some matters of a business nature, the remainder of the day was spent listening to one preacher after another. Sometime in the early afternoon, each family spread out a quilt along with their lunch, and there was much feasting and socializing among the adults. The children, when they finished eating, gathered in groups to play before the preaching began again. After the last of the preachers finished in the late afternoon, Albert and the boys hitched the mule back to the buggy, and they all loaded up to ride over to his mother's house.

Mandy had prepared a splendid supper of various meats and vegetables. After the meal, Albert joined a group of his relatives out on the front porch. Someone in the group offered him a Carolina Fields cigarette. Since Albert had only smoked a pipe before and did not actually inhale the smoke, he had no idea what to expect. Irving advised him to take a little smoke at first until he got used to it. After his brother-in-law Cleveland lit his cigarette, Albert drew in just a little of the smoke. He practically spit out the smoke, coughing so violently that several of the men jumped up and began slapping him on the back.

With urgency, someone asked, "Are you all right, Albert?"

Unable to answer immediately due to the coughing, Albert just nodded his head up and down to let them know he was okay. Finally, when the coughing subsided, he walked off the porch and threw the cigarette on the ground, crushing it with his shoe.

Albert felt the sensation of his heart beating faster, and somehow he felt different. Although he had never been much for drinking liquor, it seemed that he was getting a feeling similar to when he had tasted a little bit of moonshine. "I don't see what none of you sees in that stuff," he announced to the others upon rejoining them on the porch.

"Well, it takes getting used to," Cleveland explained. "Did the same thing you did the first time I tried it, too, but it's a whole lot easier now when I smoke one. I kind of enjoy it, to tell you the truth."

The others on the porch, who were by now blowing smoke from their own cigarettes, seemed to be in agreement.

"Don't think I want no more of that," Albert told them. "I'll stick to my pipe. I know a lot of farmers in the county are turning toward raising tobacco now, though. They must be a whole lot of folks out there that like to smoke cigarettes. Don't think I'll be one of them, though."

After a brief conversation about the tobacco growing in Johnston County, Leonard said, "Did y'all read about what's going on with the fighting overseas?"

Anyone who read the newspapers knew that war had been raging in Europe for the past two years. Most residents in Pleasant Grove had up to this point been able to remain somewhat detached from the horrific details outlined in local newspapers. Albert knew little about the countries that were fighting and felt glad that the United States was not involved, at least at that point. What Leonard was referring to was the ongoing battle between the Germans and the French at a place called Verdun, where there had been thousands of casualties.

Cleveland jumped into the conversation. "I'll tell y'all one thing. I'm sure glad none of us is over there. Couldn't imagine seeing men being killed in such big numbers. What about those things that the Germans are flying over Britain? They call them 'zeppelins,' I think."

Albert had read and seen pictures in the newspapers of the German zeppelins, and he sort of had an idea about how they worked. However, he had another grave concern about the war. "What bothers me the most," Albert told the others, "is the ships that are getting sunk. In a way, I can't believe that Wilson didn't get us into the war after the *Lusitania* got sunk by the Germans. They was Americans on that ship, you know." Albert's voice rose as he got to the last part.

Several of the other men thought that it probably wouldn't be much longer before the United States started sending men overseas to fight. Nevertheless, they all voiced their hope that the US would stay out of it. None wanted to see any of the family or anyone else that they knew sent thousands of miles away to fight.

The conversation took another turn when someone stated, "It looks like the womenfolk is going to get the vote. Saw in the *News and Observer* that all the presidential candidates and the president himself has come out for it."

Since there were only men on the porch, some felt free to express that they doubted whether women could be counted on to make good decisions when it came to political matters. It seemed all right to Albert that women would get to vote, though. He viewed Fannie as a smart woman capable of understanding most anything she studied on, and he thought that she ought to have just as much right to vote as he did.

Albert was grateful when the conversation turned away from women's suffrage to all the new inventions and conveniences that were emerging. Although most of the men on the porch still traveled by wagon or buggy, many families were now considering buying a car. They were beginning to see advertisements for telephones, and although it would be a long time before telephone service would become widely available in Pleasant Grove, most everyone had seen a telephone or witnessed someone talking on one when they had ventured into town.

Sometime well after dark, everyone bedded down wherever they could. The adults took whatever beds were available, and the children and some of the adults who didn't have a bed slept on quilt pallets that Mandy arranged on the floor.

The next morning, Mandy got up early, and with the help of some of the women prepared a huge breakfast. When everyone had washed and dressed in a new change of clothes, Albert, Fannie, and the children, along with the other family members, returned to Fellowship for the final day of the association meeting. When it was all over and Albert was heading home with the family, he reflected on how he had enjoyed the weekend, but would be glad to get back to work.

***

Toward the end of November, Annie Mae assisted Fannie in delivering another son. Fannie chose the name Albert Hugh. Albert was happy that Fannie wanted to name the new baby after him. Jasper and Myatt were so excited to have a new brother that they hardly wanted to do their chores or go to school. Every time that Albert went in the house to check on Fannie and the baby, Iva was either right by the baby's side or holding him in her arms.

Shortly after the birth of Hugh, Fannie and Albert talked about how thankful they were that the new baby had survived and seemed to be doing well in light of the unfortunate loss of Willis Chester and Mary Ann. Holding Hugh in his arms in the rocking chair by the fireplace, Albert said to Fannie, "You know, we've got a lot to look forward to."

Fannie, sitting on the davenport with Iva's head in her lap, smiled and said, "Yes, we do. We sure do."

CHAPTER TWENTY-FOUR

THE TRAIN TO RICHMOND

"Myatt got in trouble again for drawing smoking pipes on the chalkboard again today," Jasper announced at the supper table. It was early 1917, and the boys had been attending the Ogburn Grove school for a while. Myatt kept his eyes down, but Albert could see that his face had turned red.

"Well, I 'spect I know where that come from." Fannie's lips curled up in a smile as she looked over her wire-rimmed glasses. Albert knew full well that the children had seen him smoking his pipe many times and that Myatt always seemed particularly interested when he filled his pipe with the sweet-smelling tobacco.

"And he had to stand in the corner," Jasper threw in, further shaming his younger brother.

"Well, I'd say you had it coming to you, Myatt," said Albert with a harsh squint of his eyes. "Hadn't you got more to do in school than to draw such as that on the chalkboard?"

Myatt continued to look down as he finished the chicken stew on his plate. Albert was pleased that Myatt was helpful around the house, especially when outside working with him, but he knew his second child wasn't always serious when it came to his schoolwork. Since the birth of Hugh, when the boys were not inside doting on their new brother, they followed their father around while he fed the livestock. Albert often would give them a job, which they both jumped at the chance to do.

Ever since Albert had bought the farm, he had managed to keep Samuel around to help with the planting and harvesting of the crops, the feeding of livestock, and any other jobs that Albert needed done around the farm. Samuel had often talked about a brother and his family who lived down around the coast. Late into February, Samuel announced to Albert that he had decided to go stay with his brother's family. He'd received a letter from his brother stating that he could get work on a fishing boat.

"Being out on the water sounds mighty appealing to me," he told Albert. "Plus, I think a change is sometimes good."

Although Albert was a little surprised when Samuel told him of his plans, he knew that sooner or later, he would move on. Men like Samuel could only stay in one place so long, and he had been helping Albert for a good while. So, as a measure of gratitude for his years of service, Albert accompanied Samuel to Benson, where he bought him a young gelding to use for transportation. Albert figured that Samuel had been saving his money and that he would end up staying at one place or another until he reached his destination.

The next morning, after the men returned from buying the horse, Samuel rode up to say his farewell to Albert, Fannie, and the children. With his clothes packed in a brown leather bag, Samuel waved to the family as he began his journey to the coast.

Albert knew that his boys were getting old enough to help more, but he would still need the help of an adult. Through the family, he learned of a man by the name of Oscar Poole. Poole was one of those men who traveled from farm to farm looking for work. Albert's brother Charles knew Poole, so Albert told Charles that he wanted to talk to Poole about possibly working for him.

A few days after Samuel left, Poole arrived on a small wagon pulled by a mule. A tall man dressed in a long black coat, Poole stepped off the wagon just outside the barn to introduce himself. Albert immediately found him to be friendly, and by the looks of him, he would be strong enough to handle farm work. The men talked for a good while as Albert explained his crops and live-stock. Poole let Albert know that he was accustomed to doing just about everything, since he had worked on several different farms. Albert reasoned that Poole must be trustworthy, or else someone would have told his brother.

After talking about what responsibilities Poole would have, Albert told him what he would be able to pay him and that he and Fannie could board him in the house while he stayed and worked.

Albert took Poole inside to meet Fannie and the children, then showed him where he could sleep upstairs. "There's no bed up here, but we'll get one," Albert said. "You'll be able to eat here. Fannie's a mighty good cook, and no doubt you'll enjoy the food."

Albert figured that it was unlikely a man like Poole could turn down such an offer, and right he was. As soon as the men went back out toward the barn, Poole expressed his agreement with the offered pay, along with the room and board.

***

The rebound in cotton prices that Albert had betted on came early in the year. Average prices came in around twenty-seven cents a pound. This was a significant increase from when he had paid eight cents per pound for the bales he had bought from other farmers in the area. With Oscar Poole now available to help get the cotton to a buyer in Benson, Albert went about borrowing wagons from his brothers to haul as much as he could from the bales he had stored in the front part of the house.

In the fall, before many farmers would be taking their cotton to buyers, Albert led a caravan of four wagons loaded with cotton to buyer C. T. Johnson in Benson. Albert had begun banking at the relatively new Citizens Bank and Trust Company in Benson, so he made a trip by the bank to deposit his profit. *Now*, Albert thought to himself, *I can get those loans in Raleigh paid off.*

As the cultivation and growing of corn, cotton, wheat, and vegetables increased on the farm, more and more mules were needed to pull the plows, planters, harrows, and other farm equipment. Albert had been watching advertisements in *The Progressive Farmer* and talking with other farmers about how and where to get the best mules. In local papers such as *The Smithfield Herald*, he would sometimes see that dealers in Benson or Smithfield had mules for sale. The problem was that not all dealers were honest men. He had heard stories about dealers who sold mules that were older than what they claimed or sold unhealthy mules that died shortly after being purchased. Although Jack and Maude had served him well, Albert realized that the mules would never be able to handle the increased load of work he expected.

Albert had seen advertisements for the Southern Stock Yards in Richmond, Virginia, and he had heard by word of mouth that mules of a good quality and a fair price could be bought there. So, Albert made the decision to go to Richmond in the late spring of 1917. The United States had entered the war in Europe in April, and several young men from Pleasant Grove had been called to serve in the army. It was a constant topic of conversation in homes, at church, and other social gatherings.

If one discounted the time that Albert and his brothers had coasted on the boxcar down the hill between Four Oaks and Smithfield, he had never been on a train ride. Fannie was worried about his traveling alone to Richmond on the train. She said to him one morning over a plate of sausage and eggs, "I heard they's been trains that have gone off the tracks, and people's been killed."

Albert knew that to be true; he recalled that there had even been some train accidents locally. In 1906, a freight train had derailed just outside Smithfield, demolishing cars loaded with cabbage and lumber. Thankfully, that derailment had not resulted in loss of human life, but there had been other incidents in which people were killed. In addition to the possibility of derailment, since cattle often roamed freely in those days, sometimes cows fell victim to huge locomotives before they could get out of the way.

Albert tried his best to convince Fannie that despite the potential dangers, he would be fine. Another thing that she worried about, however, was the fact that he would be taking a train that left around midnight and would arrive in Richmond just before sunrise. Albert's plan was to spend two nights in Richmond in order to give him sufficient time to attend the auction at the Southern Stock Yards and arrange for the transportation of the mules before heading back south.

Since the auction was to be held on Wednesday, the seventeenth of May, he decided to leave the night before. He packed a small bag containing an extra change of clothes and other essentials, and

Fannie prepared him some ham-and-sausage biscuits that he could eat on the way.

A few days before he left for Smithfield, he had visited his mother's house to see about getting Irving to come and stay with Fannie until he returned. Irving would also come by wagon to Smithfield when Albert returned so that they could lead the mules that he planned to buy home.

By midafternoon on the sixteenth, Albert and Oscar Poole headed east toward Smithfield with one mule pulling the surrey. By the time they reached town, it was getting dark. They headed straight to the Tuscarora Inn, where Albert explained that he was paying for Oscar to spend the night and that he would be heading to the train station close to midnight. Albert also arranged for the mule to be boarded overnight in a nearby stable. With everything in place, Albert spent a few hours with Oscar in his room at the Tuscarora until it was time to head over to the station. About a half hour before midnight, Albert bid Oscar farewell and headed downstairs to a waiting hack driver, who took him and a couple of other train passengers from the inn to the station.

When they arrived at the Smithfield Depot, although it was getting close to midnight, the whole area bustled with activity. The installation of electric lights in Smithfield in 1913 had proved to be of great benefit to travelers who took the train at night.

After thanking and paying the hack driver, Albert went inside the depot to purchase his round-trip ticket to Richmond. At the ticket window, the ticket-seller told him that the train should arrive in Richmond just after five o'clock in the morning. Through talking with others who had taken the train, Albert knew not to take a train that stopped at every single town along the way.

The Atlantic Coast Line railroad had come about as a result of a merger of several other railway systems and extended up and down the eastern seaboard. Just a short while back, the railroad tracks passing through the county had been double tracked. On a trip into Benson with Samuel, Jasper, and Myatt, Albert had witnessed the big steam shovels and work engines as they dug and removed dirt in order to lay down the tracks. Albert recalled telling Samuel that he was lucky to be dealing in hogs and cows as opposed to what looked like some very strenuous railroad work.

Shortly after getting on the platform to await the train's arrival, Albert heard the huge locomotive coming from the direction of Four Oaks. The train pulled in amid billowing smoke and screeching wheels, and Albert saw the words ATLANTIC COAST LINE on the passenger cars when the train came to a stop. Picking up his bag and with his ticket in hand, he stepped on board and took a seat close to the window. Since he had never been on a train before, he had no idea that there would be lights inside the car so that he could actually see what was going on.

A woman dressed in a fine green-and-black-checked suit stepped on board and took a seat directly across from Albert shortly after he had settled in. Albert guessed that she was maybe a little younger than he was, but maybe not by much. Her hair was pulled back to reveal a strikingly beautiful face, and a bonnet-style black hat adorned her head. A crest of small white feathers arose from the top of the hat, and it was tied to her neck by a narrow black ribbon. As Albert was accustomed to the more modest dress of the women in Pleasant Grove, he was struck by her fancy attire. Trying not to stare, he pretended to be interested in the last-minute hurrying and scurrying taking place on the platform before the train pulled out.

Finally, the sound of the whistle indicated the train's readiness for departure, and the train began moving forward. As it did, Albert gradually allowed his eyes to move in the lady's direction. When their eyes met, she smiled and said, "These night trains. Never understood why they just can't run them in the daytime."

"To tell you the truth," Albert replied, "I don't know too much about train schedules and so forth. This is my first time traveling on one."

"Oh, is that so?" She raised her eyebrows a little. "Where are you going?"

"I'm headed to Richmond. Thinking about buying some mules to bring back home. I have a farm several miles east of Smithfield."

"Richmond is where I'm going, too. I live there, actually. Headed back after visiting with some family in the Smithfield area. So, this is your first train ride and first time to Richmond?"

"That's right. Looking to buy some mules of good quality at the Southern Stock Yards. I raise a lot of cotton, corn, and other grains. Have cows and pigs, too."

"So, you're a real live farmer." Although the lights in the passenger car had been dimmed, Albert could see that her eyes never wavered from him as she spoke. Her lips parted in a slight smile. Her eyes moved down to his left hand. "I see by the ring you must have a wife back home?"

"Yeah, I do. We have three boys and a girl."

"And you didn't want to bring any of them along?" The woman opened a bag on the seat next to her, as if looking for something.

"Well, the youngest boy was just born back in November, and the oldest is just eleven, so they're better off at home with their mother."

The woman smiled and nodded, then closed the bag. "I'm Libby Poe," she said, extending her right hand. "No relation to the famous writer, of course." She chuckled.

Albert had no idea what she was talking about, but nodded an acknowledgement. "Nice to meet you, ma'am. I'm Albert Stephenson." Albert reached with his right arm to clasp her offered hand.

"Stephenson, huh? I believe I heard that name a few times when I was staying around Smithfield."

"Yeah. There's quite a few Stephensons in Johnston County. I have nine brothers and sisters, myself."

"You don't say! I have three brothers and two sisters, and I thought that was a lot."

Albert found himself growing comfortable talking to Libby, and the conversation began to move from one topic to the next. Libby wanted to know Albert's views on the women's suffrage movement, as well as his thoughts on the United States' entry into the war. Although it was way past the time that Albert normally went to bed, he found that the lively conversation meant that the time passed quickly.

A little past four in the morning, the train made a stop in Petersburg. Libby leaned over and told Albert that it wouldn't be much longer until they arrived in Richmond. Realizing that he needed to try to rest a little, Albert closed his eyes for a few moments. With the noise created by the train's movement over the tracks, however, he found it difficult to sleep. Once, he opened his eyes to catch Libby looking in his direction, but when she realized he saw her, she quickly turned to face forward.

Just a few minutes outside Richmond, Albert opened his eyes again. Libby turned and asked, "Where will you be staying in Richmond, Mr. Albert?"

"Somebody told me about a hotel he had stayed in recently up there. I think it's called Murphy's Hotel."

"Oh, yes. I know the place," she replied. "It's on the corner of Eighth and Broad. It's a tall one . . . maybe about twelve floors, and from what I hear it's nice on the inside. I have a driver who is picking me up at the train station in Richmond. We would be happy to take you to the hotel."

"Oh, no," Albert said. "I can get a hack driver or someone at the station to take me. I'm sure you'll be needing to get home to your husband and family." Albert was not sure that it would be proper to accept a ride from a strange woman who was probably married herself.

Libby's eyes lowered a little. "My husband died from tuberculosis about two years ago. We have one daughter, who has been staying with my sister in Richmond while I was gone. She's nine and the joy of my life."

"So very sorry about your husband. That's a bad disease that has taken many away much too early." Albert genuinely felt sorry for Libby, especially after having lost two babies.

"I sometimes wonder how we didn't all get sick. I guess there's a lot I don't understand." For a few moments, she was silent.

Finally, she said, "Since this is your first trip to Richmond, you might be interested in seeing some of the city. Why don't you let my driver take you around on a little tour while you're in town? See some of the sights?" She sounded genuine in her request, but Albert was unsure of how long his business would take and was reluctant to commit. "It would be no trouble at all," she continued. "I have no obligations today or tomorrow, so my driver would be completely at your disposal to drive you around. I just bought a Maxwell after my husband passed away. I don't drive myself, but thankfully I was able to employ a man to drive for me, as needed."

Albert had suspected this woman might be wealthy, but these comments confirmed his suspicions. "Well, I don't know," he began. "I have to see about the mules, and I don't know how long everything will take. I appreciate your offer, but . . . " He looked out the window to avoid any further discussion.

"Come on, I insist," Libby replied. "You don't have to spend long in the car. It can be as long or short a time as you wish. Richmond's a big town, and it'd be a shame to miss seeing some of the sights."

In the back of his mind Albert was still unsure about accepting a ride to his hotel, much less accepting a city tour in a car belonging to a strange woman he had been talking to on the train. However, he then began to think what the harm would be in taking a couple of hours to see Richmond. After all, it would be just he and her driver.

As the train crossed the James River, Albert gave in and said, "All right. You've been very nice to offer your driver and your car. I'd like to wait until tomorrow, though, because I am going to need some rest today before I head over to the stock yards to find out the details on what I will need to do. Not only do I need to buy the mules, but I also have to arrange to transport them back home on a freight train."

"Well, I am sure you'll get it all worked out, Mr. Albert," Libby said. "Good, it's settled then. I'll have Charles pick you up at the hotel tomorrow. You all can work out a time."

Just before pulling into the Byrd Street station, the train came to a stop. Momentarily, a couple of policemen entered their car and began asking to see inside the bags that one of the male passengers was carrying.

"What're they looking for?" Albert asked Libby.

"Liquor," she answered. "They do this a lot. I understand some people have been trying to transport liquor into Richmond by train."

After searching through several passengers' bags in the car, the policemen exited, and Albert could see through the window that other policemen had been searching the other passenger cars at the same time. Finally, the train was given the signal to move ahead, and they pulled into the station. It was after five o'clock in the morning, and although Albert hadn't slept a wink, he felt a little excited about being in the big city of Richmond.

As Libby had stated, her driver, Charles, was waiting for her at the station. After a quick introduction, Charles led them to the Maxwell that was parked, along with several other automobiles, just outside the depot. On the way to Murphy's Hotel, Libby explained to Charles that he would be picking Albert up the next day to show him the city. Albert relayed to Charles that it would probably be best if he came in the midafternoon to give him enough time to take care of his business first.

Sometime before six o'clock in the morning, Albert stepped out of the Maxwell, thanked Libby and Charles, and headed inside to inquire about a room. A porter led Albert to one of the elevators after he secured a key to his room. This was only the second time Albert had been in an elevator, and he marveled at how the porter closed the doors, moved a lever, and up they went.

Albert was so exhausted by the time the porter showed him to his room that he took little notice of the nice furnishings and bathroom. He decided he would sleep for a few hours and then venture out to make some inquiries. It didn't take long for sleep to come once he lay down on the soft bed. There would be plenty of time for thinking later in the day.

CHAPTER TWENTY-FIVE

SOUTHERN STOCK YARDS

After a few hours of much-needed sleep, Albert got up and went in the bathroom. Unlike the Raleigh hotel in which he and the boys had stayed, Murphy's provided a private bath with a sink, toilet, and clawfoot bathtub. A white shower curtain hung from a metal rod and encircled the perimeter of the tub. Albert was unaccustomed to taking showers, but he promised himself as he washed his face that he would try it out later.

He put back on the clothes he had worn on the train and walked downstairs from his fourth-floor room to the front desk. Now that he was at least a little more refreshed, he paid more attention to his surroundings. Murphy's Hotel was considered by many to be Richmond's finest. Several tall columns, ornately carved at the top, extended from the white-marble lobby floor up to the second-floor ceiling. Comfortable, black-leather chairs were placed around each column. A few guests were seated in the chairs, while others waited at the front desk. Still others could be seen entering or leaving the hotel. Albert had heard that the hotel was a favorite of politicians and other important guests while staying in the state's capital.

After waiting in line for a few minutes, Albert approached the desk clerk with questions about where to find something to eat and how to get to the stock yards. The clerk explained that since the stock yards were a good distance away, it would be best to hire one of the hack drivers out front to take him over and back. He then told Albert that if he would walk down to the floor below, he would find a café, a buffet, and a grill, all of which served food.

As it turned out, the buffet looked so inviting that he could not pass it up. All sorts of meats, vegetables, bread, and desserts had been carefully arranged on silver platters for guests to choose from. Unaccustomed to such finery, Albert watched how other guests put whatever they wanted on their plates, filled cups with coffee or tea, and chose a table where they could sit and enjoy the feast. After a few minutes of observation, Albert followed their example and chose a small table that gave him a good vantage point to observe the comings and goings of the other guests. All the men were dressed in fashionable suits, while the women wore long dresses of a variety of colors. Almost all wore fancy hats with feathers or artificial flowers. Albert thought to himself how glad he was that he had worn one of his best suits.

At one point, a young man appeared and asked Albert his room number, which he wrote down on a little pad that he carried with him as he moved from table to table. Albert was so hungry that he returned to the buffet twice to get more meat and vegetables. This he followed with a slice of pound cake and fresh strawberries.

After savoring the last of the tasty buffet meal, Albert went out through the front entrance, where there were three or four hack drivers waiting. He approached the first one in line, told him where he wanted to go, and climbed in. As they traveled westward down Broad Street, Albert was amazed at the variety of businesses on both sides of the street. People moved about either by streetcar, automobile, or horse- or mule-drawn buggies or carriages. Richmond seemed to be an anthill of activity, Albert thought.

After passing through several intersections, the men came to an intersection with Hermitage Road, and Albert could see a long, white two-story building with the words SOUTHERN STOCK YARDS CORPORATION painted in big black letters above the second-floor windows.

As he approached the building, four or five men on horseback herded a large group of cattle into the holding pens at the stock yards. Albert later found out that the cows had arrived by train and would be sold to slaughterhouses or farmers who had come into town to buy them. Albert entered the front part of the building where he imagined the main offices were located. As he entered, he was struck by the large number of wooden desks occupied by men either deeply absorbed in their paperwork or huddled around in conversation. He decided to approach a young man with wire-rimmed glasses seated at one of the desks near the doorway to try to get some information.

Although he looked very busy, the young man rose to shake Albert's hand and ask how he could help. Albert explained that he had taken the train in from North Carolina, and that he was interested in buying some mules to take back to his farm. The young man took off his glasses for a moment and said, "Sir, you've come to the right place. Tomorrow morning we have an auction of several hundred mules that have just arrived from several states like Kentucky, Tennessee, and Indiana. Very high quality, and I am sure you'll find many to your satisfaction. I recommend you get here early, as the sale will begin around eight o'clock. The best mules always go quickly."

"Once I purchase the mules, I will need to arrange to get them on the train to go back to Smithfield, North Carolina," Albert said. "I will need some help on figuring all that out."

"Yes, sir," said the young man. "We have a lot of farmers who come in from all over to buy mules and other livestock. We have people on hand at the auction who will help you with all of that."

After thanking the young man for his help, Albert wandered outside, where there was what seemed like an endless maze of holding pens. There were sheep, cattle, horses, and even a few mules. Because it was later in the day, some pens were empty. He assumed that the empty pens had been occupied earlier in the day by animals that had been already sold. There was a pervasive smell of manure as Albert walked along the perimeter of the holding pens.

He decided that he had gotten about all the information he could at that point, so he walked back around to where he had entered and found the hack driver, who had waited patiently for him. In a short while, Albert arrived back at Murphy's Hotel, whereupon he paid the driver his fare and took the elevator back to his room.

Although he had slept a few hours that morning, he was still tired from the overnight train trip to Richmond. He decided that he would rest for a bit, get something to eat later, and go to bed early so that he could get to the sale early the next morning.

After a couple hours of rest, Albert took the elevator back down to the lobby. He decided to go back down to the lower level to get some supper at the café that he had seen when he was eating from the buffet earlier in the day.

After being seated at a small table, a young man dressed in dark pants, a white shirt, and a black bow tie approached to take his order. Albert dined that evening on a plate of fresh, fried catfish and vegetables. He then walked back upstairs to sit for a while in the lobby, where he could observe the activity of the hotel. He took a seat and watched the arrival of guests as they entered from or exited onto Broad Street. Since Murphy's had twelve floors and there were several buildings joined together, there was no shortage of human traffic to watch.

When he arrived back in his room, Albert decided to take his first-ever shower. On the shelf underneath the round, wood-framed mirror, Albert saw that the hotel provided soap. After taking a few moments to turn the round handles to regulate the water temperature, Albert stepped into the tub and pulled the curtain around him. Since he was a child, Albert had bathed in wash tubs or from a wash basin, so this new experience of showering in the bathroom tub was quite a novelty. As the water ran down over his body, he thought about how he couldn't wait to tell Fannie all about it when he got back home.

After drying off and putting on a clean change of underwear, Albert closed the window, pulled the curtain, and lay down. The next day was going to be full of activity, and for a short while he thought about everything he would need to get accomplished. Finally, he drifted off to sleep, and it wasn't until he saw the first glimmer of light from around the edges of the curtain on the window that he reached over, opened his pocket watch, and saw that it was time to get moving.

Albert washed his face, put on a dark-blue suit that he had brought in his bag, and took the elevator back downstairs to the café. There, he dined on bacon, eggs, and grits that he washed down with black coffee. Knowing that he needed to get back to the stock yards as early as he could, he finished up quickly, then hired the same hack driver who had taken him the day before.

The downtown area was already bustling with activity as they headed back down West Broad Street. He could see from a distance as they approached the Southern Stock Yards that people were already arriving to buy livestock. Albert told the driver not to wait on him, since he had no idea how long it would take to get the mules and arrange for their transportation.

Upon arrival at the stock yards, Albert followed signs to an auction ring inside the main building. A wooden fence had been erected around the ring, and a small group of buyers who had gathered to await the beginning of the auction were sitting on benches positioned around the ring. Albert decided that he would observe for a little bit first before actively participating. He knew that he wanted young, healthy mules that would last for many years, and he also knew what he wanted to spend.

Shortly, a heavy-set man dressed in tall black leather boots and puffing on a cigar entered the ring accompanied by a young man with what looked like a ledger of some sort. Another young man entered on the outside of the ring where Albert was standing with the other buyers. He gave each potential buyer a card with a number on it, and instructed the men to hold the card up when they wanted to place a bid.

The auction began with a group of five mules led in by two stock yard workers. The auctioneer announced the approximate weight and age of the mules. Without wasting any time, the auctioneer began his rapid-fire chanting of price and filler words. It was all done with a sense of urgency to try to draw the bidders into the action. Albert had seen on one of the signs that there were to be hundreds of mules and horses auctioned that day, so even though the first group of mules looked to be in good shape, he decided there would be plenty more to choose from. As soon as it was determined who the highest bidder was, the buyer was approached by one of the young men to record the number and name of the buyer. The young man inside the ring also recorded in his ledger the details of the sale.

After about a half hour of observation, Albert decided that it was time to get involved in the bidding. As fortune would have it, a group of six young mules was brought in, and it was announced that they had been shipped in from Kentucky. The auctioneer started the bidding at fifty dollars per mule. Albert held up his card, only to be quickly outbid by another man on the opposite side of the ring. When the price went up to sixty-five dollars, Albert held his card up again. A man seated just to his left moved the bid up to seventy-five dollars. Albert countered by holding up his card to raise the bid to eighty-five. It seemed that the gentleman on the other side had given up on this round, so the bidding came down to Albert and the man to his left. When the auctioneer called for one hundred dollars, the man held up his card once again. Although Albert knew there would be others to come, he really liked the looks of those mules. They still had some growing to do, he thought, but judged they would do well in the fields. When the auctioneer called for a one hundred and twenty–dollar bid, Albert quickly held up his card.

Sensing he could probably inch up the price a bit more, the auctioneer asked for one twenty-five, and the man to his left did not hesitate to hold his card up once again. Albert decided that as good as those mules looked, the price was now approaching about all that he wanted to spend. If he bid one thirty, he would be spending seven hundred eighty for the six mules. Albert held up his card and his breath. The man who had been trying to outbid him stopped and nodded in acknowledgment to Albert that he had won.

"Sold, to number twenty-three!" shouted the auctioneer, and the young man with the ledger scurried over to write down Albert's name and number. The young man explained that Albert would need to go to the front office, where he would pay and make arrangements to take ownership of the mules. Albert took out his pocket watch and saw that it was still relatively early in the morning, enabling him to have enough time to both get the mules on a freight train and see the sights in Richmond.

Albert had withdrawn cash from his account at the bank in Benson to pay for the mules. When he arrived at the counter where payments were made, he made the transaction and then inquired about transportation for the mules.

The friendly gentleman behind the counter explained, "Yes, sir, we deal with this all the time. See the man at the desk over there, and he'll tell you what you need to do." He indicated a middle-aged man standing behind his desk talking to another apparent buyer.

After he finished his conversation, Albert stepped up and asked, "Sir, I just bought six mules at the auction here. I live near Smithfield, North Carolina, and will need to get them on a train headed in that direction."

Of course, the gentleman wanted to know when Albert would be leaving Richmond, pointing out that it would be best if they put the mules on a freight train departing sometime after Albert did so that he would arrive before the mules. Since many customers used the train to move purchased livestock, the man had the train schedules ready to help Albert make a plan. After the man had gone over the details of scheduling, he went on to explain that the mules would be loaded onto a livestock car with ventilated sides. Albert asked about water and feed, and the man said that the cars were outfitted with water troughs, and that feed would be available in the livestock car, as well. The man said that since the summer heat had not yet come, the mules should do fine on the trip.

After settling on the charges for the train, Albert walked out front to locate another hack driver to take him back to the hotel. As Albert climbed into the carriage, he sighed with relief. He had imagined the process would have been more complicated than it turned out to be.

CHAPTER TWENTY-SIX

A TOUR OF RICHMOND
AND THE RETURN HOME

As Libby had promised, her driver Charles arrived at the hotel to give Albert a tour of Richmond. A porter summoned Albert down to the lobby, and he spotted Charles immediately after exiting the elevator.

"Good to see you again, Mr. Albert." Charles extended his hand with a warm smile. "Come, the car is parked out front."

There were several cars parked in front of the hotel, but Albert spotted the Maxwell right away. In the daylight he could better observe the yellow-bodied automobile with a black roof that could be folded back. The roof was not retracted today, though. As Albert approached the vehicle, he wasn't sure if his eyes were deceiving him at first, but then he could see that someone else was inside. He suspected that it was Libby.

Charles opened the door so that Albert could step up on the running board and take a seat next to him up front.

"Hello, Albert," Libby said as he took his seat. "It's so awfully nice to see you again. How has your visit to Richmond been so far?" As she had been on the train trip up to Richmond, Libby was impeccably dressed, this time in a fashionable blue dress and a wide-brimmed white hat. "I decided to join you two this afternoon since I didn't have any other obligations," Libby continued. "Charles can concentrate on the driving, and I'll tell you a little about Richmond."

"Well, I appreciate that," Albert said. After starting the car, Charles slowly moved out onto Broad Street. Albert told Libby all about the mule auction and how he and the six mules would be on their way back to North Carolina the next day.

As they proceeded down Broad Street, Libby pointed out various stores and other businesses. The car approached Fifth Street, and she called attention to the popular department stores of Miller and Rhoads and Thalhimers. "I do a lot of my shopping in those stores," she said enthusiastically. "If you were going to be here longer, you might have wanted to look for something for your wife there."

Albert nodded in agreement, but he knew that Fannie was more modest than Libby when it came to clothing, so he felt sure she would be more comfortable shopping in one of the local shops in Benson or Smithfield.

A block or two later, Libby pointed out F. W. Woolworth & Company and Hofheimer Brothers Shoes as also being good places to shop. Charles found a good spot to turn the car around, and they headed back down Broad Street in the other direction. Libby pointed out City Hall, a tall, gothic-style building that rose so high, it could be seen from a good distance away. As Libby explained, Richmond had been the capital of the Confederacy during the Civil War, and many statues had been erected in honor of the Confederate leaders. They passed a lifelike statue of Stonewall Jackson standing high on a pedestal, as if posing for a photograph. Then there was Robert E. Lee perched on top of his horse, looking as if he had just paused for a moment before galloping off into the distance.

Charles took them through wealthy neighborhoods where huge mansions dominated the landscape. Libby knew a lot about the families that lived in some of those homes, and Albert got the sense that she was a "lady of society." Even though he considered himself to be a very successful farmer, Albert was unaccustomed to the lifestyle of wealthy city dwellers.

After a couple of hours riding through the business district and several neighborhoods, Libby announced, "And that, Mr. Albert, is Richmond. So, what do you think?"

"Well, I'll tell you," he answered, "y'all have a mighty fine city here . . . nice places to do business, fine homes, and a lot of history.

For me, though, I guess it's all what you're used to, but I like the quiet, simple life of the country. Every morning when I get up, I never feel like I'm going to work, because I enjoy what I do. I guess not all folks can say that, because maybe they're not doing what they were cut out for. You know, I have a brother who told me he was called to preach while he was out plowing the fields. I feel the same way about what I do. Seems like I was just called to farm the land and raise animals. Never really wanted to do anything else."

Perhaps Libby needed a few moments to reflect on what Albert had said, or maybe she was just tired of talking for a spell, but whatever it was, they rode in silence until they arrived back at Murphy's Hotel. As Charles exited to come around and open the door for Albert to get out, Libby reached up and touched his shoulder. "I would be most honored if you would join me for supper this evening, Albert. I would enjoy hearing more about your farm in North Carolina. I can have Charles pick you up around seven. You'll be able to meet my daughter."

Albert turned around, and for a moment their eyes met. He quickly looked away. Here was a woman who had gone out of her way to offer the services of her driver and to be his tour guide for the afternoon. On the other hand, Albert knew that accepting the dinner invitation would mean that, even though her daughter might be present during the meal, there was always the possibility they would be alone at some point. This woman—a very attractive woman—had lost her husband. Being a married man, Albert was concerned about being alone with Libby. Perhaps her intentions were merely to be nice, but he decided it would be best not to put himself in a situation that could be taken the wrong way.

Albert stepped out of the car and turned around. "Libby, I appreciate your hospitality, but considering the fact that I have to be up very early to head back on the train in the morning, I think I'll just stay in for the rest of the evening."

"Aww, are you sure?" Libby said. Albert thought he could see a hint of disappointment in her eyes. "I have a very good cook sure to serve up a delicious meal."

"I thank you, but I better head on up to my room. It's been nice to meet and talk with you, though. Sure made my afternoon more interesting. I wish you and your daughter the best."

"Same to you, Albert. Your wife and children are fortunate to have you, I am sure."

Albert shook hands with Charles and thanked him for driving him around town. As he walked toward the front doors of the hotel, Albert turned around one final time to wave good-bye to Charles and Libby. It had been hard to turn down Libby's supper invitation, but Albert knew that having a meal in a widow's home could have led to some sort of impropriety that he would have been unprepared to handle. Albert sincerely hoped that Libby would eventually find a good man and perhaps marry again.

Albert never saw Libby again after that day, but later on he found that he thought of her on occasion. He wondered what she might be doing and if that made him a bad person, but he also knew that he would never be able to discuss his thoughts with anyone.

Albert, tired from the day's events, returned downstairs later for another meal at the café just as it was getting dark outside. The mule auction, making arrangements for their transport, and even the tour around the city had all worn him out, so he took another shower and climbed into bed early. When daylight appeared through the curtains in his room, he got up, got dressed, made sure everything he had brought was in his bag, and headed downstairs for a quick breakfast. Then he went to the front desk to make a payment to the hotel for a two-night stay and for the meals he had eaten.

Anxious to get to the train station on time, Albert managed to quickly hire another hack driver. A crowd of passengers had already gathered on the station platform when he paid the driver, grabbed his bag, and joined the others waiting to board the train. He had arrived none too early, because in what seemed like five minutes the train pulled into the station amidst a cloud of smoke from the engine. After boarding the train and finding a seat, he began thinking about the mules. He had to trust that everything would be handled as they promised at the stock yards. He was scheduled to arrive in Smithfield by midafternoon, so if all went according to plan, the mules would arrive not long after that.

Compared to the ride up to Richmond, the return trip to Smithfield was uneventful. A man and his wife sat across from him, but other than a cordial greeting, Albert did not engage in any sort of conversation with them. Unlike the train he had taken up that had made just a few stops, the return train stopped more frequently. Sometimes no one exited or boarded the train, and it seemed the only reason for the stop was so that mail could be handed over for transport to other locations.

Finally, sometime around three in the afternoon, the train pulled into the Smithfield station. As planned, Irving stood grinning on the platform. Of course, he wanted to know all the details about the trip, if Albert had bought the mules, and where they were. As they walked to where Irving had tied the mule and wagon, Albert filled him in on the mule auction and how the animals would be arriving in about an hour on a freight train. Albert suggested that they ride to Hood's Drug Store to have a Pepsi while they waited.

At Hood's they took seats on stools at the counter, and Albert ordered two Pepsis. Irving told Albert that all had gone well during his absence, that Oscar had taken good care of the livestock, and that Jasper and Myatt had been very helpful. "You would have thought they were two young men instead of boys," he said with a chuckle.

Albert told his brother all about riding around Richmond, but left out the part about Libby. *No need to say anything to cause gossip,* he thought to himself. Finally, after sharing as much as he could with Irving, they took the wagon back to the depot to await the arrival of the freight train.

"I know it'll be getting late," Albert told his brother, "but as soon as they get here, we'll tie them to the back of the wagon and start heading toward home." Albert saw that Irving had brought along a kerosene lantern in the event that they would be making part of the journey in the dark.

After arriving back at the depot, Albert and Irving found a bench to sit on while they waited. Albert took out his pocket watch and saw that it was about time for the freight train to come. When the train did not arrive as scheduled, he grew concerned that something had gone wrong. After another half hour passed and there was still no train, he walked inside the depot to inquire about its arrival. The rail clerk told him that they had received a telegraph communication that the train had been delayed in Richmond for about an hour, but it was on its way. Breathing a sigh of relief that there had not been an accident, Albert went back out to relay the information to Irving.

"Looks like we'll be going back in the dark most of the way," Irving said with tightened lips.

"Well, we could stay the night in Smithfield and board the mules overnight at the stable. Fannie will be mighty worried if we don't come in tonight, though. Maybe we can get by from the light of the lantern."

Finally, after another half hour had passed, the men heard the whistle announcing the train's arrival. Since this was a freight train, the train stopped before getting to the passenger-platform area. The two brothers jumped into action and headed down to find the livestock car transporting the mules. One of the railroad workers asked them what they were looking for, and after he was shown the bill of sale for the mules, he waved for them to walk down and join him in front of the car where the mules were held. Almost immediately, another rail worker came running down to assist. The two men released the bolts that kept the side door in place and gently let down the door to serve as a ramp for the mules.

One of the men signaled for Albert to board the car to identify the mules. Albert knew immediately that the mules were indeed the ones he had purchased at the auction. Although the trip from Richmond had taken quite a bit of time, they looked to be in good shape as Albert and his brother led them down the ramp and away from the side of the train. Since there was no more livestock or any other goods on board that needed to be unloaded, the train's whistle blew once more, signaling its departure from the depot. The brothers held the mules a good distance away until the train had completely left the depot area, then led them over to where they had tied the other mule and wagon to a post.

After tying the mules securely to the back of the wagon, Albert's first stop was at a livery stable so the mules could drink some water before the long journey back home. Fannie had sent some ham biscuits and baked sweet potatoes with Irving, so while the mules drank their water, the men ate in silence. *The food in Richmond was good, but there's nothing like good home cooking*, Albert thought.

With the sun getting lower and lower in the sky, the brothers crossed the Neuse River and made their way out into the countryside. Not long after, Albert lit the kerosene lantern so that they could, at the very least, see a few feet ahead and around them. The dirt road leading to and from Smithfield was well-traveled during the daytime, but with the growing darkness there was hardly anyone to be seen. Not long into their journey, they first saw the lights and then heard the engine of an approaching automobile headed into town.

Albert guided the wagon as far over to the right as possible, and as the car got closer, the mules began to whinny and heehaw up a storm. Albert and Irving went to the back of the wagon, grabbed hold of the ropes that secured the mules, and held on. As the Model T passed, a man wearing a cap and wire-rimmed spectacles smiled and waved. Thankfully, although the mules were moving about and continuing to make noise, none tried to break free. By the time the car was several yards on down the road, they calmed down, and the men got back in the wagon and continued forward.

A trip from Smithfield would take plenty of time even during daylight, but at night they moved even more slowly because of the darkness and having six mules trailing behind the wagon. After they had traveled several miles, Albert and Irving came to a small stream that was so shallow, no bridge had been built over it. As the mule Jack stepped into the stream, Albert suddenly pulled back on the reins and practically shouted, "What's that?"

Irving's eyes followed where Albert's finger pointed toward the left side of the dirt road. With only the lantern to serve as illumination, it was practically impossible to make out what looked to be some creature, about the size of a big dog, lurking in the darkness.

"I'll be John Brown if I know," Irving told him. "Can't see much of nothing in the dark."

Without a gun or anything else in the wagon to use for defense, Albert decided to wait a little bit to see if whatever it was moved on. At one point, the brothers could see what looked like two eyes looking at them through the black of night. All of a sudden, Irving jumped out of the wagon and grabbed two big rocks beside the road. After launching both in the direction of the unknown creature, they heard the sound of whatever it was taking off through the underbrush and into the nearby woods.

The encounter so unnerved Albert that he began to be on the lookout for any further sign of the animal as the mules marched forward. The remainder of the trip home was without incident, however, and long after most country folks had gone to bed, the brothers pulled into the yard.

Since Albert had recently sold all the calves he had on hand, they were able to put the mules two to a stable in the barn. They put Jack in a stable of his own. Then Albert and Irving entered the house, where they found Oscar sitting up with Fannie, who had grown worried that they had fallen victim to some misfortune. Jasper, Myatt, and Iva heard the men come in and all came to welcome their daddy home and give him a hug.

"I tell you all one thing," Albert began when everyone had settled down. "I've been a long way and I've seen a lot, but it will all need to wait. I need to go to bed."

Entering the bedroom, Albert found Hugh sleeping soundly in his cradle, but took time to reach down and rub him gently on the head. As Albert crawled into bed next to Fannie, he thought to himself how glad he was to be back home once again.

CHAPTER TWENTY-SEVEN

ABUNDANCE

After profiting so well following the rise in cotton prices and the continued sale of calves and pigs, Albert and Fannie found themselves at the pinnacle of economic success. With his loans paid off at the Raleigh banks and money saved at the bank in Benson, Albert looked for another way to increase his fortune without having to resort to a great deal of added work.

Even though Oscar continued to stay and work for many months out of the year, keeping up with all the crops and livestock often stretched Albert to the limit. Fannie continued to help by keeping records of the financial transactions. This she did despite also maintaining the household and caring for Hugh, who was not yet a year old in October of 1917.

One evening, Albert talked to Fannie about the possibility of lending money to neighbors or acquaintances. At 6 percent interest, Albert explained, they would stand to make money off any loans they might make. They would not only be able to increase their income, but they would be helping others in need.

Albert had made a loan to his brother Irving, which was co-signed by his mother, for a sum of $1,100 in January of 1917. Then, later in the year, a document of indenture was drawn up at the Register of Deeds in Smithfield on the seventeenth indicating that thirty-three acres of land were held in collateral for a loan in the amount of $800 to a Johnson family in the Pleasant Grove area. An indenture such as this would ensure that Albert and Fannie would receive the thirty-three acres if the Johnsons defaulted on repayment of their loan within the one-year time limit. Other documents of indenture followed in 1917 and into 1918: a loan of $1,500 to another Stephenson family in Pleasant Grove that was secured with forty-five and a half acres of land, as well as a loan of $1,124 to yet another Johnson family in Elevation Township. A total of ninety-six and a half acres were involved in that indenture.

As the United States was now involved in the war in Europe, Albert and Fannie, along with other residents of Pleasant Grove, began feeling the effects of rationing. Often, when Albert ventured into Woodsboro or Angier to a store carrying food items, there was no sugar or flour. He also began using commercially-made fertilizers more, but now found that they were in short supply. Despite the difficulties that arose from rationing and the fact that some of Pleasant Grove's young men had been called to serve in the army, residents of the township were glad to take a break from their daily work to attend the second Pleasant Grove Township Fair on the eleventh of October.

The first fair had been held a year earlier at the township courthouse just over a mile east of Albert and Fannie's house. Since Fannie had been just a few weeks away from delivering Hugh, she had stayed at home with Iva while Albert took Jasper and Myatt with him in the wagon. Albert had taken a couple of his Poland-Chinas over ahead of time to put on exhibit. Albert and the boys had been entertained by the Penny String Band, which included the Penny brothers Victor, Jeff, and Archie. Victor, tall with dark hair and blind in his left eye from a pitchfork accident, played the fiddle. Jeff could play any instrument, while Archie played the guitar. Rounding out the group were Carlie Parrish and Willie Clifton. Albert and Victor had struck up a conversation about the Poland-Chinas when the band finished playing, a conversation that would later lead to a trip together to the town of Coats to buy some of the breed.

The next year Albert again sent a few of his pigs to show, and Fannie sent along some canned fruit and vegetables to put on display. This time, while Fannie stayed at home with Hugh, Iva accompanied her father and brothers. The township fairs proved to be a good social gathering for the adults, and for the children it became a source of fun as they encountered cousins and neighbors all ready to play.

***

In the beginning of 1918, Albert and Fannie were unaware of a flu outbreak at an army camp in Kansas. There had been little to no mention of the flu in the newspapers, and the couple had not heard anyone talking about it. With millions of young men being called to serve in the armed forces, army camps such as the one in Kansas would eventually turn into breeding grounds for the spread of influenza.

Fortunately, over the course of Albert and Fannie's marriage, they had been mostly blessed with good health. Of course, they could not discount the loss of two infants, but for the most part, when Albert, Fannie, or one of the children had been sick, it had been because of a cold or an upset stomach.

***

Oscar Poole had stayed through the winter months with some of his family who lived not far away. He came back to work in the spring, and it seemed there was more work than ever to be done. In addition to the daily tending of livestock, plowing, and planting, Albert decided that he wanted to create a pathway leading from the house to the upper flat land. Albert recognized that to undertake such a project, he would need more than just the manual labor that he and Oscar could provide. After asking around, he was able to borrow a scraper that could be pulled behind a mule. By using a lever to dig to a desired depth in the soil, the men could scoop up dirt and dump it, or use the scooped dirt to build up areas to make the pathway smooth for traveling by wagon.

They started the project in the summer, and most days the heat was relentless. Now that Albert had more mules, he was able to change mules after a few hours of work. Albert assigned Jasper and Myatt the task of pulling weeds from around the cotton plants, while Oscar and he worked on clearing the path of stumps and using the scraper.

Even though the mules had served well in the dual role of pulling both ploughs and their means of transportation, Albert and Fannie had talked for some time about buying a car. Although Albert still saw the dirt roads as being difficult to travel on when muddy, he and his neighbors used rakes and hoes to keep the roads in the area passable. Sometimes passersby could see a group of men and boys out working on the roads in the township. It was tedious work, but necessary, not only for those who wished to travel by automobile, but also for those who continued to rely on buggies and wagons for transportation.

Sometime in late July, Albert came in from having worked outside with Oscar in the scorching sun all day to tell Fannie that he wanted her to accompany him to Benson to take a look at the cars at Parrish's. Albert told her that Oscar would be around to manage everything in his absence, and that maybe they could stop off at her parents' house to see if some—or perhaps all—of their children could stay there while they went into town.

So, early the next morning, Albert and Fannie loaded the children in the wagon and headed to the Langdon home, where they found Fannie's parents in the kitchen finishing their breakfast. They would be thrilled to have the children stay with them, they said, and Fannie's father promised to take Jasper and Myatt fishing at a nearby creek. Satisfied that the children would be well taken care of by their grandparents, Albert and Fannie headed out toward Benson.

Albert held Mr. Parrish in high esteem. The fact that Parrish was a large-scale farmer and dealt in the dairy-cattle business gave the two men much to talk about when the couple arrived. Dressed in a blue suit, gray tie, and wire-rimmed spectacles, Parrish spent a good half hour talking with Albert about farming, raising cows and pigs, and Albert's special interest in Poland-Chinas. Fannie wandered around inside the store while the men talked.

Finally, Albert turned the talk away from their shared interest in livestock and cotton. "I think I've finally decided to get a car," he said. "Been putting if off because of the roads up around where we live, but I think it won't be long before the state and the county will improve the roads to such a point that travel by automobile will be easier."

"Well, as you can see by the number of cars we have in Benson now, more men are not necessarily giving up their mules and wagons, but are buying cars to get them quicker into town, maybe to visit family or go to church," Mr. Parrish said. "The automobile has been improved over the past few years, and I would highly recommend the Ford Model T. It's a popular seller right now, and I have had good reports from those who have invested in one. Since you have several young ones at home, I believe it would be ample room for you and your wife and the children. What I'd need to do, if you decide on a car, is to order it, and it would be delivered by train right here in town. I have some pictures in a book I can show you." Parrish opened a thick book with pictures of a wide assortment of automobiles.

Fannie walked over to join the men in looking at the various automobiles in the book. Some were like the sporty roadsters Albert had seen while traveling back and forth to Raleigh. Some had tops that could be folded back, while still others had solid roofs. Parrish took a considerable amount of time explaining the advantages and disadvantages of the various features of the cars.

At one point, Parrish walked away from the couple to give them a moment to discuss what each thought would be best. Fannie offered that, even though they had the cash, it might be best to wait and sell the year's cotton harvest before actually placing the order. "We've done without a car all this time, so waiting a spell longer won't hurt," she told him.

When Parrish returned, Albert explained that they had talked it over and that they would not place the order until later in the year. "In the meantime, though," he told Parrish, "we'd like to see how that Model T you got sitting out front there operates."

Parrish told the couple that he understood their wanting to think about it some more before making such a large purchase. "I think when you see how she runs, you'll like the Model T, and you'll want one."

Said like a true salesman, Albert thought as they walked outside to take a closer look at the car.

"Now, let me show you about the controls," Parrish said, and sat down in the driver's seat. "If you look down here, you'll see three pedals. Your right pedal is the brake. The middle one is to make the car go in reverse. The one on the left is your clutch."

Albert wrinkled his forehead and squinted.

Noticing Albert's confusion, Parrish continued, "Don't worry. I'll explain everything. Now, look here. This is your throttle." Parrish put his hand on a lever on the right side of the steering wheel. "Move it down to go faster and back up all the way to put it in idle. This one here," he said, placing his hand on a lever on the left side of the steering wheel, "is your spark advance. When you're starting the engine, you'll need to move it up, but when the engine is started, you'll move it down to smooth it out."

Albert kept his eyes on every gadget that Parrish pointed to in an effort to take it all in.

"Now, I'll show you how to start it." Parrish stepped out of the automobile and walked around to the front of the car, where a turn crank was inserted into the bottom of the engine. Albert and Fannie followed close behind. "First, you'll need to prime the engine to get enough gas to fire it up. Make sure the key is turned off." Parrish motioned for Albert to move back around to look at the key inserted into the dashboard. "Then, pull on your choke." Parrish demonstrated as he explained. "Turn the crank three times in a clockwise movement."

Next, he went back to show Albert again that the spark advance was moved up and the key was turned off. Back at the front of the automobile, Parrish pulled on the choke and turned the crank three times. Then he moved back to turn the key to the start position.

"When you start the engine, be sure to turn with your left hand so you won't break any bones. One quick turn should do it," Parrish said, and with a swift movement of his arm, he turned the crank and the engine started. He went back around to the steering wheel to move the spark advance down, and as soon as he did, Albert and Fannie heard a change in the sound of the engine as it smoothed out. "Mr. Albert, you climb in on the right side, and Miss Fannie, you get in the back, if you want to ride."

Parrish went through a step-by-step explanation on how to use the hand brake and the pedals to get the car moving. First, he demonstrated the two gears that Albert would be able to use, how to use the hand throttle, and how to bring the car to a stop. Then he showed him how to put the car in reverse.

After going through all the steps and answering Albert's questions, Albert switched places with Parrish. Albert made the customary blunders that beginning drivers of the Model T generally made with changing gears, and then Parrish and the couple rode up and down Main Street so that Albert could gain confidence in the operation of the car. Arriving back at Parrish's business, Albert turned off the motor, got out, and helped Fannie out of the back seat.

"Well . . . what do y'all think?" Parrish asked.

"Seems to me to ride pretty good. It'll take some getting used to, though. A lot different from a mule and wagon," Albert answered with a grin.

"I'm amazed at how these things operate," said Fannie, her hands on her hips.

Parrish continued, "I think after you've had some time to get accustomed to the controls and gears, you'll be mighty satisfied, should you decide you want to get one of these things. As I said before, I'd recommend the Model T over a lot of automobiles out there right now."

Albert told Parrish that they were very interested, but would wait until the end of the year to place their order. So, after thanking Parrish for allowing them a trial run in the car, Albert and Fannie got back in the wagon to head back toward the Langdon home.

***

Everyone, especially Jasper and Myatt, wanted to know if they had bought a car, so over a tasty meal that Fannie's mother had prepared, the couple talked about their conversation with Parrish and their plan to wait until after the cotton crop had been sold to place an order. The boys could hardly eat for wanting to hear all about the Model T.

After thanking the Langdons for taking care of the children and for the delicious meal, Albert and Fannie loaded the children back in the wagon to head home. Thankfully, thought Albert, there was still time to get home before the sun sank below the horizon.

Though he and Fannie had agreed to wait on the purchase, he felt certain that they would end up getting the Model T.

CHAPTER TWENTY-EIGHT

THE BEGINNING OF A PANDEMIC

It was a cool September evening not unlike most evenings at that time of year. There was a hint of fall in the air. The leaves had not yet started to turn into their autumn display, but the oppressive heat of August had been replaced by a more pleasant temperature, the kind that often brought people out on their porches to sit in the early evening after a hard day's work.

Albert watched as Jasper and Myatt took turns spinning a top that he had bought for them in Angier. Iva, who had started school the year before and had learned to read some, sat cross-legged on the porch floor next to her mother, thumbing through a storybook. At the same time that Albert had bought the top for the older boys, he had also purchased a brightly-painted wooden rocking horse for Hugh. Every evening that the family came to sit out on the porch, Albert placed the rocking horse beside him. Hugh would rock back and forth until, finally, Albert would have to pull him off to go to bed. Sometimes Oscar would come down from his room and sit with the family, but this evening he had chosen to remain upstairs with both windows open in the hope of catching a breeze.

As it grew dark, Fannie went inside to bring out a kerosene lamp so that Albert could see to read *The Smithfield Herald*. Next to an article about the United States House of Representatives passing a war revenue bill was an article that caused Albert to focus his attention away from the children's amusement. "Listen to this," he told Fannie as she sat watching Iva decipher some of the words on the pages in her lap. "It says here they's a lot of people dying from the Spanish influenza in places up north and in some of the army camps. A hundred and four up around Boston . . . sixteen in Philadelphia . . . fourteen at Camp Dix in New Jersey. And that ain't all."

"Good gracious," Fannie said, turning to look at Albert. "Wonder why they're a-calling it the Spanish flu?"

Albert hunched his shoulders. "Now, I can't tell you that, but it sounds bad. Hope that mess stays away from here." Albert turned the page, and for the time being, forgot about the flu. After all, those places were far away from Pleasant Grove, and there had been nothing in the article to raise alarm for him and his family.

Three days later, however, another article appeared in *The Smithfield Herald*. This time, the situation sounded more dire. The article gave an estimate of 23,000 cases of the flu in the army camps. The flu was apparently spreading into camps in some Southern states, too, such as Louisiana and Virginia. Although both Albert and Fannie expressed their concern to each other about the contents of the article, Albert felt confident that the flu would not spread into rural areas like Pleasant Grove.

"Seems to me like it's mostly in them army camps," he commented to Fannie.

The next day, when Albert took the family in the surrey to preaching at Fellowship, there was talk among churchgoers about what they had read and heard. Albert found that most folks agreed that it was the poor soldiers who were huddled together in tight quarters in the army camps who would suffer the most from the flu outbreak.

***

In the beginning of October, with cotton-picking time bearing down on him, Albert took the wagon one morning to Woodsboro to purchase a few items that Fannie needed at the general store. Later that evening after supper, Albert opened up the *News and Observer* and saw a short article about thirty-five students at Trinity College and Trinity High School in Durham who had contracted the Spanish influenza. The article concluded by saying that there was no evidence of an epidemic in Durham. Albert sat for a moment, trying to determine whether or not to tell Fannie about the outbreak in Durham, and then decided to let it be since there was no call for precaution in the short piece.

Two days later, Albert's brother Alonzo stopped by in his new car, a Model T similar to the one Albert had driven in Benson. Alonzo had come to ask Albert about buying a few Poland-China shoats that he could fatten up for killing later in the year.

Albert walked with his brother to the pens where the young pigs that had been weaned were held. He told Alonzo that he could come back when he had time and pick out the ones he wanted. "The sows have done good, and it looks like they'll be ready to find again soon," Albert told him. "You might want to get into raising some for yourself," he added. "They's some work involved, but it'll pay off in the end."

Albert asked about Alonzo's wife, Georgianna, and their children, then shared an update on his family. Soon after, Albert changed the subject. "You heard about that Spanish flu? Looks like it's pretty bad in the army camps." Albert looked at his brother for a reaction.

"Yep, it sure looks bad in some places," began Alonzo. "I read yesterday that they're having trouble in Wilmington. The piece in the paper said some of the doctors were too sick to work, and even one doctor died from the pneumonia after he got the flu."

Albert raised his eyebrows and looked away, thinking about the other articles he had read. "I swear, I thought that mess would not get out of the army camps, but it sure looks like it's done it." He went on to talk about the article he had read concerning the outbreak in Durham. Both agreed, though, that they still felt pretty safe living out in the country. "It ain't likely to come here, I wouldn't think," Albert added, as if he were more trying to reassure himself than convince his brother.

"Was another article in the paper that was advising people to stay away from crowds, and that if anybody felt like they was coming down with it, they would need to go to bed and stay until they got better," Alonzo said.

"Well, that might be good advice for all of us," Albert replied.

"I hadn't got much need to be in a crowd, anyway. It's just us and Oscar here at home. Of course, I will be hiring a few hands to help with picking cotton, like I usually do."

After promising to bring his wife and the children for a visit soon, Alonzo left in his Model T, leaving Albert to stand and reflect for a few moments on their conversation. He made a promise to himself that he would talk it over with Fannie that evening.

As Albert readied for cotton-picking time, he continued to follow articles in both *The Smithfield Herald* and the *News and Observer* about the flu outbreak. One article talked about how the city of High Point had closed schools, churches, and theaters to try to thwart the spread of the flu. Another spoke of the disease's appearance in Raleigh at the state school for the deaf and dumb. On the fifth of October, an article told of the closing of all public gatherings in Raleigh.

Albert and Fannie spoke in low voices every evening about what they had read or heard regarding the outbreak so as not to alarm the children. "What worries me," Fannie said one evening as they climbed into bed, "is that if it's in Raleigh, it's getting mighty close."

She and Albert did not realize at that point that influenza had already begun to spread in Johnston County. Just days later, the county moved to close public gatherings, including churches and schools.

By mid-October, it was cool enough for Albert to build a fire in the sitting room after supper. With the children amusing themselves in other parts of the house, and Oscar up in his room, Albert smoked his pipe and talked with Fannie about his plans to get the cotton picked and to market as soon as he could. He then turned his attention to the latest copy of *The Smithfield Herald*. "Here, it talks about how you can guard against catching the flu," he said after reading an article in the paper.

"Well, what does it say?" Fannie looked up from sewing a button on Iva's coat.

"It says to eat a good diet, and that milk is one of the best all-around foods." He looked back down at the paper. "And it says to avoid overcrowding in the home. Well, we can't do much about that. I'm bound to have Oscar here to help me, it looks like. It also says fresh air is to be valued. We need to beware of them that coughs or sneezes and don't cover their mouth."

"I'd say that's a big problem. Folks need to carry a handkerchief, if they have to sneeze," Fannie added.

"Says here that the Pleasant Grove Township Fair is moved to the end of the month."

"I 'spect that's 'cause of the flu," Fannie pointed out.

"Hmmm . . . I would imagine that's right," Albert said. "Oh, I about forgot. I was talking to Victor Penny the other day about my Poland-Chinas, and he told me about a man over in Coats that's got some purebred ones for sale. I'm planning to get the pickers started in the morning. Oscar will be here if you need him. Charles is coming by the house, and the three of us will ride over in the wagon to talk to him. If we buy any, we'll bring them back or maybe make another trip if necessary, but we'll need to see what kind of price he's asking first."

So, just after sunrise the next morning, Victor arrived in his mule and wagon, and Charles in his buggy. Shortly, another mule and wagon appeared carrying the three men and a woman whom Albert had hired to pick.

Jasper, Myatt, and Oscar joined them at the edge of the cotton field, where Albert gave them instructions. Albert charged Oscar with weighing any sheets that got filled before the men got back, and he would need to let Fannie know each time a sheet was weighed so that she could come outside to supervise and record the weight.

As soon as Albert had everything in order so that he could leave, he hitched Maude to his wagon. Victor and he climbed up on the wagon seat, Charles sat down in the wagon bed, and the three men headed down the dirt road toward Angier. Each of them wore overalls and a jacket in the cool fall weather. Although the road was not overly muddy, Albert was concerned that they might run into some spots that would be difficult to traverse. As it turned out, Albert was able to navigate Maude around the worst spots, and they reached Coats by the middle of the day.

When they arrived in the small town, Albert stopped at a general store to inquire about the whereabouts of their destination. Not far away from the business area of town, he spotted the house and barns that fit the description given to them at the store. Albert guided Maude alongside a fenced-in area where he could see several Poland-China sows and a large boar.

After the men got out of the wagon to look at the pigs, a man in his early forties with thick, dark hair appeared from around the corner of one of the long barns. The man introduced himself as Andrew, and after exchanging pleasantries, he directed the three visitors to walk with him inside one of the barns to look at his stock. "Been breeding the Poland-Chinas for a while now and have had pretty good luck with them," he said. "What exactly are you looking for? Sows, gilts, or a young boar maybe?"

Andrew had built rows of pens inside the barn with a walkway of about five or six yards down the middle. He stopped in front of one of the pens. "This one here I call Coats Girl. Purebred registered Poland-China. She's born several litters for me. Y'all saw the boar out yonder in the outside fenced-in area? He's Mammoth Coats. He's registered, too, and a fine boar, if I do say so myself."

Albert noticed that Andrew spoke with pride about his hogs. Andrew's organization was evident everywhere. Every pen had been outfitted with feeding and watering troughs. Albert saw a man, probably a hired worker, shoveling manure out of one of the pens into a wheelbarrow.

Further down, Andrew paused in front of a pen holding five gilts. "These here are all sired by Mammoth, and the sow was Coats Girl, except for that one there." He extended his right hand to point out a gilt standing in the corner of the pen. "She came from Lady Coats, who is in the farrowing house next to us because she's got a new litter just born two days ago."

Andrew told the men to follow him to the barn next door, where several pens held sows with baby pigs. Some of the sows lay on their side while the piglets suckled with enthusiasm. Other sows stood while the offspring wandered aimlessly, grunting and occasionally squealing.

"You got a big operation here," Albert said to Andrew. Victor and Charles nodded in agreement.

"It took a while to get it going, and it takes me and three men that I hire full time to keep everything running. Some folks wants to buy young pigs to fatten up to kill, and others wants to get into raising some of their own to sell," Andrew said. "I get plenty of business, that's for sure."

Albert looked around the barn, trying to take it all in. This was the kind of operation he dreamed of having. He knew that just like raising the calves, raising pigs would be the way to increase his income even further. After looking over all the farrowing pens, Albert told Andrew that they were most interested in the gilts they had seen in the other barn.

The men reached the pen where the young females were held, and Andrew pointed out and named each pig one by one. He told the brothers and Victor what he was asking for each, and after some discussion it was decided that Albert would purchase Lucy, Fannie, and Lady King. Victor bought one named Virgin Queen, and Charles settled on Long Bess and Maud. The men then settled with Andrew on their purchase, after which he instructed Albert to move the wagon up next to a loading chute at the end of the barn, where the pigs were housed.

Like Wilbur had done when Albert had stopped with Jasper and Myatt in Wake County to buy the four Poland-China gilts, Andrew had constructed a wooden chute that allowed them to move the pigs from their pens up to a level with the wagon, which greatly facilitated the loading of the pigs they had bought. Having learned from the calamity he had faced with Jasper and Myatt, Albert told Charles and Victor to tie a rope around one of the hind legs of each pig.

After loading and securing the five gilts, the men bid farewell to Andrew and headed back toward Angier. Along the way, Albert shared with Victor and Charles how he and the boys had managed to deal with four escaped pigs in a torrential downpour. Charles and Victor could not suppress their laughter as Albert told them about Myatt saddling that pig's back and holding on for dear life. Albert found himself laughing along with them, but he recalled that the situation had not been funny at all at the time.

It was late in the afternoon by the time the three men got back to Albert and Fannie's house. Oscar met the men in the yard and helped Victor move his gilt to his wagon. Seeing that it was getting late and he still had a way to go to get home, Victor thanked the brothers for their help and headed out. Meanwhile, Albert, Charles, and Oscar moved the two pigs that Charles had bought to his wagon, then took the wagon to the barn area where Albert's two were lowered, amidst much squealing, into one of the pens. Fannie and the children came outside on the porch as the men finished up, and she invited Charles to come in and have supper with the family before going home.

"I imagine Flossie Mae's done cooked, and she's expecting me back. So, thank you, but I think I'll head on back home," Charles answered.

The family watched and waved as Charles guided his mule back out on the dirt road, and Albert paused for a moment to reflect on the importance of his purchase. He had spent quite a bit on the two gilts, but he thought about them as valuable investments that could potentially deliver some good income in the near future.

As he walked inside with his family, he looked forward to some good cooking and a quiet evening smoking his pipe and reading the newspaper.

CHAPTER TWENTY-NINE

AN EBB IN THE PANDEMIC

The news that Albert and Fannie continued to read throughout much of October pointed to a worsening of the influenza situation both on local and national levels. Since they had begun reading and hearing about the flu, they had heard of many home remedies to help ward off the sickness. Some recommended onion poultices, groundhog or goose grease, mustard packs, turpentine fumes, or zinc that could be painted on the inside of the nose. Albert had seen an article in the *News and Observer* about breathing in a product called Oil of Hyomei, which supposedly acted as an antiseptic to prevent flu germs from entering the nasal passages. As the death toll mounted, many large cities resorted to requiring the use of facial masks as a preventive measure.

Fannie believed strongly in the use of Castoria, and every so often gave the children a spoon filled with the strong-tasting liquid. "It'll clean you out good and keep you from getting sick," she told them. Filled chamber pots were testimony to the fact that Castoria did indeed clean them out.

Albert bought some mentholatum ointment at the drugstore in Smithfield, and it was good that he did, because soon pharmacies were unable to keep a supply on their shelves once the flu began spreading.

After Albert wrapped up cotton picking for the year, he told Fannie that he would not hire any more people other than Oscar to work until the flu had subsided. Toward the end of the month, articles in the newspapers presented a mixed reporting of good news of improvements in some places coupled with worsening conditions in others.

One evening, as Albert perused the latest edition of the *News and Observer*, he spotted a paragraph about how in Richmond there were over nine thousand flu cases in the city, with nearly four hundred deaths. His mind wandered back to his train trip to buy the mules, to Libby, to others he had met while there, and he hoped that none had fallen victim to the disease.

The papers remained full of suggested ways to combat the illness. There were tonics, for example, that claimed to purify and enrich the blood. One article told of the city of Winston-Salem's request to get whiskey to pneumonia victims. Pneumonia, which sometimes took hold after the onset of influenza, had proven to be especially deadly.

The Smithfield Herald often listed local victims of the flu. Albert read of people dying all around in Smithfield, Benson, Four Oaks, Kenly, and Selma. The *News and Observer* at one point reported that there were over one hundred thousand cases of influenza in the state. Fannie and Albert continued to talk about the situation away from the children. The older children were certainly aware of the flu, since schools would be closed for a while, but Albert and Fannie agreed that it was best to shield them from the most alarming details.

Albert chose to store his cotton until conditions improved so he would not be overly concerned about traveling to Benson. Working hours for him and Oscar were spent feeding and caring for the ever-increasing numbers of livestock. In addition to keeping abreast of the influenza situation, Albert often read articles about the war in Europe. As November approached, it looked as if the war might finally come to an end. Later, when it finally did, he and Fannie learned of local celebrations that brought people out from hunkering down at home for a month or more. At the same time that the war was ending, news began to appear that indicated a slowdown in the spread of influenza.

"Thank the lord, we've made it through," Fannie said to Albert one evening as they sat in front of the fireplace. "I'm getting ready to get out of this house," she added emphatically.

That they did. On the last Sunday in November, Albert took the family in the wagon to services at Rehobeth, where Leonard was preaching that day. Both Albert and Fannie were anxious to see how everyone had fared during the worst of the flu's rampage, and were happy to learn from Leonard that as far as he knew, no one in the family had been severely ill or had died from the disease.

After church, Albert took the family to his mother's house. The visit was not unexpected, since Irving had come over two days before in their wagon to check on the family's welfare, and Albert let him know that they would be coming by. When they arrived and made their way back to the kitchen, they found Amanda in her apron hovering over the cookstove. The room smelled of fried ham and fresh-baked biscuits. As soon as she saw the grandchildren, she stopped to give each one a hug and a kiss on the cheek. After getting the children seated at the dining table, Fannie helped her mother-in-law get the food into bowls and onto platters to be placed in the middle of the table.

While enjoying the abundant meal, the adults shared how they had coped with the flu outbreak during the past month. All agreed that they most likely had not gotten ill because they had stayed at home as much as possible. "I kept my windows open as much as I could," Amanda said in between bites. "That's what they said to do, and maybe it done us some good."

As Albert sat with his family savoring the delicious meal, he thought back to when all his siblings and his father had been at home. Irving was the only one left at that point who had not yet married. Albert felt thankful that he had been there with his mother through the worst of the widespread illness. "I believe we're through the worst of it," Albert interjected into the conversation. "I've been reading that it's slowed down in Raleigh and all over. I think we can get back to doing our normal business."

"I'm sure glad that war's over," added Fannie. "Looks like they're finally increasing our sugar ration, so maybe we'll be able to get some things that was in short supply."

"Yeah, with the war and the flu going on at the same time, we're all due for some better times," Amanda remarked. "I'm looking forward to everybody in the family stopping by once in a while. I'll be happy to get back to church soon, too."

After the meal, Fannie helped with the dishes while Albert joined Irving on the front porch. Iva amused herself inside by wandering from one room to the next in search of something interesting. Jasper and Myatt walked out toward the barn to look at the few goats that still remained. With the house now left to his mother and youngest brother, over time the number of animals had shrunk to a few goats, three pigs, and two mules that they kept to pull the buggy or wagon.

Albert and Irving sat on the porch for more than an hour while Albert gave his younger brother advice on cotton seed and raising pigs. Around the middle of the afternoon, Albert and Fannie loaded the children back into the wagon, and with promises to visit again soon, they headed back home.

That evening, as Albert climbed into bed next to Fannie, she turned toward him and said, "I fully believe I'm pregnant again. I've been thinking it for a while, but didn't want to say anything 'til I was sure."

Albert drew her close to him and said, "Well, I will be . . . looks like we're gonna have as big a family as the ones you and me come from!"

Fannie couldn't help but laugh. "That's all well and good," she said, "as long as they ain't born with something wrong."

Albert's mind flashed back to the two they had lost. "Well, we've had four that lived, so I think that this one will be all right. You just got to take care of yourself. You know what else I been thinking? I think we oughta go ahead and order that car. We've had a pretty good year. Even if I order it now, it probably won't be here until sometime after the beginning of the year."

Fannie agreed that the time had come to go ahead with the purchase. So, a couple of days later Albert went into Angier and made his very first telephone call to Parrish in Benson to place his order.

Being that Oscar was a traveling farm worker, he had not

stayed with Albert and Fannie for an entire year since arriving for work that first time. This year, however, Albert convinced him to stay on to help with his ever-increasing number of livestock. Oscar, seeing that he could use the money during the ordinarily slow winter months, agreed. As December came, so did the cold weather, and the two men found themselves doing everything they could to keep the younger pigs warm. Frequently they took the wagon down the road to get fresh pine straw and hauled it back to make bedding under lean-to shelters and inside the pens in the barn.

Finally, the schools reopened, and Jasper, Myatt, and Iva walked to Ogburn Grove every day that it wasn't too cold or rainy. On those occasions, Albert would take them in the wagon or surrey. Hugh was left behind in the house with Fannie, and when he was not on his rocking horse, he would search for other ways to amuse himself. The family looked forward to Christmas now that things had started settling back into more of a normal routine.

On the days leading up to Christmas and for several days afterward, Albert and Fannie visited with both the Stephenson and Langdon sides of the family. Some days they were surprised by visits from family members at home. This was a source of delight for the children, who got to see and play with cousins they had not seen in a while.

During the course of a visit by Albert's sister Callie, her husband, Allie Austin, and their children, Callie gave Fannie a copy of a Santa Claus rhyme that she had saved from the paper years earlier. "My children know this by heart," she told Fannie.

Fannie kept the paper, and on Christmas Eve Fannie read the rhyme to the children:

This is the Pack
That Santa Claus brought at Christmas
This is the Sleigh
That carried the Pack

That Santa Claus brought at Christmas
These are the Reindeer
That drew the Sleigh
That carried the Pack
That Santa Claus brought at Christmas
This is the house
Where the Reindeer stopped
That drew the Sleigh
That carried the Pack
That Santa Claus brought at Christmas.
(*The Smithfield Herald*, December 26, 1913)

After Fannie read the rhyme twice, Iva asked, "Is there really a Santa Claus, Mama?"

"I 'spect so," Fannie smiled and said, "way up north somewhere."

All the children, even Hugh, sat wide-eyed as they pondered the possibility of a sleigh pulled by reindeer. "Them reindeer must be like that big buck we seen on the way back from farm when we had them gilts in the wagon," Myatt suggested.

Albert looked up from a copy of *The Progressive Farmer*. "I imagine you're right. And I'll tell y'all another thing. If you want Santa Claus to bring you something in that sleigh, you better get to bed and be good, 'cause he don't bring a thing if he sees that children have not been good." He did not have to say another word. They all stood and hugged their mother and father, then went to put on their nightshirts and crawl underneath the covers. "It's a pity Santa Claus don't come every night," Albert said to Fannie with a wink after the children had left the sitting room. "Maybe we'd have less trouble getting them into bed."

Albert had gone to Smithfield two days before and had bought a basket of fruit, a twenty-four-inch bicycle, a tricycle, and a red wagon for the children, along with a handsome new parlor lamp for Fannie. The lamp had painted flying geese on the top and bottom portions, and a fringe of translucent beads hanging from the top. He had managed to get Oscar to distract Fannie while he had hidden the gifts, except for the basket of fruit, in the smokehouse until Christmas day arrived.

On Christmas morning, Fannie arose early to begin preparing breakfast and to get a start on the midday meal, as well. When the mouth-watering smells of breakfast began to waft through the house, the children got up to see if Santa Claus had left anything. Albert was sitting by the fire smoking his pipe when they made their way, still in their nightshirts, to the sitting room. "Look here what Santa Claus brought y'all," he said. "A big basket of fruit."

It was not customary for children to receive much of anything during Christmas. Therefore, when Albert announced what had been left by Santa Claus, their smiles indicated to Albert that they were happy to have received anything at all.

About the time that Fannie placed a heaping breakfast on the table, Oscar came downstairs to join the family in the dining room. With everyone seated, Albert asked to say the blessing. Normally he allowed Fannie to say the prayer, but today he felt especially grateful that they had made it through the tight grip that influenza had held over the community, and that he and the family continued to benefit from the prosperity brought about from his investments in the farm.

"Let's bow our heads," he began. "Lord, we thank you for this food we are about to eat, that we are all well, that all of our families are well. We thank you for the help that Oscar has provided, and we look forward to a good year to come. In Jesus's name, amen."

With that, the family dove into the sausage, ham, eggs, grits, and biscuits that Fannie had prepared. As Oscar finished, he excused himself under the pretense that he was going to check on the livestock. Instead, he went to the smokehouse and brought the gifts Albert had bought onto the back porch. Just as the children finished their meals, Oscar, wearing his long black coat, came back in the dining room. "It looks like to me Santa Claus must've left something else," he announced with raised eyebrows and a slight smile.

All the children jumped up from the table, except for Hugh, who was not quite sure what Oscar was saying.

"What?" asked Jasper.

"Where?" Myatt wanted to know.

"You'll have to go out on the porch," Albert said.

As if someone had declared the house to be on fire, Jasper, Myatt, and Iva raced to the back door. Albert scooped up Hugh to carry him outside. Oscar had placed the bicycle, tricycle, and wagon on the porch next to the back door, but had left the lamp in the smokehouse so that it would not get broken in the excitement. At first, the children seemed awestruck by what they saw. None had ever ridden a tricycle or bicycle before, and they had never had a wagon.

"Which one's mine?" Jasper asked his father as he and Myatt ran their hands over the bicycle.

"Here's what I was thinking," Albert explained. "You and Myatt can take turns riding the bicycle. If you're good, maybe later on I can get another one so you'll have one apiece. Iva can ride the tricycle, and all of you can help pull Hugh in the wagon some." He lowered Hugh into the wagon. "How do you like that, son?"

With a huge grin on his face, Hugh said enthusiastically, "Pull me, Jap, pull me!"

Jasper took hold of the handle and pulled the wagon around the corner of the porch and back.

Meanwhile, Oscar lowered the bicycle to the ground and began giving Myatt some instructions on how to ride. "Now, you're prob'ly gonna fall off," he told Myatt, "but just keep getting up and trying again. That's how you learn." He held the bicycle steady so Myatt could try riding. Sure enough, after a few feet the bicycle fell over on the side, and Oscar rushed to help the boy up.

Iva climbed on the tricycle and began moving her feet on the pedals. In practically no time, she was riding around the wooden porch. The children were so excited that they paid no attention to the cold temperature. Finally, Fannie told them they needed to get back inside and put on some warmer clothes and a coat. "You'll catch cold, and then you won't be able to ride anything."

As Fannie followed the children back in to see that they put on the proper clothing, Albert went to the smokehouse and brought out the new lamp. When Albert entered the sitting room with the lamp, Fannie and the children paused what they were doing to admire the beautiful addition to the room.

"Albert, you ought not to have spent so much," Fannie said, but Albert knew she was happy about the lamp. After running her hands over its porcelain, she placed the lamp on a small end table next to the davenport. It became a conversation piece in the days following Christmas when family came by to visit or to share a meal.

Gradually, Jasper and Myatt got the hang of riding the bicycle without toppling over. This was after both had suffered a few scrapes and bruises, of course. Despite the cold weather, Fannie often had to force the boys and Iva to come inside as they enjoyed their Christmas gifts.

***

The end of World War I in November had brought masses of people back together as they celebrated victory. The reopening of public places and the Christmas season also served to bring those who had lived in isolation back side by side. What Albert, Fannie, and their children did not realize as January 1919 came is that this bringing of people back in proximity to each other served as a breeding ground for a third wave of the influenza pandemic. What lay ahead would prove horrifying, and would change the course of events for the family in ways they could not have imagined.

CHAPTER THIRTY

LA GRIPPE

With the wartime rationing behind them, Albert sent Oscar on the twelfth of January by mule and surrey to Angier to purchase a few items that Fannie needed for baking. As Oscar stood waiting to pay in the general store with the money Albert had given him, another man stepped up behind him to wait his turn. Oscar never turned around to look at the heavy-set, bearded man whom he could hear coughing and sneezing intermittently.

After the woman ahead of him had completed her business with the clerk, Oscar stepped forward and asked for sugar, flour, baking powder, molasses, and a tin of tobacco. As he stood waiting for the thin young man behind the counter to round up his order, the portly man behind him continued to cough. It was a deep cough that sounded as if the man had a severe case of bronchitis.

Once the young man had brought everything to the counter that Oscar had ordered and payment had been made, Oscar turned to exit the store. Simultaneously, the man behind let go a huge sneeze with no effort to cover his nose. Oscar returned to the mule and surrey that he had tied to a post just outside the store, and slapped the reins to get the mule moving back home. The ride over had been a cold one, and not only had he worn his long black coat, but also a scarf to keep himself as warm as he could.

In a short while he was back at the barn, where he unhitched the mule and led him back to one of the stables. Then, he carried the items he had bought at the store into the kitchen, where Fannie was busy cooking. When the children realized that Oscar had returned, they all came to the kitchen to see what he had brought back. "It's mighty cold out there, Miss Fannie," he said after removing his hat and scarf. "It'll be a wonder if I don't catch cold. They was a man in the store coughing and sneezing up a storm."

"Well, you go on in there and get warm by the fire. I'll have you something to eat in just a few minutes."

The children, who enjoyed hearing Oscar tell stories, followed Oscar into the sitting room. Somewhere Oscar had learned the story of old Brer Rabbit and the Tar Baby, so after pulling off his coat and sitting down in one of the rocking chairs in front of the fireplace, he retold the story, changing voices with each of the characters to the delight of all. Just as he finished up the story, Albert came in from the barn, and Fannie called everyone to the dining room.

After Fannie said the blessing, the children all wanted to let their father know about the story Oscar had told them. Even little Hugh got caught up in telling how Brer Rabbit had gotten stuck to the Tar Baby. Laughter erupted from the children each time one jumped in to tell what was remembered about the story.

The next day, Fannie and Albert decided to remain at home rather than attend church. Except for helping Albert with the feeding of the livestock and coming downstairs down to eat, Oscar spent the day in his room. Jasper and Myatt took turns riding the bicycle up and down the path that Albert had created from the house to the flat land, while Fannie insisted that Iva and Hugh stay inside, where it was warmer.

Rather than spend the entire afternoon inside, Albert decided that he would hitch Jack to the wagon and take a ride over the land to think about what plans he wanted to make for the year to come. First, he went on his new pathway to the flat, where he rode around the perimeter of the cleared land. Upon reaching the Caudill cemetery, he brought Jack to a stop and got out of the wagon to look at the gravestones. So far, there were only two infant graves, along with that of Mathias' first wife. Albert's mind wandered back fondly to the time that Mathias had spent helping him in so many ways on the farm and accompanying him on trips here and there.

Getting back in the wagon, Albert thought about the possibility of getting into raising tobacco. Once, he had visited a neighboring farm to watch how a mule would drag a sled up and down the tobacco rows as men picked the leaves and placed them in the sled to haul to the tobacco barn. He had observed the workers at the barn stringing the tobacco onto sticks that would be later hung in the barn for curing. *It would be a big shift for me,* Albert thought as he rode along, *to go from depending mostly on cotton to raising tobacco.* Always on the lookout for the next way to expand his operation, he felt confident that he could learn.

When Albert came back to the house, instead of unhitching Jack, he turned the wagon to head toward the westward boundary of his land. He pictured how perhaps a pond might be added to provide a source of water, and how more land might eventually be cleared for planting. It had been a little over fifteen years since he and Mathias had gone to Smithfield to sign the agreement for the purchase of the property. Albert could not help but bask in the knowledge that he had met with so much success in that period of time.

When he finally returned to the barn, Albert unhitched Jack, led him to the barn, and patted the faithful mule on the rump. It would turn out to be the last opportunity that Albert would have to ride in the wagon.

As the sun got lower in the western sky, Albert called Oscar downstairs to help him feed the calves. Putting on his coat, Oscar followed Albert out to the barn to mix some water in with the food that they gave to the two calves Albert had not yet sold. As the men worked together, Albert noticed that Oscar seemed less energetic than normal. When Albert asked if he felt all right, Oscar replied, "Not feeling the best in the world, Mr. Albert. Head's been hurting a little bit, and I've been coughing some. I imagine I'm a-catching cold."

"I can finish this then," Albert replied. "You go on back in the house and tell Fannie to give you some of that Jack's Powder that we keep in the cabinet. It does me good if I have a headache."

"I hate to leave you with the work, but I ain't feeling like I can do much of nothing right now. Maybe with a good night's rest,

I'll feel better in the morning." With his head hanging down, Oscar turned and walked back toward the house. When he came in the kitchen, he told Fannie that he did not want anything to eat for supper, but would be obliged to her if she could give him some Jack's Powder for his headache.

"Lord have mercy, I hope you ain't catching something, Oscar," Fannie said as she reached in one of the kitchen cabinets to produce a blue-and-white packet. She opened the packet, gave Oscar a paper wrapper containing the white powder, and handed him a glass of water to wash it down. As soon as Oscar swallowed the powder, he disappeared up to his room.

When Albert came back in from the barn, Fannie said softly, "Oscar sure don't seem to be doing too good. Do you think he could be coming down with the flu?"

Albert narrowed his eyes and furrowed his brow. "Well, it's hard to tell, but maybe it's just a cold. He might've caught something when he went to Angier. It's best he stay up in his room, though. You might want to put his food on the steps so he won't have to come down to the table."

"He said he don't want nothing this evening," Fannie said. "We'll see about tomorrow, when it comes."

That evening was uneventful as the family gathered to eat supper and sit by the fireplace afterward. Although Albert had not wanted to unduly alarm Fannie, privately he wondered if Oscar had caught the flu.

Oscar was an early riser, and often he would be dressed and ready for work as soon as Fannie could get breakfast on the table. The next morning, however, in spite of the breakfast smells and the noises Fannie made with pots and pans in the kitchen, Oscar did not appear downstairs. Albert walked halfway up the stairs and called to him, "Oscar, are you all right? Do you want some breakfast?"

A somewhat weakened, raspy voice answered, "Thank you anyway, but I ain't hungry. Felt pretty bad all night. Might be best if I just stay here 'til I can get to feeling better."

"I can put you some food here on the steps where you can get it," Albert offered.

"Thank you, but I can't eat a thing right now. Maybe later."

Albert backed down the steps. Fannie turned around from the stove, and the two looked at each other without saying a word. They both knew. Oscar had the flu, and they might have been exposed to it. Neither said anything to the older children, who went on to school as usual while Albert tended to the livestock on his own.

Once, during the late morning, Fannie called up the steps to ask Oscar how he was doing and if there was anything he needed.

"I'm feeling mighty low," he answered back. "Don't think I can eat a thing, Miss Fannie. I'll let you know if they's anything I need."

When Albert came back inside from feeding, he and Fannie talked quietly about Oscar's condition. Fannie expressed her worry that the children would get sick.

"Well, the good thing is that ain't none of us, except for Oscar, that's sick, so maybe we'll be all right," Albert said reassuringly. "I'm telling you one thing, though. Since you're carrying that baby, you better be getting plenty of rest. Let these children help you as much as they can when I'm not in the house. It won't do for you to get sick." Albert worried that if Fannie got the flu, that might bring harm to the unborn child, not to mention the danger the illness could bring to her.

Two days later, Oscar still remained in his room. Albert insisted that he put his chamber pot on the steps so that he could empty it, since he imagined that it must be full. Thankfully for Albert, Oscar had put the lid on top, and though the smell was vile, he was able to carry it outside and dump the contents far away from the house. Finally, Oscar agreed to eat a few bites of food that Albert placed on the steps, but he was unable to consume much, saying that he had no appetite.

Albert took the surrey to pick up the older boys and Iva at the Ogburn Grove school, and as soon as they got in, Jasper began complaining that he did not feel well. Albert tried not to sound worried in front of the children, but his mind jumped to the thought that perhaps Jasper had contracted the flu from Oscar.

By the next morning, all of the children, including Hugh, were sick. Jasper was having chills, and Fannie wrapped him in quilts and put him close to the fireplace to try to calm the effects. Iva and Myatt stayed in bed, refusing any food or drink. Finally, Fannie insisted that they drink at least a little water. "You need to drink something," she told them, "to make you feel better." When she touched her hand to their foreheads, she could tell that all had a fever. Hugh, not old enough to fully understand what was happening, cried and fretted.

Albert did no more than was necessary at the barn to take care of the pigs and calves, then hurried back inside to help with the sick children. At times he was so absorbed with dealing with chills, high temperatures, and coughing among the children that he forgot about Oscar, who remained in his room all day and night, silent except for his coughing that could be heard downstairs.

The next morning, Albert opened his eyes and turned over to see Fannie still curled up in the bed. Normally she would have been up by then preparing breakfast. Albert reached over and touched Fannie on the arm. Without moving, she spoke in a near whisper, "I think I might have it, too, Albert. I don't think I'm able to even get out of the bed right now."

Albert felt his blood run cold as he realized that everyone in the house, except for him, was now stricken with the flu. He wondered how much longer he would be able to go on before he fell victim to the illness himself. How would they manage? Who would feed the animals? How would they eat? Who would look after the children? The alarming thoughts running through his mind were dizzying.

"You stay in bed, and I'll see what I can do," he told Fannie. After pulling on his shirt and overalls, Albert went to check on the children. All were still asleep, and Albert was glad, for that gave him a few minutes to try to figure out what to do. He knew that they needed help. The cows and hogs needed to be fed and watered.

In the kitchen, he found a couple of leftover biscuits. As he ate what would be his breakfast for the morning, he made the decision to let someone in the family know that help was needed. Hoping to find Oscar awake and some better, he climbed halfway up the steps.

Shirtless, Oscar was sitting up on the side of the bed. Albert detected the unmistakable smell of sickness. A quick interchange between the two revealed that Oscar was still feeling poorly, but as he told Albert, he thought he might be just a little better.

"The whole family is sick," Albert said. "I'm going to Mama's house to let her and Irving know, and see if they can get word to some of the family that we need some help. I don't feel sick right now, but I'm liable to get it, since everybody else has. Fannie and the children are still in the bed. Don't try to do anything 'til I get back. I don't plan to be gone long."

After returning to the bedroom to inform Fannie of his decision to go get some help, Albert hitched Jack to the surrey and struck out toward his mother's house. When he arrived at the back door, he cracked it open and told Mandy and Irving that he would not be coming in, and that everybody at home was sick with the flu. "Fannie won't be able to do much," he explained. "We'll need some help with food mostly. I don't want anybody else to catch it, so tell everybody not to try to come in the house. We'll look after the children as best we can. Oscar's been real sick, but he might be getting a little better. I'll do the best I can to feed the cows and pigs."

Irving promised to get the word to some of the family. Amanda said that she would send some food later with Irving.

Albert could tell by his mother's tone that she was worried. "We'll be all right, Mama," he told her. It would be the last time that Albert would speak to his mother.

After arriving back home, Albert went about trying to do his best to wait on Fannie and the children by offering water or warm milk. Coughing could be heard all over the house as he went from room to room to check on everyone and offer something to drink. In about an hour, Albert heard what he thought was the sound of Oscar coming down the steps to the kitchen. Albert left the bedroom and walked to the kitchen to find Oscar dressed as if he were going to go outside and work.

"I thought I'd see what I could do to help," he said in a still-raspy voice. "Looks like you got your hands full with trying to look after everybody."

Surprised yet grateful, Albert responded, "Now, I don't want you to try to do nothing 'til you're well. You might take a backset, and then you'll be back where you started."

"Well, I thought I could at least help you feed, and then maybe I'll go back to bed. I figure I ought to be rid of this mess in a day or two."

Albert conceded that he would welcome some help, given the circumstances, so the two men bundled up and headed outside to take care of what they deemed necessary. When they finished the feeding and watering, Oscar returned to his bedroom.

As Albert walked back toward the house, it struck him that he somehow didn't feel the same as he had when he and Oscar had headed toward the barn earlier. He brushed it off as being tired from worry. However, by the early afternoon he could no longer attribute what he felt to worry. He was getting sick himself.

La grippe, some had called it. The Spanish influenza.

Sometime around half past one, he heard a knock at the side door leading to the sitting room. Through the window he saw that it was Irving, who had arrived by mule and buggy. Albert raised a window just enough so that his brother could hear him. "I'll be dog if I'm not feeling sick myself now. Don't come inside, 'cause I don't want you to catch it and carry it back to Mama or anybody else."

Irving told Albert that his mother had sent some food and that he could pass it through the window. Albert stood by the window until Irving brought a large basket covered with a red and white–checked cloth. Albert raised the window just high enough so that his brother could pass the basket through, thanked him, and promptly lowered it back down. It would be an action that repeated over the next several days as neighbors and family tried to assist with food as best they could.

CHAPTER THIRTY-ONE

TRANSITION

Throughout the week, although both were almost too sick to do anything, Albert and Fannie attempted to care for their ailing children. Family and a few neighbors who had learned of the family's plight showed up regularly to pass food through the window, as Irving had done. Despite Albert's feeling of discomfort, he insisted on accompanying Oscar at least once a day to the barn to try to help a little with the feeding.

On Saturday evening, Albert came into the kitchen from feeding the hogs. Though the children were still feeling the effects of the flu, they all sat around the kitchen table as Fannie dipped chicken broth into individual bowls. Albert did not speak, but went straight to the bedroom, where he disrobed and crawled in under the covers. Every part of him ached, and chills racked his body.

As soon as Fannie and the children had eaten what they could manage, Fannie put Hugh back to bed and saw that the other three children got settled in for the night. Fannie then turned her attention to Albert. She placed a damp rag on his forehead and spread salve on his chest. Perhaps because he realized that he was in trouble, Albert opened his eyes and looked at her as she stood over him. "Take care of yourself, Fannie," he managed to get out. Those were Albert's last intelligible words to his wife, as his condition grew worse during the night.

Hardly knowing what to do, Fannie decided to fold out the davenport so that she could lie down with Iva next to the bedroom. All through the night, she was up and down. At times Hugh would awake and call out for something to drink. Iva tossed and turned. Worst of all were the sounds of deep coughing and heavy breathing coming from their bedroom.

The next morning, Oscar got up early to feed and water the livestock while Fannie did her best to prepare something from the food that had been passed through the window. She went to the bedroom first thing, where she found Albert on his back with his eyes closed. Fannie thought that his breathing rate had increased, and when she touched his head, she felt the heat of an intense fever. She brought some water and milk for him to try to drink, but he was unresponsive.

During midmorning, her brother Cleveland came to pass them some food. Standing back from window, Fannie expressed her deep concern about Albert, and told Cleveland to let her side of the family know.

As Albert grew worse, the rest of the family began showing signs of improvement. By Sunday afternoon, Jasper and Myatt wanted to go outside, and even though Fannie was concerned that they were not well enough to go out, she recognized that they needed to get out of the house and away from what they heard coming from their father's bed. Years later, Myatt would tell the story again and again of how, despite being outside in the yard, they could still hear their father's breathing.

Desperate, Fannie began to try everything to ease Albert's suffering. She tried dissolving Jack's Powder in water. She tried giving him a spoonful of Hicks' Capudine, something that claimed to lessen the effects of the flu. Albert had picked it up at the drugstore in Smithfield when he had bought the Christmas gifts. She kept applying salve to his chest. None of these seemed to have any effect.

By midafternoon, Fannie began to notice that the mucous Albert coughed up was no longer greenish, as it was in the beginning of his sickness, but now a dark red. Although frantic with worry, she managed to keep the children away from their father's bedside so that they could not see his suffering, even though they could clearly hear it.

Oscar, who had accepted the full responsibility of looking after the animals, opened the bedroom door to ask Fannie if there was anything he could do. "Yes, there is," she answered, applying a damp cloth to Albert's forehead. "Go hitch up one of the mules to the wagon and see if you can get word to Albert's mother that we need a doctor."

Without hesitation, Oscar sped out the back door, ran to the barn, and hitched one of the mules that Albert had purchased in Richmond to the wagon. As the wagon rolled out of the yard, he called to Jasper and Myatt, "You boys better go on back in and stay with your mama 'til I get back. I'm going to see about getting your daddy a doctor."

With the sun getting lower in the winter sky, Oscar arrived at Mandy's to find Albert's brother Leonard and his family visiting in the front parlor. After explaining the dire situation, Leonard said, "I'll go see if I can get Dr. McLemore." Oscar left everyone with worried looks on their faces as Leonard, accompanied by Irving, took his mule and buggy to Dr. McLemore's house.

Dr. George McLemore, who had studied at Wake Forest and the University of North Carolina Medical School, had established his practice in nearby Cleveland Township in 1906. By the time that Leonard and Irving arrived at the doctor's home, it was already getting dark, and the temperature had dropped. Leonard knocked on the door, and a man still dressed for church opened the door. Leonard and Irving could see the doctor's wife, Nellie, standing behind him in a long blue-and-white dress. Leonard knew Dr. McLemore from a previous visit to his office that sat to the left of the main residence, so no introductions were needed.

"Sorry to bother you at this hour, Doctor Mac," he started, "but my brother Albert is bad off with the flu, and his wife has tried everything, and he's not getting any better. We wanted to know if you could please come to see if there's anything you can do."

Dr. McLemore turned and said something to Nellie that the two men could not hear. The doctor then told them that he would be ready as soon as he hitched his horse to his cart and grabbed his bag.

With the horse and cart now ready, Leonard and Irving led the way toward Albert and Fannie's house with Dr. McLemore following close behind. When they arrived at the side entrance that led directly to Albert and Fannie's bedroom, the men saw someone standing on the porch. As the three men stepped up on the porch, Leonard recognized the man as Fannie's father.

Leonard, Irving, and Mr. James Langdon stood on the porch, shocked by what they heard coming from inside, yet concerned about catching the flu themselves. McLemore went into the bedroom, pulled his stethoscope out from his black bag, and listened to Albert's chest. He asked Fannie some questions about when he had first gotten like that and what all she had tried to do to help him.

Meanwhile, Leonard and Irving had stepped back off the porch and were standing next to the doctor's cart, talking. Fannie's father looked through the window to try to see what was happening, and after about fifteen minutes, he saw the doctor and Fannie emerge from the bedroom. Dr. McLemore was talking quietly to Fannie, but Mr. Langdon was unable to hear what he was saying.

When the doctor opened the door to come back out on the porch, Mr. Langdon asked, "Isn't there anything you can do for him?"

Leonard and Irving came back up on the porch to hear what was being said.

"Well . . ." Dr. McLemore took in a deep breath. "He doesn't just have the flu. He has pneumonia, and his lungs are full of fluid. I don't know if it would have made any difference if I had gotten here any sooner, but he's in such bad shape now. I don't think he'll make it another twenty-four hours."

All the men could do was look down.

"I hate mighty bad that there's nothing I can do for him, but once the flu turns into pneumonia, it can be and has been deadly for many an unfortunate soul," Dr. McLemore said.

"Well, we thank you for coming anyway, Doctor Mac," Leonard said, his eyes growing misty. Leonard reached into his pocket and produced the money to pay for what Dr. McLemore normally charged for a home visit, and with that the doctor was on his way back home. Dr. McLemore would later log the visit in his ledger along with the five-dollar charge. Yet before he left,

McLemore said to the men, "I know you all are probably afraid to go inside, but I'm going to leave these masks here for you to put on. Keep your hands washed with soap and water, and you ought to be all right."

After talking with Irving, Leonard announced that he would be staying the night because, as he said, "Fannie ought not to be left by herself with just Oscar and the children."

Fannie's father decided to stay, as well, and after both men put on the masks that Dr. McLemore left them, they went inside to take turns sitting by the bedside so that Fannie could try to get some rest.

Irving, on the other hand, went back home to relay what the doctor had said. He would check back sometime the next day.

By midday on Monday, the news had spread that Albert was dying, and his other brothers began to appear one by one. All put on masks and went in to see their once-handsome brother. He now looked nothing like how they had last seen him. His face and extremities were turning blue, and his mouth was agape as he gasped for air.

Around two thirty in the afternoon, the sound of the rapid, heavy breathing that had filled the house since the worst had started was replaced with the death rattle. Fannie had tried to prepare the children for the inevitable. When they were brought by their father's bedside in his final moments, all they could do was stand and stare, transfixed in disbelief that the man who had shown such strength and resolve had been reduced to what they now saw before them.

At approximately three thirty in the afternoon, with Fannie and Albert's brothers by his bedside, Albert's soul departed the earthly form it had taken and went toward the light. Fannie lay her head down on his chest and wept. No one spoke for what seemed a very long time, until finally Leonard asked that they all bow their heads as he delivered a short prayer.

Now, they would need to plan for a burial—a burial that they never could have imagined for a man so young. Willis Albert Stephenson was only thirty-seven years old.

CHAPTER THIRTY-TWO

BURIAL AND AFTERMATH

Shortly after Albert made his transition, his brothers jumped into action to take care of burial arrangements. First, they used a basin of soapy water to clean up the body. A table that sat on the porch was brought in to the front unfurnished room, where they placed the body that they had covered with a sheet. Alonzo and Charles appointed themselves to the responsibility of going to pay a visit to Rose and Company, a business in Benson that had gotten its start in selling furniture, but had added the sale of caskets.

The next morning, the two brothers left early in Alonzo's automobile to make the arrangements with Rose's. Fannie told them on the evening following Albert's passing that Albert had the money saved to pay for a nice burial, so when Charles and Alonzo arrived at Rose's, they ended up getting a copper casket and vault.

Meanwhile, on the home front, everyone was assigned the task of spreading the word that the burial would take place in the Stephenson family cemetery later that afternoon. Around noon, a black hearse pulled by two rather handsome brown horses appeared in the front yard of Albert and Fannie's house. The hearse had two large windows on each side, and black curtains extended across the top and sides of each window. There was enough of an opening to give a partial view of the vault inside. Two men dressed in black suits, white shirts, and black hats stepped down from the wagon and were met by Charles and Alonzo, who directed them to the front room, where Albert's body lay.

The men removed the sheet to inspect the body. They explained that once they were given the clothing the family had chosen for Albert, they would dress the body, place it in the casket, and allow the family to view the corpse before taking it to the cemetery.

Charles found Fannie sitting by the fireplace, exhausted from having been sick and from enduring watching Albert's suffering in his final hours. "They want to know what you want to bury him in," Charles said softly as he touched her on the shoulder.

"Well, he always felt proud when he was wearing his black suit and bowtie." She rose to search the bedroom closet and chiffonier to locate everything the men from Rose's would need.

After about an hour, one of the men helping to prepare the body emerged to speak to Alonzo, who was sitting with Fannie and the children. "Somebody'll need to sign the death certificate," he said quietly. Alonzo took the small piece of paper and entered his name in the box indicated by the man. At the bottom, the undertaker was listed as Rose and Company. No cause of death was written on the certificate. "Miss Fannie, you, the children, and anybody else in the family who wants to may come to view the body, if you would like," the man continued.

Fannie walked into the chilly front room and stood in front of the opened casket. Iva clung to her side, just barely tall enough to see her father's body inside the casket. Charles lifted Hugh up into his arms, while Jasper and Myatt stood quietly next to their mother and Iva. The men from Rose's had done their best to make Albert's body presentable. They had dressed him, combed his hair, and rubbed something on his face to make it look a little less dark. One of Albert's classic black hats rested on his abdomen.

For a long time, no one spoke. It was almost as if everyone had been frozen and was unable to move.

Finally, one of the men who had prepared the body spoke. "Miss Fannie, at about two o'clock or so we will take the body in the hearse to the cemetery. You and the family will follow behind us. Do you know who you want to say a few words at the gravesite?"

Fannie nodded. "Yes, Leonard's a preacher. He'll be the one to speak."

Over the next couple of hours, family from both the Stephenson and Langdon sides arrived to view the body and offer their condolences to Fannie and the children. Some brought food and left it in the kitchen so that when the family returned later, there would be plenty not only for that day, but for some time afterward.

At the chosen time, the two men approached Fannie to let her know that they were moving the casket to the hearse. Some of Albert's brothers helped to remove the vault first, upon which they placed the casket inside and then covered it with the vault again until they arrived at the burial site. Climbing up on the hearse, the two men led a procession of buggies, wagons, and even a car or two on the journey to the cemetery.

Upon their arrival, Mandy and a few of Albert's siblings who had not gone to the house earlier to view the body joined the gathering. First, the men withdrew the vault and casket from the hearse, and after placing the vault to the side, they brought the casket around to the gravesite that had been dug earlier in the day by neighbors and any men in the family who had been available. Wooden planks had been placed around the grave forming a rectangle, and two long ropes extended across the grave opening. As the casket was brought and held over the grave, a group of men held tightly to the ropes. Gradually, the casket was lowered into the ground.

Leonard called for the family to gather around the gravesite as he spoke of Albert's goodness as a man, of his faith, and of all he had been able to accomplish in such a short life. He would later summarize that eulogy in an obituary published days later in *The Smithfield Herald*.

Fannie wiped away her tears with a white handkerchief, and the children—except for Hugh, who was perhaps too young to fully comprehend what was happening—wept over the loss of their father. There was not a dry eye among Albert's brothers and sisters, either, who had long looked to him for advice and leadership, and who had shared many wonderful memories growing up.

Following Leonard's eulogy, most everyone headed back to be

with Fannie and the children. The men from Rose's, after helping with lowering the vault on top of the casket, departed in the hearse as the sun descended in the sky.

***

Over the course of the next few days, family members came and went to offer solace and assistance to the bereaved family. One of the most pressing matters at hand was how to handle the remaining livestock and how to help Fannie run the farm. After talking with her sister Elizabeth, who had married James E. Olive, Fannie arranged for her nephew James R. Olive to stay with them and help run the farm for a while. Fannie let Oscar go, thanking him for all the work he had done, especially for the help he had provided during their illness.

Four days after Albert was laid to rest, another horse-drawn hearse pulled into the yard in the early afternoon followed by a carriage and a buggy. A man Fannie thought she recognized stepped out of the carriage and held out his hand for a woman dressed in all black. Fannie could hardly believe her eyes. It was Mathias' wife, and as others began stepping out of the carriage and buggy, Fannie saw that other members of the Caudill family had come, as well. The one that Fannie did not see was Mathias.

Fannie invited everyone to come inside and warm themselves by the fireplace. The women followed Fannie and the children inside, while the men took a spot in the wagon to head up to the Caudill cemetery. Mary explained that Mathias had also caught the flu, followed by pneumonia. As Mary tearfully told the story of his illness and death, Fannie shared their own tragedy. The two women held hands as they sat side by side on the davenport and wept. Fannie expressed to Mary how much Mathias had meant to them over the time he had stayed on to work with Albert, and how she could not believe that both men had passed away almost at the same time from the same illness.

Fannie called to her nephew, who had moved into the upstairs bedroom after Oscar's departure, to ask him to come down and stay with the children. Then she put on a long coat, scarf, and hat, and followed the Caudill family outside to ride with them to the cemetery. There, with a cold, northerly wind blowing over the open field, Fannie watched as yet another coffin was lowered into the ground.

After the Caudills left that afternoon, Fannie never saw them again, though she often thought of them fondly.

Shortly after the burial of Mathias, Fannie received word that the Model T that Albert had ordered had arrived in Benson. Knowing that she did not want to go to Benson alone or even with the children to get the car, she talked with Charles and Alonzo about going to bring the car to the house.

On the day the brothers came with the car, the children gathered with Fannie on the front porch to watch as Charles drove the handsome black automobile under a wooden shelter close to the oak tree. The car sat there for a good while, until one day in late February a few of Fannie's sisters and brothers, along with their families, came to visit. As the women sat inside talking with Fannie, the men roamed outside, looking over all that Albert had left behind. There were cows, pigs, farm equipment, the wagon, the surrey, and of course, the Model T.

Fannie's nephew James told the men that the automobile had sat there since Charles and Alonzo had brought it. "Nobody's touched it, and it probably needs cranking up and driving a little bit," he said to those gathered around the rear of the car. "Does anybody know how to crank it?"

Everyone just looked at James and either hunched their shoulders or shook their head. Finally, James went in the house to tell Fannie that they wanted to start the car, but that nobody knew how. Without saying a word and not stopping to put on a coat, Fannie strode out to the shelter and sat down in the driver's seat, where she followed the steps Parrish had demonstrated when she had accompanied Albert to Benson. She stepped around to the front and turned the crank three times, starting the motor on the first try.

At first the men were in awe at how Fannie took control of the situation. When she stepped back in the house, James said to the others, "Aunt Fannie's a tough woman. I don't think there's anything she couldn't do."

Fannie would rely on a lot of that grit to get her through the coming months and years. In July, she gave birth to Myra Ann, bringing to five the number of children she would need to raise on her own.

***

Eventually, Fannie and the children moved into the house that still stands overlooking Highway 210 near the intersection of Interstate 40 in Johnston County. While there with their mother, the older children began attending the one-room Rohobeth School. There, Myatt met his future wife and the author's mother, who would go on to tell many times over the years how he drew tobacco pipes on the chalkboard. Myatt and his wife, Flossie, later moved into the same house where Albert and Fannie had lived through the fourteen years of their lives together.

The house, located on present-day Landmark Road in Pleasant Grove, has undergone remodeling several times over the years. The couple raised six children in that house: James E., Jay, Bobby, Max, Linda, and the author, Randy. Myatt raised cotton, corn, and other grains, and for many years cultivated and harvested tobacco. Somewhat following in his father's footsteps, he raised cows for a while, and then got into raising pigs on a large scale. Unfortunately, as a result of financial problems, the house and most of the land were sold shortly before Myatt's death in 1991.

Jasper, who also became a farmer, went on to marry Beulah McGee, but like his father, he passed away at a young age in 1943. The couple raised five children: Helen, Grady, John Albert, Jasper S., and Larry.

Iva married S. S. Sauls, a successful farmer, and they resided in the McGee's Crossroads area north of Benson for many years. They had three children: Norma Grey, June, and Sidney. Iva passed away in 1979.

Hugh married Mary Ryals in 1935, and they resided in the same house with Fannie for years. There, they raised their children, Kenneth Hugh, Nadine, Judy, and Sue.

Some years after Albert's death, Fannie had Albert's grave and those of the two infants moved from the Stephenson family cemetery on present-day Sanders Road to the one at Fellowship Primitive Baptist Church. Fannie passed away in 1974 at the age of ninety-two. Many remember her as "Grandma," the soft-spoken lady who always had a piece of peppermint candy to hand out when family came to visit.

Myra Ann, born in July of 1919 following Albert's death, married Sherwood Lassiter in 1936. Myra gave birth to four children: James Jr., Joy, Bertha Anne, and Jane.

If Willis Albert were alive today, he would likely be amazed at the number of his descendants. Many have gone on to have successful lives and careers. One of Albert's grandsons, Jay Stephenson, is especially remembered for developing a highly successful farming business, much like Albert had done.

It is unknown how the family's history might have changed had Albert lived into his older years. Would he have continued to expand his land holdings? Would he have ventured into raising tobacco? Would there have been more children?

The flu pandemic that raged through the United States and around the world is estimated by some to have killed up to 50 million people. The sheer number of victims is astounding. Medicine was on the verge of having many breakthroughs at that time, but it would be too late for Albert and for many flu victims, as there was so little that doctors could do for severe cases of influenza and pneumonia back in 1919. Since the great flu pandemic, there have been additional flu epidemics that have proven costly in terms of human life. Other diseases such as Ebola, AIDS, SARS, malaria, and tuberculosis have all taken their toll.

It is often repeated that one must live life to the fullest, for it cannot be known what tomorrow brings. There is no doubt that Willis Albert Stephenson did just that in his own way, for he accomplished more in his thirty-seven years than some are able to accomplish in a much longer lifespan. He understood the power within him to do exactly what he wanted to do—not only to be a highly successful farmer, but also to be a good person. He held a vision that enabled him to manifest prosperity.

Perhaps his ability to both envision what he wanted and bring that vision forth into fruition serves as his greatest legacy.

W. A. STEPHENSON PASSES AWAY

On Monday, Jan. 20, one of Johnston County's best young men, W. A. Stephenson, passed away, having been sick only a few days with influenza. He, together with his whole family and a hired hand, were sick at one time. The following account of his life was furnished us by his brother, L. H. Stephenson:

Albert was born April 22, 1882, and was the second oldest child and son of the late Nimrod Stephenson. There was a big family of ten, and this the first death since father.

At twenty-two, after farming one year for himself and receiving $325 and a mule from mother he had some supplies and $600 in money. He married Miss Fannie Langdon, a daughter of Mr. and Mrs. J. M. Langdon, of the county. He bought a run-down farm, invested every dollar of his money and went heavily in debt. Then he worked himself through and to show to the world what a working man could do was his motto. Hard work, honest dealings, and skinning no man soon lifted him to the confidence and esteem of the outside world.

Albert was foresighted and saw the need of farmers raising cattle; so he set out and soon became an extensive cattle raiser and dealer. He has built up one of the finest and most productive farms of its size in this county, not only making it profitable and beneficial for himself and family, but also for his neighborhood and county.

Albert was liked by everybody who knew him, was always about his own business and never meddling in others. He had nothing too good to lend a neighbor and has helped many financially. A few years ago when cotton went down to 5 and 6 cents, having gained the confidence of two of the leading banks of Raleigh, he went out among his neighbors and told them that if they had to sell their cotton at such prices to take it to him and he would pay them eight cents, and at that price he bought 100 bales, and this, with his own crop, he stored away for two years, during which time cotton rose to a triumphant level.

Albert never wasted a dollar, but when he made one he put it out to help him make another. By his hard work and saving he has, during his fourteen years of farm life laid up for his family an estate at around forty thousand dollars. Not many young men advance so fast osn the farm.

For the past few years Albert was keenly interested in his friends and more especially in his brothers and sisters. He wanted them to do well, he aided us and would encourage us to buy real estate, and in these ways he was more to us than a brother, he was our main brace post. Therefore, we all feel keenly our great loss.

Albert believed in improved seeds, especially cotton, and by it was a great benefit to his neighbors and friends by loaning them the best seed to plant in the spring and buying them back in the fall at a fancy profit above the ginners. He delighted in fine cotton and leaves around him about 100 bales old and new.

While he was so much interested in cotton and corn, he was becoming interested in the future meat situation, and had decided to convert a part of his farm into hog raising in connection with his cattle. He had chosen as his choice the Poland China, and for the past few months had bought a dozen of the best sows he could get, and had already started raising pigs.

Albert was a very homey boy, never leaving except on business, and to church or to visit friends. We have no knowledge of his ever riding on a train but once, and then he was in need of more and better mules, and went to Richmond and brought back six of the best mules he could buy.

He never visited a show, but occasionally went to the State Fair at Raleigh purely for agricultural benefit, and then he would make other business to the market to make the trip pay him.

He was a daily reader of the News and Observer, Progressive Farmer and other local papers, but never took any part in politics except to go and vote and hurry back to his work. He was fast advancing in the idea of good roads and was building one through his farm. In every way Albert was an ideal young man.

Albert was not a member of any church, but had a sweet hope in Christ and was a believer in the Primitive Baptist, and I am informed today that the last words he ever spoke just before the last he spelled his own name as though he was reading and this confirms our satisfaction that he saw his name written in the Lamb's Book of Life and is at rest.

He breathed his last Monday at 3:30 in the afternoon, January 20, 1919, leaving a wife, three little boys and one little girl (having lost two children in childhood) and also five brothers and four sisters.

He was laid to rest at the old homeplace of his birth in the family burying ground Tuesday, January 21, at 4 p.m. in a double copper casket.

Though we did all for him we could, his family and physician, yet we would that we could have done more. We now have to bow down to God's will, and say "Thou knowest best." Though we loved him, yet we part.

A grieved brother,
L. H. STEPHENSON
Jan. 22 and 23, 1919

ABOUT THE AUTHOR

Randy Stephenson was raised on the same farm in western Johnston County, North Carolina, that was purchased by his grandfather Albert Stephenson in 1903. Upon graduation from Johnston County's original Cleveland High School in 1969, he went on to receive a bachelor's degree in English from Appalachian State University in 1973. Randy moved to the Atlanta area in the early 1980s, where he furthered his education at Georgia State University by obtaining both master's and specialist in education degrees. After teaching in several school systems, he retired from public education in 2010 and spent the next seven years teaching English as a second language to immigrants in Atlanta. Now fully retired, he serves on the board of directors for Friends of FORMA, a nonprofit organization that seeks to provide educational opportunities and improved nutrition for impoverished youth in Guatemala. *The Last Wagon Ride* is his first published work.

www.ingramcontent.com/pod-product-compliance
Lightning Source LLC
Chambersburg PA
CBHW050244110726
47898CB00007B/2266